HIJAB

HIJAB

A Novel

Guruprasad Kaginele

Translated from Kannada by
Pavan N. Rao

SIMON &
SCHUSTER

London · New York · Sydney · Toronto · New Delhi

A CBS COMPANY

First published in India by Simon & Schuster India, 2020
A CBS company

1 3 5 7 9 10 8 6 4 2

Simon & Schuster India
818, Indraprakash Building,
21, Barakhamba Road,
New Delhi 110001

www.simonandschuster.co.in

Hardback ISBN: 978-93-86797-79-7
eBook ISBN: 978-93-86797-80-3

Typeset in India by SÜRYA, New Delhi

Printed and bound in India by Replika Press Pvt. Ltd.

MIX
Paper from responsible sources
FSC® C016779

Simon & Schuster India is committed to sourcing paper that is made from wood grown in sustainable forests and support the Forest Stewardship Council, the leading international forest certification organisation.
Our books displaying the FSC logo are printed on FSC certified paper.

‘Words, as is well known, are the great foes of reality.’

— Joseph Conrad, *Under Western Eyes*

For
Padma, Pranita and Prabhav

PART 1

Two Years Ago...

Prologue

My name is Guru. That is not my given name. Yet, that is how I'm addressed by my friends, my co-workers, and my patients. I do have a first, middle and last name. I live in a small town called Amoka in the state of Minnesota, working as an emergency physician in the only hospital in town.

Nobody here can pronounce my full name. They inevitably call me Guru, and I, instinctively respond to it. Don't go looking for Amoka, Minnesota on Google Earth or Google Maps. You'll never find it.

I am also a writer. I've written a few short stories and novels in Kannada.

This is one story that I feel compelled to tell.

In a town like Amoka which is right in the American heartland, you see a few Indian doctors like Radhika and me and many Sanghaali immigrants like Fadhuma, Rukiya, Abdhi and Kuki—sometimes more than you would expect.

Again, don't go looking for Sanghaala on Google Maps either. You will not find this country on it. Sanghaala could be any country in Africa—like Sudan, Ethiopia, Kenya or Uganda. It really should not matter much when all the immigrants from these countries look the same, eat alike and speak alike.

There are many Sanghaali immigrants in Minnesota. In fact, according to a census report from the United Nations, the highest number of Sanghaalis outside Sanghaala live in Minnesota. Many of them speak little to no English!

They all came to America for the same reason.

Their homelands failed them.

This story is about them.

This story is about us.

Where shall we start? We can start anywhere. Let's begin with Fadhuma's incident.

1. Fadhuma

'Name?'

'Fadhuma Hassan.'

'How far along are you in this pregnancy? How many kids do you have?'

'Fourth month ... three babies.'

'Do you speak English?'

'No.'

'What language do you speak?'

'Sanghaali.'

'Does your belly hurt?'

'No.'

'Any bleeding?'

Fadhuma shook her head. She looked like she was about twenty-four or twenty-five years old, with dark skin, a glowing face, and sparkling eyes. She had applied her eyeliner with utmost care, almost like an artwork, without any smudges or overflows, eyelashes nicely groomed with mascara and her eyebrows shaped like an arch. A Hijab covered her head, with no glimpse of even a single strand of hair. Even in this touch screen age, she carried an old-fashioned flip phone with its slim ear-piece tucked into her Hijab. Her lips were lightly painted. The colour of her lips and the mascara paled against the brightness of the eyeliner and the Hijab, which had an odd brownish purple colour. The mobile phone's speaker was on and her husband Hassan was at the other end of the line. He interpreted my questions in English into Sanghaali language for her.

I asked her, 'Fadhuma, what brings you to the hospital?'

'I've been vomiting all day and my belly hurts.'

'Are you hurting right now?'

She shook her head.

'Not this belly, but this one,' she showed her protruding abdomen.

'I have to examine you to find out what's wrong.'

'No, not possible. I want a lady doctor. Interpreter, interpreter,' she screamed with impatience. The operator had paged the hospital's Sanghaali interpreter as soon as Fadhuma arrived but she hadn't arrived yet.

'Fadhuma, there are no female... sorry, lady doctors here today. I am the only doctor here who can examine you. I'll not look down there. I'll check if the baby is alright. If I sense that there is a problem, we can get Dr Radhika. Were your first three deliveries normal or did you have cesarean sections?'

Fadhuma did not respond to my question right away.

The husband and wife conversed in Sanghaali for five minutes. I continued with my examination. It was a full-term pregnancy. On her lower abdomen there were horizontal surgical scars. I suspected that her previous deliveries were all done by C-sections. I held the probe soaked in gooey gel against her abdomen and looked at the baby on the ultrasound monitor. The baby was breech—its head was up. Fadhuma's contractions were very unsettling for the baby. I figured that the chances of a normal delivery were slim.

Fadhuma had not replied to my question yet. She was still talking to her husband.

I asked again, emphasizing each word, 'the... first three... deliveries... were by... cesarean section... right?'

She spoke with her husband again for a few minutes. I didn't understand any part of their conversation.

'No,' Fadhuma's husband spoke cautiously over the mobile.

'What?' I asked, a little surprised at the delayed response.

'The first three children were delivered normally. No surgeries.'

Fadhuma made a futile attempt to conceal the scars on her lower abdomen.

'This one?' I pointed at the scar.

Fadhuma was embarrassed. Her husband intervened quickly, 'That...that...there was a growth in her tummy and that mark is from when they took out the growth.'

I decided not to say any more. I called Radhika, the hospital's obstetrician, on her mobile and gave her a quick summary of what had transpired so far.

'Let me guess, the husband and wife are refusing cesarean section, right?'

'I briefly raised the possibility of a C-section. I didn't say it was one hundred per cent necessary. I think the baby is breech. I also think that her previous deliveries were all by cesarean sections. But both the husband and the wife deny this. They insist that the children were delivered normally. Fadhuma's husband is not here in the hospital. She does not speak any English. He is interpreting everything over a speaker-phone. I am waiting for the hospital's interpreter. She should be here anytime. Fadhuma is demanding a female doctor. She says that if we cannot provide that service, she will leave against medical advice.'

'Welcome to my world. This is what I have to deal with every day. This has been these people's jig-and-dance now-a-days. No matter what, they insist that they will not get a cesarean done. Apparently, "cutting the belly open" and taking the baby out is against their cultural beliefs. There was another Sanghaali patient of mine who complained that we do unnecessary surgeries all the time, only to make money! None of them have health insurance. Neither the hospital nor I make a single penny by treating them. And if something goes wrong, I have to deal with these "Human Rights" and "Patient Rights" groups. They come chasing you at the drop of a hat. Guru, don't try to be a hero. I will come and take over.' Her tone made it clear that she was getting a bit antsy.

'Hurry up, Radhika. What if Fadhuma starts to deliver here in the emergency room?'

'Don't worry. If she delivers normally, all you have to do is watch. If she needs a cesarean section, no one can convince her to have one, not even her good Lord Allah!'

'Why?'

'Trust me on this, I have no idea. Just hold the fort. I will be there as soon as possible,' she hung up.

2. The Land of Ten Thousand Lakes

The State of Minnesota is well-known as the 'Land of Ten Thousand Lakes'. The state is dotted with lakes. The land is luscious green as far as one can see. Those who visit the state in the months of July or August are so enthralled by its tall maple trees, the fawns that stray onto the backyards, the clear blue sky and the lakes and streams along its many walking trails, that they easily forget the '10 below' temperature and piles of snow in the winter that follows. We too were enticed by this weather. The fresh verdure of Minnesota was a welcome change for people like us moving from a concrete jungle like New York.

Situated in its Fair Blue County is the small town of Amoka, with a population of ten thousand. In the town's only hospital, three Kannadiga doctors—I, Radhika, and Srikantha—served as the chief of medical staff, chairman of the department of obstetrics and chairman of the department of medicine, respectively. We didn't earn these professional titles at the young age of thirty-two because America recognized exceptional leadership potential in us. And neither was it sheer serendipity. According to Minnesota State's Gazetteer, Amoka was a medically underserved town. A recent census had reported that the ratio of patients to physicians was highly disproportionate—for the town's population of ten thousand, thirty doctors were just not enough. Amoka barely held on to the new world order with its free Wi-Fi zones, two huge satellite dishes, mobile phones and a single two-lane road. No wonder that 'American' doctors, regardless of the perks offered, didn't want to move to this 'metropolis'. It was on folks like Srikantha, Radhika and me who were on J-1 visas and waiting for their green cards that the American government set its sights. We were their back-up, contingency 'just-in-case' MDs.

The J-1 visa is one of its kind. A foreign-born physician needs to do three years of residency to practice Medicine in America. Specialty practice needed further training. Doctors, scientists, pharmacists and other professionals can come to America on this visa. One can stay for a total of seven years. Getting a green card while on J-1 visa is extremely difficult. One cannot work other than in the enrolled training program. After seven years, these professionals are required to return to their home countries, live there for two years, and then find another job on a work visa again to return to America. Then, they are eligible to apply for their green cards. At times when America changed its foreign policy with countries like Pakistan, Iran and Syria almost daily, no residency trained doctor from these countries wanted to go back to their homeland. J-1 visa waiver program is the only saviour for most of us. Radhika, Srikantha and I were no exceptions.

Under this visa waiver program, doctors on a J-1 visa could stay if they served in government-declared underserved areas like Amoka for three to five years. That would get them their green cards expeditiously. Hence, Amoka had doctors from countries like India, Pakistan, Mexico, Columbia and the Dominican Republic.

Radhika, Srikantha and I came to America together. We did our residency training in the same hospital in New York. As we were about to complete our residency, we saw an advertisement for three jobs in this remote town. So remote, we had noticed that we didn't have access to any mobile network when we visited the town for the first time for our interviews. This did not stop us from accepting the jobs, and within ten days of finishing our residency we started working without any qualms.

Thirty years ago, Dr Smith, an obstetrician, founded the Amoka General Hospital. He still practices here with Radhika. Amoka, like any other small Midwestern town, had transformed and developed significantly when people from countries like Sanghaala, Mexico and Cambodia started immigrating. Development here really meant the coming up of a multiplex cinema, a mall and a couple of Starbucks look-alike mom and pop coffee houses. The joy of Muskie fishing and snowmobiling or ice skating hardly had enticed US citizen doctors. Apart from Smith and a few other native Amokans, all other physicians were from foreign countries.

Radhika used to joke, 'If thirty to 10,000 physician to patient ratio is considered medically underserved, then by that definition, except for Bengaluru, all other towns in Karnataka are underserved.' She always had thought that Amoka was underserved because of the surge of Sanghaali refugees and Mexican minorities who had none to minimum health insurance. According to her, 'If you are uninsured or underinsured you are always underserved.'

Srikantha and I had decided to share a house. We were delighted when we found a four-bedroom house for a mere five hundred dollars rent. Radhika had rented a small apartment for herself.

That didn't last very long. Apparently, she was freaked out by the eerie silence of the nights where she couldn't hear even the buzz of fruit flies. One day, she showed up at our house and said, 'Guys, I am moving in. I will cook for you if I must. Why do you need this big house, anyway? Are you worried about how a single sexy girl like me could live with studs like you? I'm sure you are not scarier than these lonely nights. Moreover, neither of you is sexier than my Giridhar!

I am taking the master bedroom.' She had moved in without so much as waiting for our consent.

Radhika was engaged to a boy from Mysuru who worked for Intel in Austin, Texas. They lived on the opposite poles of the country. The lovebirds communicated on Skype and Facetime. Giridhar already had his green card. Radhika had thought that she could apply for hers as Giri's dependent if they got married soon. But she had learnt after talking to an immigration attorney that since she was on a J-1 visa, she had to work in a place like Amoka for five years before she could apply for her green card even if she married an American citizen. She was frustrated and lamented, 'Coming here on this visa is like doing time. There's no way out. Instead of getting stuck in this shit hole for five years, had we been to Bengaluru and worked at the Central Jail for a couple of years, and applied for our green cards, we could have got it by now. At the very least we would have had the satisfaction of living in Bengaluru for two years.'

Her sweetheart Giridhar had visited us at Amoka once. This past Christmas, he had taken a flight from Austin to Minneapolis. On his way from the Minneapolis airport, he was caught in a severe snow storm. Roads were closed, and he was forced to stay in a motel right outside Amoka. He could see the town but couldn't get on the only highway to Amoka which was dangerously icy. Apparently, Radhika had requested the Highway patrol guys to drop her off at his motel. The patrol guys had declined. 'Ooo... she is coming hard you know. She is a tough one.' Radhika was stumped. She had no idea that Minnesotans personify their cars, snowstorms, and tornadoes as *she*. The Skype connection was down, and the lovebirds had to settle for their smartphones. Emojis and succinct LOL, TTYL texts had served as poor substitutes for an encounter and they bid adieu over their mobiles alternately sobbing and exchanging greetings for a Happy New Year. Since that visit, Giridhar had never ventured into another trip to Amoka. Radhika used to visit him at Austin.

Even at thirty-two, Srikantha was single like me. When asked about the reason, he always had the excuse that his parents hadn't found the right girl yet. He relied on his parents to find him a match. A Mysuru native like Giridhar, he grew up in Birmingham, England. His father had moved to England when he was twelve years old and they had stayed there for the next ten years. He completed his college and subsequently went to medical school at Birmingham. After their retirement, his parents had returned to Mysuru for good. Apparently, they had hoped their son would stay back in England. Srikantha had realized very soon that he would be a *staff grade doctor* at best, always sucking up to the English physicians, no matter how long he worked in England. He had pondered over returning to Mysuru and practicing medicine there. His parents had advised him not to return. He had ignored their advice and had moved to Mysuru, worked there for about six months in a medical school, and had realized that the medical practice in India was not as easy as he had imagined. He had gone back to England. He had realized soon that he didn't belong there either. The answer out of this limbo was America. But his MRCP from England hadn't given him any advantage over us. He too had come to America on this 'Doing Time' visa.

Srikantha was nothing like what I had imagined him to be. My initial impression of him was that of an English bloke who had grown up in Birmingham eating Fish and Chips and drinking Lighthouse beer. My clichéd stereotype was soon found to be wrong when we saw him doing the *Trikala Sandhyavandhyanam,* the traditional three-times-daily prayers, and having conventional Indian breakfast like *gojjavalakki* with *mosaru*-spiced ground rice flakes with yogurt. His mom would often WhatsApp him traditional Indian recipes from Mysuru and he would cook for everyone. Radhika hadn't cooked for a single day.

Srikantha used to thank all the gods for his fortunes, after drinking a couple of Kingfishers: 'Man, we should all be thankful for what we have. Thanks to Amoka and the comforts it has offered us! We can amble to work at nine in the morning and still no one will question us. We can go home for lunch in the afternoon and pinch a round of golf before getting back to work. We can come home in the evening and have another cup of coffee or a mug of beer. Thanks to you Guru, no need to stress about going back to the hospital at night. You guys at the emergency room will take care of everything, true nocturnists you are—saving lives when the rest of the world sleeps. God bless you. Not bad for doing time, huh!' This had made me think that we need to get him out of Amoka as soon as possible. Otherwise, instead of a Mysuru girl he would end up finding someone here and settling down as 'The Indian Doctor'.

There is a popular saying in Kannada: *haaloorige ulidavane gowda.* 'In a deserted town, the lone survivor will himself be the chieftain.' In a similar sort of way, I was promoted to be the chief of emergency medicine and later, the chief of medical staff for the Amoka General Hospital within two years of my joining the job. I still had to work full time in the emergency department. We had eight full time physicians. All of us worked three twelve-hour shifts a week. Thanks to a highway passing through the town and a few skiing resorts in the vicinity that attracted a lot of people, the emergency department was busier than what I had expected it to be. Even after a forty-hour work week, I had three days off in a week. In a town like Amoka, since there was nothing else to do except play golf, I had accepted the chief of medical staff position.

The chief's main duty was to oversee that the hospital staff followed the guidelines laid down by the state's medical board and to sit down in monthly meetings with other department chiefs to talk about important sounding stuff, such as a five-year road map to make us a state-of-the-art facility in the state of Minnesota. The 'overseeing' part was more about working with Carla, the chief of patient services—a sixty-five-year-old Administrative Assistant who had memorized every by-law of the hospital. My job was to sign all the papers at places the stickered post-it arrows pointed.

The department of obstetrics and gynecology had three doctors: Radhika, Smith and a Pakistani by the name of Abdul Razak. Razak also had come to Amoka just like us, seeking a green card. He too had completed his residency along with us in New York. After doing their residencies in family medicine, Radhika and Razak had gone on to do a one-year fellowship to learn how to perform C-sections. Since this training licensed them to do Cesarean sections on their own, they both functioned as OBGYN specialists. Radhika was the town's only female obstetrician. With Smith's retirement around the corner, she was the uncrowned queen of that department.

Razak was married to Zeba, a very pretty Karachi girl. Srikantha used to tease them, 'Razak, when I heard that you guys were from Pakistan, I had expected your wife to look like any other Begum. Nice catch, buddy. And Zeba, you have a fine taste for selection of your outfits. You remind me of Zulfiqar Ali Bhutto's wife when she was young. Watch out, guys. Your Mullahs will order a Fatwa if they see you walking around, without a burqa.' Razak and Zeba had a two-year-old girl, Reshma.

Razak had absolutely no interest in hospital administration. He mostly kept to himself and lived comfortably with his wife and daughter. His only complaint was that no halal meat was available in Amoka. He was surprised that despite the presence of so many Sanghaalis, there was no one selling it here.

The prospect of a green card looming large, added to the fact that we landed these 'chief' positions within two years of completing our Residency meant that we were having a good time. In terms of rank I was the boss to both Radhika and Srikantha. In meetings—when I used management jargon like 'Healthcare Reform', 'Strategic Planning', 'Creative Destruction' or 'Affordable Care Act'—Radhika would joke with me, 'Guru, we will be getting our green cards in a couple of years. You look like you are getting comfortable here. Listen to me, if your mom pairs you up with a nice-looking girl, just get married. Think of an exit plan from Amoka. Keep New York and Chicago in mind when you try to settle down permanently. You look like you are never going to leave this place.'

Those were happy times. We were cruising along, like a ship sailing on a calm sea, like an aircraft flying at thirty thousand feet.

3. The Original Sin

Fadhuma's pain had worsened. I had ordered for some blood work and asked the nurse to give her four milligrams of morphine and was anxiously waiting for Radhika's arrival. I was a bit nervous about my expected actions as an emergency physician if Fadhuma were to deliver in the emergency department. I remembered Radhika's words—'Things will go just fine if it were to be a normal vaginal delivery. Normal babies will "pop out" like slippery blobs with or without your help.' However, I had an intuition that Fadhuma's case wouldn't be 'normal'.

Dr Carlos Alvarez, another immigrant physician from Mexico was working the shift with me. It suddenly occurred to me that this was a good time to respond to Human Resource's emails. I asked Carlos if he would mind keeping an eye on Fadhuma as she was my only patient. I told him, 'She is thirty-nine weeks into her pregnancy. She has mild lower abdominal pain, these could be labour pains. She had a few contractions when she came in, but nothing now. The baby is doing fine. I have paged Radhika. She is on her way. There are some emails that I must respond to. I will be in my office. Call me if you need anything.' I was surprised at my own voice when I signed my patient out to him. The breech presentation and Fadhuma's obstinate opposition to C-section had conveniently slipped out of my mind. I went into my office before he could ask any questions. Perks of being the boss, I chuckled to myself.

I went inside my so-called office, which was only a wee-bit bigger than a fifty-six-inch TV box, and started going over my e-mails. I was a bit uneasy about delegating Fadhuma's case to Carlos at a crucial moment. I consoled myself, since Carlos loves delivering babies, he might be better suited than me for this job.

One email caught my attention. It was from a certain address Abdhi.Abu-Bakr@yahoo.com and was forwarded to me by the hospital's human resources department. Abdhi had complained against Radhika to the hospital. The email that started with the salutation 'To whom it may concern' could be paraphrased as: 'My wife Rukhiya Abu-Bakr was admitted for delivery to the Amoka General Hospital on 20 June. This was our first baby. We were as excited about this delivery as we were anxious. Our family physician, Dr Mohammad Mohammad had told us all along the pregnancy that we had nothing to be concerned about. We were skeptical about having our first baby delivered in a small hospital like yours. But, at the end we had no choice as Rukhiya's labour pains were so bad that driving to Minneapolis was impossible. As luck would have it, I wasn't in town at that time. A few of our relatives had accompanied Rukhiya to the hospital. None of them could speak English. Apparently, Dr Radhika insisted on doing a C-section right away. The baby was delivered by C-section within fifteen minutes of Rukhiya's arrival at the hospital. We feel that we were given no other options. As there were no interpreters around, we could not make out who said what to whom and when. Later, we spoke with Dr Mohammad Mohammad and he told us very clearly that this was an unnecessary surgery. Our culture does not support cutting the belly open and taking the baby out. If either the mother's or the baby's life is in danger, as the baby's father I should be the one to make the call on who gets to live. We believe it is wrong to not have given us this choice. Rukhiya, amongst all people, didn't want her baby to be delivered by C-section and this unfortunate event has made her go into severe depression. She is not letting the baby near her. We would like to request a meeting with the hospital board members or anyone else who can dispense justice for us.'

I was a bit surprised by this email. Abdhi sounded like a Sanghaali name and I felt it was impossible that he could have had this kind of command over the English language to surmise his thoughts into such an articulate complaint. Even if he did, he must have approached another doctor for an opinion.

I was surprised by the coincidence and timing of the events. Rukhiya had her C-section a month ago. Now Fadhuma is declining hers.

I tried calling Radhika on her mobile. She did not answer. I went out and checked on Fadhuma. She was somewhat calm. Morphine was doing its trick.

I went to my office and looked up Rukhiya Abu-Bakr's records in the computer. Twenty-four-year old Rukhiya had recently immigrated to Amoka as a Sanghaali refugee. She had checked into the emergency department with labour pains on 20 June at 4:10 in the morning. The emergency physician who saw her had immediately sought expert help by paging Radhika and had asked her to come to the hospital immediately. According to Radhika's notes, Rukhiya had severe abdominal pain. The fetal heart rate was very irregular with very little variability indicating fetal distress. She was very clear in her documentation: 'Family was explained of imminent danger to mother and baby including but not limited to fetal and maternal death at the worst.' I chuckled at the use of language—'not limited to fetal and maternal death'? Can there be anything worse?

She had also documented that since the hospital's

interpreter was not around, she had used interpreter services over the phone. Rukhiya was accompanied by her mother and a couple of young men who had identified themselves as her cousins. These two could speak spotty English and had apparently threatened Radhika that if she did any kind of surgery on Rukhiya, people would die! Scared by their words, Radhika had summoned the hospital's security and had them escorted out, before performing the C-section. She had made a note, 'Due to an anatomical distortion of patient's genitals, a vaginal delivery is unlikely.' This sentence made me wonder for a moment, but I did not think too much about it and made a mental note to ask Radhika once she arrived.

I felt that anyone in Radhika's place would have performed a C-section on Rukhiya. Since this was beyond my expertise, I thought of showing this complaint to Smith or Razak from the same department and getting a courtesy review from them. I hoped that they would agree with me and officially certify that Radhika had acted in the best interest of the patient. I forwarded the relevant documents to Smith and Razak and a copy to Radhika as well. I needed to send a response to Abdhi immediately.

In hospital administration, managing such complaints is an art by itself. All these shenanigans of patients complaining about doctors and their care were something that neither Radhika nor I was familiar with before coming to America. Once here, I had learnt to respond to our patients who complained about trivial things like non-availability of cable television in the waiting rooms. My response would invariably start with, 'The hospital apologizes for not meeting your expectations.' Patients and their relatives always would like to watch their favourite show on cable television in the waiting rooms, but the Amoka General Hospital was operating in 'red' every year and we had no money to entertain our patrons.

However, I could not directly tell them so. I had to use my administrative skills to communicate this message tactfully. If my answer was a firm 'no' I would lose all my 'sniffles', 'sore throats', and 'cuts' to the hospital next town. At the same time, I could never convince the hospital's financial officer why we needed a nice TV with satellite or cable connection in waiting rooms to attract our customers. The only solution that I had for this was to say sorry and apologize.

I therefore apologized to everyone with no exception whatsoever with a hackneyed 'sorry'. I used this 'sorry' word so much that the word had lost its meaning. Both the apology monger and the giver were aware of this. It had turned into a ritual: they complained, and I responded with an apology letter!

I did the same with Abdhi's complaint. After the usual 'sorry', I wrote, 'We regret the inconvenience. Your complaint has been forwarded to our hospital review committee. We will get back to you after the concerned personnel review your case.'

What surprised me was that Radhika had never talked about Rukhiya's case with us. While the patient privacy laws prohibit discussing our patients' histories outside work, it hadn't really prevented us from our dinner table gossip about 'interesting cases'. My stories from the emergency department were always the best. They spanned from the unbelievable to the ridiculous. For instance, the story of a man who had come holding one end of an iron rod with the other end speared into his chest, or that of a blonde girl who couldn't stop grinning after sudden detumescence with her boyfriend in tow. They were apparently trying a brand-new Kamasutra position when her 'dude had broken his dick'. She had splinted his bruised, limp manhood with two plastic knives and a rubber band and had brought him in.

Radhika would invariably say, 'Man, your stories are

always dirty' and would laugh hysterically. But as far as I could remember, Radhika had never raised Rukhiya's topic either at home or at the hospital. I thought of asking her, 'What else do you gossip about?' I wondered why she had not spoken with me about it. I started reading Rukhiya's records all over again.

Just then Radhika stormed into the hospital, after hurriedly parking her car in the parking lot. She poured herself a cup of coffee from the coffee maker. She was drinking the stale coffee while reading Fadhuma's records 'Hasn't Duniya come in yet?' she turned towards me and asked. I could sense some unrest in her voice.

'She may be here at any moment. I've sent word for her.'

Duniya is the hospital's Sanghaali interpreter. It has been twelve years since she left Sanghaala and immigrated to Amoka. She is about twenty-five years old. Since she attended high school in Amoka, she spoke English very well. This job was especially created for her at the hospital to meet the needs of the growing Sanghaali community. She also worked part-time jobs at places like Amoka's paper mill, chicken farm, and packaging as an interpreter. She was the only interpreter for all of Amoka's Sanghaali community. At times when she was unavailable, we used interpreter services on telephone or via Skype. My question in English would get interpreted on the computer screen and the answer would be delivered back in English. Sometimes we had live interpreters on screen; sometimes we only heard voices. Several times these faceless voices consoled the patients more than me and my Medicine. We could sense jitters in their voices and see sweat on their foreheads when we couldn't get any interpreters; especially if the telephone lines did not work or if the Skype connection was down, then all the assurances that I gave came to no avail and with the refrain of 'Interpreter, interpreter', they panicked until they could see another Sanghaali face or hear another

Sanghaali voice. This was a new experience for someone like me who firmly believed that a doctor is someone who saved lives by prescribing drugs.

'I read Rukhiya's husband's complaint,' Radhika said looking at her phone. Radhika had already read the email that I had sent just five minutes ago. I thanked these smartphones silently in my mind. I didn't say anything but gave her a puzzled look.

'Guru, have you seen her records?' she sounded scared.

'Don't be scared Radhika. You have done your job. You'll not be in any trouble. Anyone in your place would do the same. I've sent the records to Razak and Smith for review. This is only to appease the clients. I'm certain their opinion would be no different from mine.'

'I hope so. Don't you ever try to help anyone. Seriously. You will land yourself in deep trouble. God knows why these Sanghaalis are so rabidly against C-sections! Fadhuma says no to C-section too, doesn't she? She is a breech. She will never be able to pop that baby out. She insists that I turn the baby downside up. Apparently, her mom did this to her sister in some refugee camp in Kenya and claims that the "baby came out just fine". This is America. No real doctor does this here, especially at full term! In fact, it is against the law in some states. Now, what kind of antics should I pull off to get this baby delivered?'

Babies naturally settle into a head-down position which we call vertex presentation and come out with their heads leading. If by the ninth month the baby isn't 'vertex', there is a chance to turn it 'downside up', by gently squeezing and turning the baby from outside. This is called 'External Cephalic Version' in medical jargon. This is the technique that Fadhuma was referring to. It was Radhika's opinion that using this technique in her case was not only difficult but extremely dangerous. I offered my advice, 'Why don't you send her to the University and wash your hands off?' Since Amoka was a rural hospital with no specialty care, we often sent our patients to the University Hospital in Minneapolis. Radhika said, 'Guru, we can send patients to the University when we have complications or when we cannot absolutely handle them. There is nothing that they will do there that I can't. After all, this is a simple C-section. If we send her to the University, folks there will raise a ruckus and complain to the government that we are dumping our cases on them. The problem is not that we can't do it here, but convincing Fadhuma of getting it done. Our hospital has a team of three gynecologists, social workers and interpreters. We should work on finding a way to convince her.'

'Why is this a problem now? Weren't Sanghaalis living here even before we came here? Didn't doctors perform C-section before you?'

'This problem has been there for long. I'm not aware of the reasons. There has been a deluge of three thousand Sanghaali refugees to Minnesota this year. Fadhuma and Rukhiya have also arrived this year. Perhaps, they are not familiar with the culture here. And it is very difficult to make them understand.'

'Why don't you ask Smith? He has been here at Amoka for a long time.'

'Smith flatly refuses to see any Sanghaali patients, even daring people to slap discrimination suits.'

Not having any comment to offer, I said 'Good luck'.

Duniya came in, walked over to Fadhuma and wished her, 'Assalam Walekum.' She, poured two cups of coffee, for both of them, and sat next to Fadhuma. She looked at me, 'Doctor, good morning. *Kahaani* is playing in Regal Cinemas at Minneapolis. Have you seen the movie? Very nice movie, Vidya Balan is pregnant in the movie, kind of like this.' I didn't know what to say about the Bollywood obsession of these Sanghaali girls. I remained quiet knowing that this was not the time to talk about *Kahaani*.

Radhika said disapprovingly of Duniya's liberty in the department, 'Guru, you are a bit too easy on these people.' And went to Duniya and told her curtly, 'Fadhuma is not allowed to eat or drink anything till I examine her. Duniya, you are supposed to know this.' Duniya and Fadhuma looked at each other, talked to themselves in Sanghaali, and started giggling.

Radhika said, 'Duniya, your job is to interpret what I say, not to make fun of me.' They both appeared a bit stunned. Despite Radhika closing the door behind her, I could hear the conversation quite clearly.

'Fadhuma, I've told you very clearly before that you need a C-section. The baby is breech. We are not even sure whether your earlier three deliveries were normal.'

Duniya was interpreting Fadhuma's responses into English, 'I've told you before. My first three were normal deliveries. I've told this to the other doctor too. The scar you see on my belly is because I had a tumor taken out.'

'Letting you have a natural delivery poses significant danger to the baby. And to you too,' Radhika told her directly and clearly.

Fadhuma responded, and Duniya interpreted, 'There is no danger to the baby. I can feel the baby move in my belly very clearly. My mother had fourteen babies and there were all kinds of deliveries—feet first, hands down, and I was told my twin sister and I were hugging each other and refused to come out. My grandmother delivered us. No surgery.'

'Whatever, let me examine once.' I heard Radhika's dejected voice. Ten minutes had passed, and I heard Radhika telling Fadhuma hurriedly, 'I have to get an opinion from another doctor. I've to get my colleague, Dr Razak, here.' And she rushed out. Her face was pale. 'Guru, I'm not sure how much you know about it. Fadhuma is circumcised, just like Rukhiya. She had come to see me twice for prenatal visits, and on both occasions refused to let me examine her below her waist. I suspected that there could be something like this. This is the first time I'm doing a pelvic exam on her, which is highly unusual. I think we need to take a chance and try 'Version' at least once before taking her to the operating room. I don't have much help upstairs in the labour ward to sedate her. Can you sedate her here in the emergency department? I'll try to get Razak here and ask him to convince her to be ready for C-section if this doesn't work. I am almost positive that a normal delivery is impossible for her. At least let her have the satisfaction of a sincere attempt from our side.'

I had heard about the Female Genital Mutilation of women from this part of the world but despite working in the emergency department, I had never seen one. I felt uncomfortable. I started to wonder if Radhika could pull this off by herself. Razak arrived within five minutes of paging him. Radhika brought him up to speed on the situation. Both of them went into Fadhuma's room and started discussing the plan. I went inside the procedure room to get ready with all my equipment and medications needed for sedation, in case Radhika and Razak delivered Fadhuma's baby right there in the emergency department.

Radhika said, 'Guru, we are ready. Give her some morphine and anything else you choose to sedate her with. We will give it our best shot. We will try Cephalic Version and try to move the baby to the right position. If this does not work, we will have to perform the C-section.'

'Radhika, don't you think you are taking too much risk? I can get the chopper here in ten minutes. Any doctor at the University will admit her. Nobody is asking you to try this at Amoka. You are holding yourself to an unreasonably high standard of care. Stop trying to be a hero. She can be in Minneapolis in thirty minutes.'

Radhika replied, 'It will be too late by then. We do not have that much time,' and went into Fadhuma's room. I followed her. Duniya and Fadhuma were conversing in Sanghaali when I went inside. Radhika asked Fadhuma, 'Look Fadhuma, they have cut you down below. Why didn't you tell me before?' She gestured with her index and middle fingers to simulate a scissor-cutting action. Her desperation to communicate her thoughts to Fadhuma was quite evident. I couldn't help but snigger even in that situation.

'What does it have to do with what you are doing today?'

'Where do you think the baby comes out of? Your distorted anatomy makes it impossible for you to have a baby the normal way.'

'Not true. What was done to me was Sunnah. I delivered my first three children normally. Only those who have had Pharaon will have difficulty bearing children. My mother did not have a Pharaon done on me.'

Radhika was speechless. She obviously had no clue what these Sunnah and Pharaon are. She persevered, 'Fadhuma, I have told you more than once, the head upward position of the baby and your "cutting" below makes it impossible for you to have a normal delivery. I will try my best to turn the baby around. The baby's heart rate is all over the place. Anytime during the procedure, if I feel that the baby is in danger, I will have to perform a C-section.' It was not clear how much Fadhuma understood what Radhika said via Duniya's interpretation, but she nodded her head in agreement to everything that Radhika said, and signed all the papers placed in front of her.

I felt that Radhika was taking a huge risk. But she was the

specialist and supposed to know more than me on child births and I had no say in the decision making. I had to defer to her decision. I went out to check on Fadhuma's husband. He had not returned yet.

I asked Razak, 'What do you think?'

Razak was changing his gloves, 'Radhika is way gutsier than me. I would never even think of venturing into something like this if I were in her position. But this is not the time to analyze what's right and what's wrong. We don't have the time to think. Could you push something into Fadhuma to make her sleep?'

I asked him while drawing Propofol into a syringe, 'How long do you think you guys need to turn the baby around?'

'Guru, if everything goes well, it should be fifteen minutes. I have never done this procedure before. This task is even more difficult when the baby is fully grown. In fact, there are lots of medical articles advising against attempting Cephalic Version at full term. My gut says that the chances of Radhika's success with this procedure are very slim.'

'Then why is she attempting it?'

'Who knows Guru? I'm only a second assistant here. I have no idea why Radhika does certain things sometimes. May be she is trying to prove her point. This is her way of telling Fadhuma that she tried everything before taking her to C-section. Anyway, Fadhuma is her patient. Let's keep everyone happy. I have already told you what I think. There is no way out here. She will end up getting a C-section.'

I started injecting the Propofol into her vein and asked, 'Razak, what are these Sunnah and pharoan?'

'I'll explain in detail later. Where did this Radhika go?' He went out looking for Radhika.

I spoke to Fadhuma through Duniya, 'Now, slowly close your eyes. Think of something pleasant. The medicine I'm about to give you will make you sleep. You can even sing one of your favourite songs.' Radhika was standing behind me, 'Yo, Guru, dude. What are you doing? Trying to hypnotize her? She is already asleep. Move aside.' She looked at Razak. 'Are you ready?'

He replied, 'Yes ma'am.'

And they started the procedure of reversing the baby's presentation by dexterous manipulation. Using the grainy black and white image on the ultrasound scanner as the guide they started working their hands on Fadhuma's belly to bring the baby's head down.

It is an irony that humans who live with their heads held high and up all their lives, come out of their mother's womb with their heads down! And Fadhuma's child did not want to let go even here. It was as if the baby sat there stubbornly cross-legged. Radhika and Razak continued their masterly art of belly massage for fifteen minutes. At the end, Radhika was profusely sweating. For someone like me, who had never witnessed this procedure before, the whole affair was a strange, almost surreal experience.

No matter how hard they tried, the baby did not move an inch. Radhika looked at me, in an accusatory way, 'Guru, you have to give her something more to relax. What can I do if the uterus is this tight?'

I threw my arms up, 'I've given her the maximum dose. If you need more medications, then you should call the anesthesiologist. I don't have the license to administer anesthetics.' The baby monitor made a loud ringing noise and turned silent. I was a little scared and looked at Radhika, 'Don't you be scared, Mr Doctor. Why fear monitor beeps when you can see the baby's heart beating so well on the ultrasound?' she commented rather patronizingly and pointed to the ultrasound monitor. Fadhuma started moving her arms and legs slowly. I suspected that Propofol was wearing off and she may wake up any minute. I told Radhika, 'Look, whatever it is that you are trying to do, please do it fast. I mean it. If not, please call the anesthesiologist. This procedure is taking longer than expected.'

Razak yelled suddenly pointing at the ultrasound machine, 'Radhika, the baby is crashing. Look at the heart rate. The umbilical cord is coiled around its neck. I don't think Version is possible. You've got to stop the procedure now. Let's go to the operating room and take the baby out like RIGHT NOW! I don't think the baby will make it.' Duniya stood there dumbfounded. I had absolutely nothing to say.

Radhika wasn't ready to give up. She started yelling at everyone there, 'Razak, I understand. But keep this in mind, if I do the C-section she will curse me for the rest of my life. Let's try once more. If I fail, then we have no choice but to take her to surgery. She has signed the consent for surgery. I wonder where her husband is. My god! Look at the baby. How can a thing be so chubby and beautiful but stubborn at the same time? Guru, what kind of doctor are you? Relax her a little more. I can reposition the baby in a minute.'

I said, 'No, it's not an option, Radhika. I've given her the maximum dose and why are you being so difficult and want to do the impossible? Razak says that the baby's cord is coiled around its neck'.

'Look, I don't have time to argue with you. The baby is in distress now as Fadhuma is waking up and is feeling the pain. If mom is not happy, baby is not happy. Give her another five ml of Propofol. I just need five more minutes to do this job. I promise, if things don't work out, I will take her to the operating room on this very stretcher.' She said firmly. She sounded very confident. I had no doubts in my mind on her competence either. But then this was an unusual situation and I could sense the mild quiver in her voice.

I had to be stubborn, 'No, Radhika, no matter what, I'm not willing to give another millilitre. This medicine will slow down the baby's heart rate and I'm not prepared to take that risk.'

'If you don't want to do it, I'll do it myself,' she grabbed the syringe from my hand and pushed the remaining Propofol. Fadhuma stopped moving.

I was furious. 'Radhika, you take care of the baby. I will take care of the mother. If anything happens to Fadhuma, it's my head on the line.'

Razak said, 'Grow up, doctors. Don't act like babies. Guru, another five ml. won't kill her. Consider the situation. Radhika, can you please stick to your job? You guys, don't forget that there are others in this room, not just you two.' He glanced obliquely at Duniya. He was clearly implying that our childish behaviour was inappropriate in Duniya's presence. I was quietly observing Fadhuma's breathing on the monitor. Radhika and Razak were both looking at the baby on the ultrasound. Radhika was hard at work, sparing no effort to turn the baby around. The baby did not seem to cooperate. As a last effort, she grabbed the baby's head looking at the ultrasound monitor and tried to turn it around gently but firmly.

'Radhika, What are you trying to do? No, you can't do that. The umbilical cord is stuck there…' before Razak could complete, blood started oozing between Fadhuma's thighs. The monitor went berserk displaying all sorts of numbers.

Radhika yelled, 'Oh my god! I might have cut the cord prematurely. We need to go to the operating room right away! Razak, call the crew. Tell them we are on our way. Not sure what the baby's condition will be when we are done here. We might need to do CPR. Guru, could you also join us, please?' She grabbed the stretcher and started pushing it and running towards the operating room. Razak and I followed her.

The C-section was over in thirty minutes. The umbilical

cord was not torn, contrary to Radhika's fears. Since the umbilical cord was coiled around its neck, the baby's heart rate had slowed down to the red zone. Somewhat like suffocating by squeezing one's neck. Everything was back to normal in five minutes once she uncoiled the cord.

The incidents had unfolded rather dramatically. All of us were apprehensive about Fadhuma having a normal delivery. But none of us thought we would need to rush her to the OR and do an emergency C-section like this.

All I did was stand there. Fadhuma and the baby were doing well. The baby cried loudly right away. I stayed in the operating room for just about twenty minutes and came out to the emergency department to check on my other patients. Radhika came out after wrapping up her work, 'Guru, I would like to speak with you for a moment.'

I came out and went to the break room and brought her a cup of coffee.

'Sorry, I was a little rough on you. I was a bit stressed out.'

I did not respond. I looked at her and saw beads of sweat, as if strung together, on her forehead. She looked tired and I told her, 'Radhika, you should know better by now. Things will never be under your control at all times. Why were you so stubborn?'

Radhika gazed at the sky, 'Guru, I wanted Fadhuma to have at least one chance at a normal delivery. Just one chance. That did not happen. They are scared Guru, they really are. And, you know Rukhiya's case very well. Do you remember that I had mentioned that there were two young men who had accompanied her to the hospital? These two had threatened me that if I do a C-section, someone will die.'

I nodded.

'I thought they were trying to scare me and so I had the security escort them outside before Rukhiya's surgery.'

I looked at her, lost and not comprehending much of what she said.

'Now when I think about it, they were possibly more scared than me and the threat to my life was just posturing.'

'What do you mean by that?'

'These Sanghaali women vehemently oppose C-section. It's a virtual death sentence to some of them. This is perhaps what those young men were implying when they said that performing the C-section is nothing but taking Rukhiya's life.'

'What does that mean?'

'Guru, I'm still trying to understand their situation. We are doctors. All we care about is the mother and, of course, her baby. We never think of what happens to them after they go home. These Sanghaali women, I think their issues are totally different. I guess, their problems start when they go home. They must face their families and their community. I can only document the reasons why I need to do a C-section and do the surgery and feel good about saving both the mother and the baby. This is all good, legally and ethically from my side. The Sanghaali women, however, have to deal with completely different problems. We have no clue what those are.'

I didn't know what to say. Just then Razak came out, 'Radhika, Fadhuma is awake. She is screaming and yelling without a break. According to Duniya, she is saying that she did not know you were doing a Cesarean section, and that you got her consent without explaining to her properly. Her husband is also here, and both are making a big scene. I scooted out telling them that I will talk to you. Please do not drag me into this. You are on your own,' and left immediately.

'Guru, welcome to my world. This has been my shitty story all along. It was Abdhi then, and now this. This saga never ends—I must fight to deliver babies! I'll go inside and talk to them.' She got up to go inside.

'Shall I also come along?'

'Are you going to save me?' She laughed. 'Sure, come along. I may need your help.'

Radhika and I went into Fadhuma's room. Fadhuma's husband Hassan was also in the room. He was quite a hunk. He had grown a beard right up to his chest. The beard was dyed with mehndi. He wore a pair of jeans and something that looked like a kurta.

Radhika came to the point right away, 'Hello, I'm Dr Radhika. This is Dr Guru. I'm the doctor who operated on Fadhuma. If you have questions on what was done, I can answer them. Do you know English, or do we need Duniya here?' I shook hands with Hassan.

Hassan, who had apparently come from Sanghaala nearly two years ago replied rather angrily, 'I know enough English to talk to you. Look doctors, we're not sure how much you know about us. Let's be clear about one thing. Nobody does any surgeries on our women. We are ready to face any consequences that it might lead to. You have acted against our beliefs and cut my wife's belly open to get the baby out.' Duniya was certainly helping.

'Hassan, I did try my best to deliver the baby normally. The baby's head was up and had we been able to turn the baby around, we might still have had a normal delivery. Unfortunately, the baby did not move. I did everything I could but I was not successful. I had to operate as the baby wasn't doing so well. Please don't call it as cutting the belly open. This is a medical procedure.'

Fadhuma was crying all along and talking gibberish which I suspected that even Duniya could not understand.

'You can give any number of reasons, but this is our baby. Fadhuma is *my* wife. And you have had her sign on papers she did not understand. This is wrong. I'm not going to spare you.'

I asked him, 'Hassan, what can you do? Are you taking us to the court?'

Hassan said, 'Who are you?'

'I'm this hospital's chief of staff.'

'What does that mean?'

I was not sure how to respond. 'That means a kind of boss for all the doctors.'

'Then, are you the boss of this doctor also?'

I looked at Radhika and said, 'Yes.'

'Then why have you kept such doctors on the job? Fire her today. We know about Rukhiya's case. We will not let go of that easily.'

'Sorry, we cannot discuss Rukhiya's case here. That is against our privacy policy. Let's talk about Fadhuma.'

'Then write down my complaint. It was wrong to have operated on my wife. You had no authority to force her to do anything that she didn't want.'

'Look, write down on a piece of paper all your complaints and I'll pass that on to the concerned authorities. We have no intention of being unjust to anyone. Let us sit down and discuss calmly,' I said.

Radhika looked at me and said, 'Thanks.'

'Of course, I will,' Hassan retorted. 'We will first consult our doctor, Dr Mohammad Mohammad. And then write my complaint.'

Radhika addressed Hassan, 'Look, Hassan, I can understand your concern. It would be helpful if I speak to Fadhuma alone.'

Hassan responded, in an authoritative voice, 'What is there to talk with her? She doesn't want to speak with you, guys.'

Radhika said, 'Look, this is important. I have to speak to her alone. If you do not agree, I'll have to get the hospital security, and have you escorted outside.'

Duniya took Hassan aside to a corner on the far side of the

room and whispered something to him. Hassan started yelling in Sanghaali and walked out.

Radhika grabbed a chair and sat next to Fadhuma. I was not certain if I needed to be there. I couldn't help but feel that I have got myself into a pickle. I felt that I should have left them to their ways. As I turned around towards the door and started to leave, Radhika waved at me signaling me to stay.

I stood there.

Radhika held Fadhuma's hand and asked, 'Does it hurt?'

Duniya interpreted that to Fadhuma.

Fadhuma was about to say something but was interrupted by Duniya's voice. She didn't bother to continue.

I felt that Fadhuma didn't need an interpreter to appreciate Radhika's concern, but her language came in the way of what could have been a real moment of solace and consolation and instead, lent flippancy to it. Radhika's touch of healing appeared frivolous. Duniya kept quiet as if she had done something wrong. She probably felt that she was in the way of something that could have been so natural, so simple.

Radhika continued, 'If I had not operated, the baby would not have survived.' Duniya interpreted that again.

Fadhuma replied, 'You are thinking only about this baby. What about my future babies?'

'What I did was a C-section, not a tubal ligation. There should be no problems for you to have more children in the future.'

'Doctor, my mother has told me that babies can be taken out by cutting the belly open once or twice but not many times.'

'What does that mean? How many babies are you planning to have?'

'Everyone in our family has eight to ten children. Tell me, can you cut my belly eight times and deliver my babies?'

Radhika could not answer right away but spoke after about

a minute, 'Again, please do not call it cutting the belly. It is a medical procedure. Anyway, I've not done C-section on a single uterus ten times. It is possible that other doctors may have done that. I'll check and let you know.'

'Can you tell me if I can have children later? We plan to have ten children. Hassan says that more children means that we get more money from the government.'

Apparently, there's a law, a welfare scheme, which required the government to pay an allowance of $200 per child for low-income households that have more than two children. Radhika and I had no idea what Fadhuma was talking about.

Radhika was speechless.

'Doctor, I know that you cut our belly for the first one. You say since the first one was an operation, the second one also must be an operation. How many times can you do this? Three? Four? And then warn us that our lives will be in danger if we get pregnant again.'

Radhika was at a loss for words. I believe she did not expect this from Fadhuma—from a woman who just had a baby!

'So, in your opinion, what should I have done?' Radhika asked in a quiet voice.

'You should have left it to god and not done anything.'

'The situation would have turned serious then.'

'So, what if the situation had turned serious?'

'The baby could have died, and your life could have been at risk too.'

'If the baby were to die inside the belly, wouldn't it be easy to turn the baby?'

'But...that would be a dead baby!'

'If this baby dies for the future children, I would take that as god's will and go home. If not this baby, then the next, then the next after that...'

I was shaken for a moment. Radhika also looked stunned by this answer. She did not speak either.

The just-born infant was joyously sucking the milk from her breast. I was shocked at this utter indifference of this woman talking about the possible sacrifice of the very infant that she was breastfeeding as god's will. Duniya showed no emotions and continued to interpret Fadhuma's words.

Fadhuma's calm, detached answer angered Radhika. She said, tersely, 'Fadhuma, what kind of motherhood is this? Isn't this like sacrificing the baby in the belly to others that may or may not be born later? And isn't this illegal? What kind of a person keeps having babies for the sake of money? Who taught you to speak like this? Is it your husband?'

'Yes doctor, I know nothing. Nobody has taught me anything. We have delivered and raised children in wars and refugee camps and jails where we had no proper food and water. Did you know that?'

'Fadhuma, these are completely different situations. You are in America now.'

Fadhuma continued not paying any attention to Radhika, 'You doctors need to have patience. If you had waited, the baby would have come out by itself. You have no patience.'

Radhika persisted, 'What if your life were to be in danger?'

Fadhuma replied with no emotion whatsoever, 'That will be decided by my husband, Hassan. I know that he will protect me from any kind of harm.'

I thought it was futile. I looked at Radhika. She was getting ready to leave. Fadhuma was screaming, 'What do you people know about the consequences of your actions? Don't you ever do this to any Sanghaali mother again! I did not want to have this baby. Doctors always tell me that my life will be in danger. How do I make you understand? Whether I get surgery or not, my life will always be in danger.' There were only three of us in the room. But Duniya was interpreting Fadhuma's outbursts in the same angry tone that could be heard all over the hospital.

I wondered if Fadhuma could really say the things that she did while feeding her newborn or was it a faulty translation.

I tried to console Radhika, 'You are a good doctor. You did everything you could. The circumstances were beyond your control.'

'What can I say, Guru? She says that she is fine having a dead baby so long as it is a normal delivery! She is what, just a twenty-five-year old? She believes that she can have ten more children. Didn't I tell you? This C-section is like a death sentence to them. If they have one C-section, it is considered an affront to their motherhood. They seem set on the belief that if they can't deliver normally, then life is not worth living.'

'My god, Radhika! What kind of logic is this?'

'Guru, I only work here. I'm not an anthropologist. I've not studied their culture in depth. Neither am I interested in doing so. And I was totally unaware that this child allowance can be a factor!'

'What kind of reasoning is this? The government doles out money only if the baby lives, not when it dies.'

'Well, what do I know? She wants ten children. Since we can't operate ten times, she perhaps wants to keep her uterus strong for the remaining nine children.'

'Come on Radhika, I don't believe any mother will sacrifice her child for the sake of money.'

'Guru, we think of this as sacrifice, but they look at it as saving their next ten children. All I do is deliver babies. Sometimes normal ones. Sometimes Cesarean. It shouldn't be this difficult. I would be happy if I can stay in my job for the next three years. I do not know the reason for their shenanigans. I wish I did, my job would be much easier. Apparently, Hassan determines if she lives or dies. I'm not even clear about what he understands, and what he does not.'

I was concerned that if we stayed there any longer, she would break down. I drove Radhika home in my car.

4. O Sanghaala ...

'Sanghaali refugees started migrating to America in the 1920s. It began as a trickle at first and then went up substantially in the 90s owing to the internal strife in the country and conflicts with neighboring countries. Most of them live in Minnesota, almost to the tune of at least one hundred thousand,' Srikantha was trying to explain the demographic and social changes in Minnesota after the surge of Sanghaali immigrants. He was reading us a United Nations Report, Radhika and I listened quietly. She was picking at her food. Srikantha had cooked greens curry for supper.

Srikantha was trying to educate us. He was preparing us for a meeting scheduled for the next day with Dr Mohammad Mohammad. Srikantha continued, 'Decades of poverty, civil war, famine, violence, and ethnic cleansing have made the citizens of Sanghaala very tough and resilient. Now this freedom here has overwhelmed them, and they are having a tough time handling the very freedom that they fought for. It is like if you let a bird out of a cage after long captivity, it will bite the savior. I've been observing them since I came here, they are extremely suspicious of everyone, sometimes even paranoid. When my parents moved to England, they were first generation immigrants too. They were educated and well employed, but they did not exercise any entitlement just because they came from a foreign country. Most importantly, they listened to their doctors' advice and complied with their treatment. And these Sanghaalis? No. Never. They always act as if someone is trying to harm them.'

It was a month since Fadhuma's incident. Things had taken a turn for the worse. Hassan had called the Human Resources for as many as ten times and demanded justice. In addition, apparently, he had written long emails to the chief administrative officer of the hospital, Jack Powell. Powell had no idea what these emails meant. He asked me to either help him understand the issue or take care of it by myself. I called Hassan and enquired what exactly was he looking for and how we could help him. He demanded that copies of Fadhuma's records be sent to their family physician, Dr Mohammad Mohammad. They would seek his opinion on the appropriateness of Fadhuma's care at Amoka General Hospital. I did try to explain what happened at Amoka General Hospital as best as I could. It was as if all my explanation fell on deaf ears. Neither Fadhuma nor Hassan was convinced. Haplessly, we ended up sending copies of her medical records to Hassan.

There was a meeting scheduled in the hospital to discuss their grievances. Fadhuma and Hassan were scheduled to meet with us along with Dr Mohammad Mohammad. We were very uncomfortable meeting someone not directly related to the case. I told Fadhuma and Hassan, that it was not only inappropriate but illegal to discuss patients' case histories with parties not related with patient care. Hassan surprised us by putting an end to our legal conundrum by declaring that Dr Mohammad Mohammad was his cousin.

This precipitous morphing of Dr Mohammad into Hassan's cousin remained an enduring mystery. We had to agree to include him in our meeting. Patients have the right to bring their family members to such meetings.

Besides, now aware of the lack of English language skills of Hassan and Fadhuma combined with their questionable understanding of the gravitas of the situation, I reasoned, looking at Radhika, 'That might be the reason they are bringing along Dr Mohammad to the meeting.'

To which Radhika said, 'I could care less about who they bring along. I'm convinced that I've done nothing wrong.'

I looked at her with a mentor's pride, approving of her assertiveness. She looked the other way indicating that she detested my appreciation as rather bossy and patronizing.

'I've seen many Sanghaali immigrants while I was in Birmingham, but not to this extent,' Srikantha said.

'Why do these people move to other countries and make our lives miserable?' Radhika deplored.

'Radhika, we have no moral right to raise this question.'

'But we are different. We went to college. We all have jobs. We pay our taxes. We are not refugees. And we have not illegally crossed the border like the Mexicans. Once they are here in America, they should live like Americans. If they continue to display their entitlement—likes, dislikes and what not—and turn into stumbling blocks, how are we supposed to do our jobs?'

Srikantha smiled, 'We eat rice and curry. Radhika, are we living like Americans here?'

'I don't think you guys are getting my point. You do what you want in your home. It's not okay to decline scientifically proven treatments like C-sections in the name of faith. What do we do then?'

'We can argue both ways, Radhika. You may be familiar with a group called Jehovah's Witness. They never consent to blood transfusions even when lives are in grave danger. Well, even in India, people don't always agree with what doctors recommend, especially surgeries.'

'There is no point in talking to you two. My only concern is that I should be able to do my job with no hassle.' Radhika got up, went in to her room and locked the door.

Srikantha looked at me. I looked at him hoping that he may have more information to share. I asked him, 'Do you know anything about this Dr Mohammad Mohammad?'

'Not much, but as far as I know he is kind of a godfather to all the Sanghaalis here. He has been living in the Minneapolis area for the last fifteen years. He did his Residency here. Of course, he is a Sanghaali and is believed to understand their special health needs. In fact, this was the reason that the Minnesota Department of Health hired him as an immigrant health officer in 2003. He has since quit the job and was moonlighting in other hospitals. For the last four years, he is into private practice. Almost all the Sanghaali residents of Minneapolis consult with him. There are also some shady secrets about him.'

I continued to listen.

'It is rumoured that in his clinic, he cuts Sanghaali women below. About six months ago, there was an article about him in *Tribune*. He apparently has ties with some Sanghaali terrorist organization. It was mentioned in the article that he recruits Sanghaali young men from Minneapolis and sends them to Syria, Sudan and Sanghaala to fight against their governments. In fact, this article was written by another Sanghaali. Dr Mohammad Mohammad took the author and *The Tribune* to court and filed for damages. He won the case. He is supposed to be highly active and rather flamboyant in their community.'

I said, 'Sounds like a character straight out of a Tom Clancy novel. You had mentioned that you did not know much about him?'

'Everyone living in this area will be aware of at least this information about Dr Mohammad Mohammad. Just Google his name.'

'This "cutting below" that you referred to, is this circumcision? Do women get this thing done too?'

'You work in the emergency department and you ask me?'

'I have heard about it. I haven't seen it myself, even once.'

'Dude, that is a sexy topic. I do not know much about it. You must ask Radhika. It's getting late. I've got to go. I've outpatient clinic tomorrow.' Srikantha went to bed.

I was curious about Dr Mohammad Mohammad and wanted to learn more about him. I came up with about one hundred and sixty-four hits when I googled 'Dr Mohammad Mohammad Minneapolis'.

Dr Mohammad Mohammad migrated to America in 1993. He wasn't a refugee like other Sanghaali immigrants in Minnesota. Apparently in the seventies, his father had worked as Secretary of Commerce under Syed Abdallah, the notorious dictator. Mohammad was born in 1958, the year Sanghaala got its independence. His elementary schooling happened at the boarding schools of Italy and England. In the fifties his father served as a high-ranking officer in the Sanghaali army at a time when Sanghaala was an Italian Colony. In 1972, Syed Abdallah came to power in a military coup. Mohammad's father was very much impressed by Abdallah's socialist ideas and with a strong conviction that Abdallah's socialism held a bright future for his country, he started serving the Abdallah government. Abdallah had a grand vision for his country. He was greatly influenced by Karl Marx's 'Scientific Socialism'. His vision was to have socialism and Islam as the two main pillars that framed the identity of Sanghaala as a country. His statue stood grandly shoulder-to-shoulder with those of Stalin, Lenin and Marx in the country's capital, Dahir-Bar.

Another important change brought about by Abdallah was to make the Sanghaali language the country's national language. This policy made the Sanghaali language mandatory in its schools, colleges and government offices. In the chaos that these policy changes engendered, it was difficult for the administrative class to shed its influence from the colonial languages of Italian and English that were in usage for decades. All the important and plush jobs went to those who were well-versed in Italian and English. The Sanghaali language remained a common man's language. No one, least of all people like Mohammad's father who served in government jobs and who educated their children in Italian and English, was convinced that higher education was possible in the Sanghaali language and children could have a bright future there. The very freedom that they fought for did not make their country worthwhile for their children to have a bright future. Mohammad's father sent him to England's boarding schools. He then went on to study at the Cambridge Medical School.

Further details about him were hazy. He had somehow managed to migrate to Italy. It is rumoured that he was radicalized around this time. For someone who was pub hopping in a pair of denims and Harley jackets, he had suddenly transformed into a character straight out of a radical's playbook, at least in appearance: shaven moustache, hanging beard down to the chest, mascaraed eyes, tikhiya on the head. He was arrested in connection to a couple of small terrorist operations in Milan but was later acquitted for lack of evidence. He moved back to Sanghaala after a year and started practicing Medicine there. Further details were few and sketchy.

Those were the last days of Syed Abdallah's rule. There were escalating internal conflicts all over the country. Small terrorist groups across the country challenged the country's sovereignty. There was a likelihood of a war with the neighboring Ethiopia or its ally America or with both in tandem. Mohammad's father had suspected very early that there was a clear existential crisis for the Abdallah government. He advised his son, 'Governments which come to power with guns in their hand are never secure. Leave this country if you desire a better future.'

The very next year Dr Mohammad Mohammad had enrolled at the University of Minnesota for his residency.

I culled all this information about Dr Mohammad and Sanghaala from Wikipedia. The authenticity of this information was, of course, questionable, and I was uncertain whether to believe it or not. The very fact that there is information on Dr Mohammad online was a merit in itself. In fact, I typed mine, Radhika's and Srikantha's name. Sure enough, nothing came up.

I got a hold of the *Tribune* article that Srikantha had referred to. There were some discrepancies in the details that Srikantha narrated. There was no mention of Dr Mohammad going to Sanghaala to recruit young men from Minnesota. Instead it talked about various fund-raising activities he organized in Minnesota, flying to Dahir-Bar and personally handing over a big amount of money to a terrorist by the name of Aftikar. There were heated discussions about this incident all over the internet and on social media. The person who authored that article had clarified that his article was well researched. Apparently,he had hacked Mohammad's computer and accessed an email sent to Aftikar. The email supposedly talked about Dr Mohammad affirming that their enemies' destruction was their goal. Later, in another article *Tribune* published its editor's mea culpa. The editor had cited the FBI findings that Dr Mohammad Mohammad was organizing these fundraisers for an NGO who rehabilitated Sanghaali refugees in the city. Dr Mohammad Mohammad was acquitted of all charges and, in addition, *Tribune* offered him a compensation of twenty-five thousand dollars. That this Mohammad could go up to the FBI's attention made me more curious about the man.

I looked out of the window. It was a moonlit night. It was muggy and hot inside the house. I opened the window. Being the month of June, even the breeze that drifted inside at ten in the night was warm. There was deathly silence all around. No sound of a vehicle honking, no bird calls, not even the buzz of flies. This weather would only last for the next four months. Later, it will be bone chilling cold. One cannot venture out without an armor of coats. The cold would be intense enough to freeze tears.

What am I doing here? In a town like Amoka fighting to save people who do not want to be saved—people cavalier enough to drive drunk in below temperature on dangerous icy roads, people swimming in enough alcohol to make a breathalyzer tipsy, people reciprocating with a 'Fuck you dude' just because they had to wait for an hour in the emergency department before getting their nasty head gashes sutured.

Boy, I hate my job!

Is this why I am seeking out Mohammad Mohammad? To give myself a worthy excuse to sleep better at night?

Does this elevate my job? Does it invest more nobility into it?

Why am I doing this?

Is this because Amoka is in America?

5. Dr Mohammad Mohammad

The next morning, I was getting ready for work. I didn't have to see patients in the ER. My calendar showed a meeting with Dr Mohammad Mohammad lined up for the first three hours of the day. This was my administrative day.

Radhika was up early at five and feverishly washing the dishes in the sink.

I handed her a cup of fresh coffee and asked, 'Did you talk to Giri?'

'I did. He cannot make sense of anything that is going on around here. He naively asks me, like a child, "You haven't done anything wrong, have you?" What can I tell him? Guru, I've been wanting to ask you for a while. Why do we need to meet this Mohammad Mohammad guy? The complaint has been filed by Fadhuma and Hassan. My business is with Fadhuma. Technically I don't have to talk to Hassan either. Then, why not handle everything officially? Why doesn't Dr Mohammad come through the proper channels? Why do we have to meet with random people, as if we did something wrong? '

I could not come up with a response. I thought for a moment. I felt that Radhika made sense. 'Radhika, our best bet is to exercise restraint and be a little tactful. After all, we do not have to apologize to anyone. All we need to do is explain that what we did was what is considered as standard of care. He will understand. He is also a physician. He also underwent residency training here in America, just like us.'

'I do not know who understands what. My gut says that this is not going to be as simple as you think.'

I assured her rather pompously, 'Don't worry Radhika, I'm here for you. I'll take care of everything.'

She laughed and left. It was obvious that she neither had the belief in my words nor the bravado they sought to express.

Meanwhile I noticed that Srikantha was getting ready to leave. I told him, 'I need your help. Please make yourself available at ten. Call me if possible. I will keep my mobile on.'

Srikantha said, 'Dude, keep me out of this. I'm an Internist. I have no idea about child births, let alone Sanghaali ones. If you need any help with some research and pulling up relevant background information, I am your guy,' and left.

As soon as I arrived at the hospital, I went directly to the conference room on the third floor. Radhika went to see a couple of her patients. To me, the most perplexing part in this sordid affair was that Dr Smith as the senior-most physician in Radhika's department had nothing to say. Dr Smith has been practicing in Amoka long before any of us came to this town. I had reached out to him the previous week thinking that he might have some answers.

'Look Guru, I'm gonna be blunt. I've seen Amoka change colours in the last ten years. I've stopped treating *them*. I have heard that their anatomy is different. And weird. Weird maybe a politically incorrect term. I don't want to pretend to understand their unique distortions or anomalies or by whatever fancy words you call it. "Female Genital Mutilation." Yuck! I hate even saying that word. I am too old for this bullshit. At my age buddy, I have no interest or the energy to learn either. I'm not sure if this whole business of "cutting" is their culture or their religion. I always fear that I may end up doing something wrong. And I'm very close to retiring! As the old saying goes, "You should earn your keep". I simply am not looking for any trouble. That is why you have Radhika and Razak. Please ask them.' He washed his hands off.

Dr Mohammad Mohammad arrived ten minutes prior to schedule. We had asked Duniya to attend the meeting as well. I had invited Razak to the meeting. He declined initially but later, when I told him that he didn't have much of a choice since his name is also on the medical records, he had agreed to come with some reluctance.

Ever since I woke up in the morning, a mysterious anxiety came over me, I felt uneasy and nauseated. I had used the restroom four times. I couldn't help feeling like an upstart, not equipped to prepare for a meeting like this. Had I known that Mohammad was coming over to discuss only the case of his cousin I would have possibly felt differently. After all he was also a physician, a kindred spirit for most of us. This sketchy awareness that Mohammad was not just a physician, but perhaps had other indulgences made us apprehensive and intimidated. Besides Razak and I weren't fully convinced that Radhika had followed the standard of care. We thought she had stepped out of her comfort zone when Fadhuma's care needed expertise such as Version. I had not seen Radhika try a Version before.

Could she have agreed with Hassan and Fadhuma and not done the surgery regardless of the outcome?

I didn't know what my role was. What kind of power did I have as the chief of staff? Nobody had explained this to me and I couldn't find the right answer in the hospital bylaws. I had contacted the hospital board before the meeting and they had given the go-ahead. But should I have reached out to our legal counsel? Why did we need lawyers for this kind of a meeting? Isn't this supposed to be an informal, cordial affair?'

I could sense that I was sweating lightly before the meeting. And I had two more restroom visits after coming to the hospital.

Dr Mohammad Mohammad looked pretty much the way I had imagined him to be. I had looked at his picture on the computer the previous night. His beard was grayer than that in the picture. He was dressed in a spiffy suit. The tint on his eyeglasses quite clearly adapted to the ambient light inside. He held a Starbucks coffee cup in his hand. Fadhuma and Hassan were with him. There was no sign of the baby.

'Hello, how do you do?' Dr Mohammad had a clipped British accent.

I shook his hands, 'Please take your seat,' and addressed all three. 'Would you like some coffee?' even as I was pouring a cup for myself. Dr Mohammad flashed his Starbucks cup. The coffee in the Styrofoam cup that I had filled from the old coffeemaker in the conference room looked bland against his bubbly cappuccino. Radhika declined the coffee and sat down and straightened her eyeglasses. She looked sharp in her new suit and makeup. Razak arrived a bit late and took his seat. Dr Mohammad spotted Razak's name tag hanging down his neck and extended his hand, 'O Dr Razak, assalam walekum brother!' Razak hesitated for a moment, and said, 'Hi.'

I adjusted my tie knot and addressed the group, 'I call the meeting to order. Tell me gentlemen and ladies, how may I help you?'

Dr Mohammad Mohammad smiled, 'Hello doctors, it is unclear as to who can help whom, who should be helping whom, but let us help each other.' I was not expecting this philosopher-like posturing to my general conversational opening to the meeting. I simply nodded and looked at Radhika and Razak. They stared back at me. An awkward silence filled the room along with a strong odor emanating from Hassan and Fadhuma. Dr Mohammad was chewing gum and looking at us with a smile on his face.

I thought to myself, 'This guy can create a great first

impression on people.' It occurred to me that this meeting could drag along with no end in sight. I said, 'Dr Mohammad, let's cut to the chase here. Why are we here today? What is the agenda for this meeting? If Hassan and Fadhuma have grievances against us, we have a department that can handle them. We have our own Standard Operating Procedure. Instead, you have asked us to meet here. We have squeezed some time out of our schedule to get to this meeting. Please tell us, what can we do to help you?'

Mohammad got up from his chair and said, 'Doctor, are you suggesting we come through the proper channels? Certainly, by all means. I can find the right channels.'

Radhika curtly raised her voice, 'Dr Mohammad, let us stop this nonsense and get it over with.'

'Dr Radhika, have you read Sun Tzu's *Art of War*?'

'What?' Radhika was taken aback a little.

'*Art of War*? Sun Tzu? Do you know what he says? "In order to defeat your enemy, you must become your enemy first."'

'What's your point?' I intervened. 'Are you implying that we are your enemies? I'm sorry, we won't get anywhere with this kind of attitude.'

'Well, you might not consider us as your enemies, but we may not be generous enough to share the same feeling. I bring this up because in our Sanghaali community, there may be a few who may hate you, right? And for their own reasons ... isn't it?

None of us spoke.

'You see where I'm coming from? I agree "enemy" may be a bit melodramatic. If you want to take care of our patients, you need to know them better. I'm here today to make you aware of that. If you have no idea who you are treating, there can be a lot of misunderstandings.'

I got a sense that if left to himself this guy can go on and on. Before I could say anything, Radhika interjected, 'Let's keep this discussion confined to Fadhuma. We have enough resources to learn about the Sanghaali community. I'll read about them and if I do not understand, I will reach out to you on my own.'

'Ok, let's start from there. Alright? Let me ask you a question. Do you watch Bollywood films?'

His elliptical style of speaking around the topic annoyed me. 'Dr Mohammad, I think it is better not to lose focus as much as possible.'

'I'm asking this question precisely because these things are related. Please do not get me wrong. But you should know one thing, we Sanghaalis watch a lot of Bollywood movies. I watched a movie last year with my daughter. I don't recall the title of the movie. The lead star of the movie is a college student who gets coached over the internet to deliver a baby with the help of a vacuum cleaner.'

Radhika smiled, 'Dr Mohammad, what's your point? Are you suggesting that I use a vacuum cleaner?'

'Of course not! That is in the movies, and this is real life. All I'm trying to say is that this phenomenon of childbirth is so natural and so beautiful. This has been happening for a long time and will continue in the future. Whether it is Cesarean or Vacuum or anything else, it *will* happen. As doctors, all we do is grease and ease. And that pain! Ah that labour pain! The *fifth* vital sign; we control it a little.'

'Dr Mohammad, just because things were done in a certain way in the past does not mean we should do the same now. Do you know how safe the deliveries are now? I can reel out the statistics to show this clearly.'

'Ok. Statistics. Ah, the numbers! I love numbers. Dr Radhika, do you know what percentage of the American babies are delivered by Cesarean section? '

'I can't tell you right off the bat. Maybe 10 to 15 per cent?'

'32 per cent! I am not pulling this number from my ar... sorry.' He winked. 'This is the WHO report. This includes all women. This number is much more for Sanghaali women. I've not come here to bore you with these numbers. For a variety of reasons, in America, C-sections are done much more frequently than in other countries. There might be plenty of reasons for this, including Friday evening date nights of OB GYN docs. Do not laugh, there are lots of surveys to prove this. Anyway, let us not solve all of world's problems today. Fadhuma, who's here, is my cousin Hassan's wife. What was your reason for doing a C-section on her?'

Radhika said, 'I cannot discuss this without Fadhuma and Hassan's consent.'

Then Dr Mohammad talked to Hassan for a bit in Sanghaali.

I said, 'Dr Mohammad, whatever it is that you wish to speak, please do so in English. We have Duniya here to interpret.'

Then Hassan said, 'Dr Mohammad can ask any question on my behalf.'

Radhika said, 'I've documented everything in the chart. She had a breech; the baby's head was upright in her uterus. Usually it is down, as you are aware. We tried everything we could, including external Cephalic Version, which is to turn the baby upside down, without success. We didn't have any choice other than C-section.'

Dr Mohammad asked, 'Dr Razak, do you agree?'

Razak said, 'Yes. I was there too. Now, Dr Mohammad, why do we have to answer all of your questions?'

'So that you don't have to answer in the court later, Dr Razak. Anyway, ma'am, on the records you have also documented that since Fadhuma was *cut* below, it is impossible for her to have a normal delivery.'

Radhika was annoyed. 'Guru, how is this related to the case in any way? I will not talk about it. What's going on here? Who is he to question my competence? Is this a courtroom? Should we be sitting here tolerating all his shenanigans?'

I spoke to Radhika in Kannada, 'Radhika, the board members have given their approval to this meeting. Please cooperate. Let's have a quick chat and wrap up. I do not know what his agenda is. Razak is here, anyway. Srikantha is one of the members of the medical staff. I'll page him. We can answer questions that we would like to and ignore the others. Let us tell everyone that a provisional meeting was held, send out the minutes and make this official. I'll also inform Karla. Once these board members read these minutes, they will get out of your hair. This can save us the hassle of internal enquiry and outside review. What do you say?'

Dr Mohammad looked at us and laughed. 'Hello, now I've to ask for an interpreter.'

Radhika did not say anything. She and Razak excused themselves for five minutes and left the room. Once they returned, Radhika said, 'Alright, I'm ready. But only on one condition. I will only speak about those issues that are relevant to Fadhuma's case. I don't want to listen to any lecture on Sanghaali culture.' I paged Srikantha and asked him to get there. I needed at least another doctor to get the right quorum to the meeting. But he did not answer at all.

Radhika spoke, probably realizing that there is no point in waiting for Srikantha anymore, 'Ok, without getting into too many details, I can only say this much. But, before we start, we all need to know that we shall be discussing Fadhuma's C-section. Has she consented to discuss her case?' and looked at Fadhuma. Fadhuma said yes once Duniya translated Radhika's question to her. I had completely forgotten the fact that Fadhuma did not understand English. This entire meeting was supposed to be about Fadhuma, it was surprising that everyone except her spoke and made their points.

Radhika had to respond, 'Fadhuma has had a circumcision. She cannot have a normal delivery.'

Dr Mohammad said calmly, 'Don't get me wrong. I have spoken to Fadhuma about this. What she has had is sunna, where they take out just a little skin outside the vagina, to be specific the vulvar area. There will not be any problems for her to have a natural delivery. Child births are difficult only for people who have had Pharaonic circumcision which is otherwise called infibulation. Do you know what that means?' he directed his question to both Radhika and Razak.

They shook their heads. I said that I did not know anything about it.

Mohammad said, 'I apologize for discussing these sensitive issues here. In Pharaonic circumcision, all soft tissues in and around the genitals including clitoris and labia are excised and the edges of the vulva are stitched together. Only a small opening is left for passage of urine and another one for menstrual blood flow. One could say it is a kind of physiologic chastity belt. Those who are totally ignorant of these practices think of them as cruel and a severe type of female circumcision. It is not clear where this practice originated. One of the beliefs is that this started in the jungles of Egypt to prevent the rapes of women from marauders. All Sanghaali girls have had some sort of circumcision. There are several reasons for this. Community pressure or peer pressure is one of them and possibly the most important one. It's like everyone does that and so shall we. And the second reason is that, all Pharaons are virgins unless proven otherwise. In fact, mothers on their own initiative get Pharaonic circumcision done to their daughters to protect their virginity. Let alone bear children, these girls cannot even have intercourse. Sometimes they need surgical procedure called deinfibulation before childbirth. Yes, Pharaons always find a way around, have sex and get pregnant, which you Americans classify legally as rape because of the act. What can I say? Law is only provincial.' We looked at each other as the only American in the room was Dr Mohammad himself.

I asked, 'Is this a religious practice?'

'Doctor, it is interesting that you ask this question. In my opinion, nowhere in Islam is this practice prescribed. In fact, several religious clerics oppose such practices. Only a few women may contend that getting a Sunna done is a religious practice. As they say, "Belief: To each, his own".'

Razak, 'Not true. This has nothing to do with Islam, let's not bring in religion here.'

'Dr Razak, I thought you did not know how to speak at all! Look, I said the same thing. Did I not say that religious clerics oppose this practice? But isn't it fun to put a religious spin on everything? The idea of religion is scarier than faith or culture.'

I was getting a feeling that the discussion was going a bit off-track. Even Radhika who had professed to discuss only Fadhuma's case and nothing else, sat there listening with complete attention to Mohammad's words.

'Look. I'm a physician too. I've given several seminars on this topic. This practice is illegal in America. In the seventies, people's awareness of Sanghaala was through *National Geographic* magazines and the BBC. And even this awareness, which was not flattering to the country, was mainly centered around two things. The misery of its people with pictures of young children with bloated abdomen and emaciated bodies displayed prominently, and, of course, this practice of female circumcision. Back then, everyone assumed that these are medieval practices of underdeveloped tribes living in caves. Now these people live right here in America and, they practice what they believe. Here in Minnesota, you see circumcised women visiting hospitals. It is tough for doctors, who are ignorant of this practice of circumcision, to handle their pregnancies, and their child births. Please excuse me, if this makes you doctors uncomfortable, how would Fadhuma and Duniya feel about it? Fadhuma and Hassan are simple folks. They are not smart enough to speak with you. That's why they come to me and I represent them. Now, you decide if this discussion is relevant to Fadhuma's case or not.'

It seemed a little surreal and I felt I was in some unfamiliar world. I was at a loss for words. Radhika herself continued, 'Dr Mohammad, thank you for enlightening us with all this information. But I did a C-section not just because of her abnormal genital anatomy but the baby was a breech. No matter how hard we tried, normal delivery would have been impossible.'

'Dr Radhika, let me ask you a question. Is the baby's life more important than the mother's?'

'Both are equally important to me.'

'Ah, this is how America has brainwashed you. On the way from Minneapolis to here, there were at least ten billboards. Each one displayed anti-abortion messages. These neon-lit billboards probably sponsored by local churches—that looked like commercial—almost proclaimed that if you get an abortion you'll go to hell. Since when did the baby turn more important than the mother? When did we forget that someone pregnant is also a human being? Why do you spend millions of dollars trying to save a five-hundred-gram baby born to a teenage mom? Just because it is against your religious beliefs? Isn't it a Christian belief that people go to hell if they get an abortion? Why do we not circumspect why a mother would take the extreme step of sacrificing the baby in her belly? Instead we tag such women as murderers and Sanghaalis oppose such blind labeling.' Radhika remained stunned. Seeing this, Razak chimed in, 'Dr Mohammad, we doctors are always trying to save lives but when the life of a mother or a baby is threatened, we have to do whatever we can. Shouldn't we?'

'Tell me frankly. Was Fadhuma's life in any danger here? Or let me ask the same question in a different way, if you decided to get a court order to get this C-section done on her if it was against her beliefs, do you think any judge would have granted you the permission to perform C-section against her will?'

'We can't discuss just keeping this one case as a reference. There was nothing wrong in saving the baby here.'

'Ah! this is clearly what I call cultural imperialism. It's not just the current pregnancy that is important to the Sanghaalis. But they care for their next ten pregnancies. And so is the mother who can bear them. They value the land more than its harvest. They oppose anything that reduces their fertility. So much so, that they are ready to sacrifice their pregnancies. Just like the way weeds are cleared from the land before healthy crops can be grown. They oppose America's health care system that exploits this science to cater to its "lesser the better" culture. But they are not able to express this sentiment. It is somehow gone into their heads that only weak women get operated to have children. I'm only asking you to respect their beliefs.'

Radhika asked, 'Is there a connection between this and the government's child allowance?'

'How dare you? You are a woman too. Do you seriously believe that a woman sacrifices her baby for money?' Mohammad's voice was shaking.

Radhika did not flinch, 'Fadhuma herself told me about it.'

'What would she know? She is an illiterate woman.'

'Exactly my point.'

'What do you mean?'

'Dr Mohammad, don't you think that this child allowance the government pays for every child is more relevant and makes a more compelling case for her to have more children than any of these cultural reasons that you are giving us?'

'You can make whatever sense you wish to out of this but let them be themselves.'

'Meaning?'

'If she does not want an operation, don't do it.'

'The baby has rights too.'

'That baby is yet to be born, doctor.'

I was a bit shaken by this whole line of argument, 'As a doctor what do you feel about this whole affair?'

'I don't feel anything. I serve my clients. My job is to serve them by giving them what they are looking for. Do you know my clinic is also licensed for doing abortions?'

I sensed that this fellow is not an ordinary person. He does abortions. He has declared a virtual war against Cesarean sections. May be he does circumcisions too. I asked him softly, 'Why don't you deliver babies?'

'Do you think that I haven't given it a thought? But what can I say? You can't teach new tricks to an old dog.'

This meeting needed a closure. Not knowing what else to say, 'Dr Mohammad, now what do we have to do to make Fadhuma and Hassan happy? Should we apologize? Should we assure them that we will be more sensitive the next time? Would they believe us if we did so?'

Radhika, who was quiet till then said, 'Guru, I have done nothing wrong. I'm not going to apologize to anyone. Dr Mohammad, I do not know who you are. I think you are a big crook. You have brainwashed these people. No matter what, I'm not going to change the way I practice Medicine. It's not just me but all the other doctors and the medical community agree that I am doing the right thing. I'm not going to apologize to anyone. Neither will I promise anything about my future practice. Do whatever you guys want to do. If you want to take us to court, go ahead.' And she got up.

Hassan, 'You have to apologize to us. You have operated

on my wife. And not just that, you should not do any more operations on us Sanghaalis in the future. If you do, there will be consequences.'

Radhika said, 'What? Will you sue us?'

Hassan replied, 'No. Lives will be lost. Heads will roll.'

'Do whatever you want. I'll keep doing my job. You can look for other doctors if you don't like me. How dare you threaten me? I can report you.'

Hassan was continuously blabbering in Sanghaali.

Dr Mohammad said, 'Ma'am, nothing can be accomplished with this rage. He is not a harmful person. I will talk to Hassan. Give this matter some thought. Nobody is dictating anything to you. Keep today's discussion in mind when you do your work in the coming days. And everyone can be happy.'

Radhika said, 'Whatever happens, I'm not going to apologize.'

'In that case you shall be responsible for any disasters that may happen in the future. Thanks for your time,' he picked up his water bottle, drank from it and walked out. Fadhuma and Hassan followed him. A little later, Duniya also left. I noticed that on the sign-up sheet for the day, she had not signed her name.

6. Postpartum Depression

Dr Mohammad Mohammad was right.

Within three weeks, some dramatic events beyond our wildest imagination, beyond anybody's comprehension happened in Amoka.

A news report was published in *Amoka Daily Herald*, the town's only newspaper:

> A twenty-four-year-old Sanghaali woman named Rukhiya Abu-Bakr was found dead in her home. She had hanged herself. Paramedics had rushed to the scene when her husband Abdhi Abu-Bakr called 911 for emergency assistance. Despite their best efforts, they could not save the woman. Police are conducting further investigation.

In a strange way, I was expecting this news in the paper. I was working in the emergency department on the day Rukhiya died. Since the hospital owned the ambulance, I had expected that the paramedics who responded to the emergency call would bring Rukhiya to the hospital. According to the protocol, even if Rukhiya had the faintest signs of life, she had to be brought to the hospital. After hearing on the ambulance radio: 'Amoka ambulance arriving at the scene for a twenty-four-year-old woman ... who is unresponsive after an attempt to hang herself from the ceiling ... no further history obtained because of significant language barrier'—I was anticipating Rukhiya to show up. I had the nurses ready, with X-ray and lab technicians on standby.

Rukhiya never arrived.

The paramedics who returned after completing the paperwork said, 'Doc, I wish you were there. You should have seen the chaos. It was quite a scene. When we went there, they had already brought her body down and had laid her on the floor. Talk about keeping the crime scene intact, doc. They had even started to pray! When we said we were going to check her pulse to confirm if she was alive or dead, her husband looked at us strangely and started crying. I initially thought it was ok, the poor guy is grieving or what not. But you know, I got to do my job, right? I told him, I hear you fella. But I got to know what happened so that I can write my report, you know. But the strangest thing happened, doc. Poor fella who was praying and all, started swaying his body back and forth. I thought he was having a seizure or something. I told him straight out, "Hey buddy, all we are trying to do is to help the lady in case she is still alive." To which he said, "Please do not do anything else. It's been a long time since she died. Where are the police? I called the emergency only so that the police can come and do their work. Why are you here?" As if police are the only ones who show up when you call 911. But I have to say doc, I didn't disagree with him and all, but we had to do our jobs. We called the coroner and waited. Once he arrived, we got the hell out of there.'

The newspaper report read:

> The deceased Rukhiya is survived by her husband Abu-Bakr and her two-month-old infant. When our reporter contacted her husband, he refused to comment. We have learnt from unconfirmed sources that the police had responded to few domestic disturbance calls during the last month. Police said that they were considering all angles. When specifically asked about domestic abuse, they said they haven't ruled out anything. It is still unclear at this

> point whether Rukhiya's suicide was due to repetitive abuse by her husband. Her husband Abdhi was arrested and released after a day of interrogation. Minneapolis' well-known physician Dr Mohammad Mohammad has bailed him out.

I had not uttered a word. I did not know what to say. I was thinking about how Radhika would react to the news.

As soon as she heard the news, Radhika had rushed to the hospital. 'Oh my god, Guru! It's a disaster. Did you watch the news? I'm done. They will deport me to India.' She started rambling and her eyes welled up. 'Guru, has anybody mentioned in the news that she killed herself because I performed a C-section on her? What do they mean by all angles? They said that her husband was physically abusing her, and she killed herself unable to tolerate that. Even when the police interrogated her husband Abdhi, he didn't say a word about the C-section. If she didn't want the C-section, she could have been more assertive and not consented to it at all, right? Instead, if she takes her own life like this, what shall I do?' she wailed.

I was at a loss for words and softly whispered, out of earshot of the patients and nurses around, 'Don't cry Radhika, people may think that you did something wrong,' and led her to the breakroom.

She appeared extremely traumatized, 'Guru, let's say that Abdhi tells the police that his wife took her life because I performed the Cesarean section against her wishes, where would that lead? Are they going to arrest me? My god! I can't believe that she is dead. I can't understand what I did wrong. You were with me. You will testify for me, right?' and she started crying again.

She seemed convinced that Rukhiya had committed suicide because of the Cesarean section. When it comes to death, reactions can be varied. I work in the emergency department where dealing with deaths, many a times sudden or unexpected, is a part of the job. I have seen rare, almost surreal ways in which people die. I've seen burly young men come in with minor fever or body aches and die of something like dengue fever or pneumonia. I have seen patients walk in for what seems to be trivial migraine, get a couple of painkillers, and stroke out in the hospital parking lot! Hence, like all emergency physicians, I assume the worst while treating my patients. My job is not just to rule in or rule out a heart attack in a patient presenting to ED with chest pain, but also to assure him that he won't have a heart attack once he is out of my ED. This is a statistical game that I play. Most of the times I play it well. Thanks to all the tools of modern medicine. So, when patients come with headache, chest pain, abdominal pain or any sundry complaints, I end up doing all sorts of tests whether they are needed or not. It is easy to confirm the presence of a disease, but insanely difficult to confirm the absence of it. We fancily call it as ruling in and ruling out. I do see a lot of hypochondriacs who strongly believe that there is something wrong with them despite ample evidence to the contrary as shown by a battery of tests. They want something to be wrong with them and are very much disappointed to hear that all the tests are normal. Even god cannot convince that there is nothing wrong with them!

It is perhaps for this reason that we emergency physicians believe in the 'act of god' towards unexpected medical gaffes. If a patient who is given antibiotics for ear ache later dies after gushing blood and pus out from his ears, we console ourselves with a prophetic resignation that the patient died because he might have had brain abscess or mastoiditis. It is a sad fact that we accept death easily premised on a rationale that anyone who comes to the ER might end up dying. This easy acceptance of death is unfortunate but something necessary to maintain our sanity. However, Rukhiya's death did shake me up a little. It was not so much her death but the reason that drove her to it that troubled me.

Radhika, on the contrary, is an obstetrician. Everything in her work has a happy ending. The ambience is that of joy and anticipation of a new arrival. Mothers who sport a grin despite their excruciating labour pains, fathers who are ready to welcome the new born with a video camera, a home with grandpa and grandma waiting to welcome the new family member with its nursery ready, the excitement of selecting a name, and nurses getting an imprint of the infant's feet on a white paper. There is no sadness here. Even the mother forgets the pain she has gone through. Only merriment everywhere. It's as if there is no such thing as death. This is possibly the reason that if there is a death—of an infant or of a mother—the doctors and the medical staff treating them are devastated, some go into depression, and some even quit their jobs.

Therefore, Radhika's reaction to Rukhiya's death was quite different from mine. I suspected that my senses were numbed due to working in the emergency department as compared to Radhika's. At that time, it occurred to me that I may not cry even when my parents die.

I must admit that even in that situation, I suspected the sincerity of Radhika's grief. In retrospect, I've felt that this was a shameful thing to do.

I sincerely thought that her grief was not so much for Rukhiya's death as much as for the fear that she may be responsible for her death and anger towards the way the events unfolded. She didn't want to even imagine her life as a physician in India. The ridiculous possibility of an investigation which could lead to her deportation had made her miserable. So, her crying and wailing was more due to anger and helplessness rather than gloom over Rukhiya's death. If she so much as even got a hint of my thoughts, her reaction would be par for the course: she would agonize with extreme guilt holding herself accountable for Rukhiya's death. Knowing this, I tried to console her to the most extent possible.

We were yet to recover from this shock when another incident happened. Fadhuma drove to Minneapolis alone from Amoka and in broad daylight, even as people around watched, jumped into the Mississippi river. She had driven slowly to the bridge, parked her car on the side of the road, walked gingerly and jumped into the water. There were people all around who watched her jump. Every little detail of this event was telecast on TV. I couldn't help but feel that among those who just stood there watching her jump, even if one had ventured to help, she might very well have been saved.

After someone from the crowd called the police, their department's expert divers arrived on the scene and brought her body ashore. When the local TV interviewed a passerby near the incident and asked 'You could have tried to save her instead of taking a video of the incident, right?' he replied sheepishly, 'Are you kidding me? I shot that video from fifteen feet away. I was afraid that the bridge may explode once she jumps. Who knows what they hide underneath that garb?'

I accepted Rukhiya's death, against my instinct, as a coincidence. I coaxed myself into believing it.

Now Fadhuma's dead. And how? In the middle of the day, in a busy place, by jumping into the Mississippi river! All the local channels are playing this on and on. They suspected her to be a suicide bomber!

It was apparent to anyone that these two deaths were related in some way. I felt bad for Rukhiya and Fadhuma's deaths but as the hospital's chief of staff I didn't know what I was supposed to do? Should I call a staff meeting? Should I talk to the board? Should I contact both Hassan and Abdhi? Should I consult Dr Mohammad Mohammad for advice?

I wondered what Radhika would say about this second

death. She was perhaps clueless. We had not met in the recent past due to our overlapping work schedules. I decided to call her. There was no answer.

Two days had passed. Radhika and I had not seen each other yet. Since I was working the night shifts, when I was at work she would be at home, and when she worked, I stayed home. And she was not answering my calls. When I checked with Srikantha, he said, 'I haven't been able to get hold of her either. But I feel she is handling the situation well.' I was not able to talk much with Srikantha too.

The newspapers and the TV channels had not mentioned our names or that of Amoka General Hospital. The media had not established any connection between Fadhuma's and Rukhiya's deaths. We had a gloomy sense that something bad was about to happen. The impact and the scale of this was something we couldn't predict, and it made us even more helpless.

I thought hard, but I could not figure out what to do. My wiser instincts prevailed, and I kept to myself and my job.

On that day, when I came home, Radhika had finished her supper and was busy with some kitchen chores. I wondered if she was the same person who came running to me after Rukhiya's death. She was unusually calm and was busy with her daily chores as if nothing had happened.

Srikantha too was at home. And as always, he had his head buried in his laptop. My head was overwhelmed with hundreds of thoughts and questions that begged for answers. Echoes of Radhika's assertion that 'This is like a death sentence to them' and Hassan's threats that 'Heads will roll' filled my mind. Why did these girls commit suicides? What did they accomplish by doing that? They are against a clinical procedure validated by science the world over. Why so? Is it because of a baseless belief that, once operated, a woman cannot get pregnant? What role has Dr Mohammad Mohammad played in these murky set of events? These women died within a few days of his visit and meeting with us. What does it mean?

Srikantha suddenly looked up from his computer and exclaimed, 'My god! Guru, look here!' Before I could get to him, he shouted, 'A Sanghaali woman named Asha Ali has committed suicide in Columbus, Ohio.' I went up to him quickly and looked at the website he was culling this information from. He had googled for 'Sanghaali suicide'. Asha Ali, a Sanghaali girl, had taken her life with a magnum 33 pistol—quite unlike Rukhiya and Fadhuma. A local newspaper also reported that she too had a three-month-old infant. Nowhere was it mentioned that Asha Ali had a Cesarean section. For some reason, I glanced at the news report date.

That news was six months old!

I felt like punching Srikantha right there. 'Srikantha, what the hell are you doing? I know you are curious. But this is not the time, dude.' I told him after restraining myself. I showed him the date, 'Look, this incident happened six months back. What would you gain by prying this open now?' The distance of this death, both in time and space, provided some solace. Srikantha too was surprised at his oversight. He had not observed the date. 'Sorry, Guru. But so what if this incident is old? Don't you think that Minnesota's incidents and this death in Ohio are related?'

I had not responded.

Radhika was standing at the door. Neither of us had noticed her. She seemed to have had a reasonably good inkling of what we were discussing. She moved over to Srikantha, pushed him aside, sat on his chair and started reading, taking in all the details. I suspected that she may start crying at any moment.

I said, preemptively consoling her, 'Radhika, there is absolutely no relationship between this incident and the events at Amoka. This incident happened in Columbus, six months back!'

Even as I said this, for some vague reason, I had an instinct that all these incidents were somehow related. Radhika had not uttered a word. This silence was surprising. Srikantha was standing behind me and not knowing what to say, asked her, 'Did you call Giri?' Radhika nodded her head. I said, 'Radhika, why don't you take a week off and go to Austin. I'll talk to Smith and Razak. We can manage here.' Radhika went straight to her room. She had not responded to the news in Columbus. She was talking to someone on the phone for about nearly half an hour. I assumed that she was talking to Giri.

She was surprisingly calm later when we sat down for a cup of coffee. In fact, she was the first one to talk. 'Duniya was at the clinic today, and we were talking casually, Fadhuma's topic also came up. I was talking to her again.' I realized it was Duniya that she was talking to, not Giri.

Srikantha and I waited for her to continue. Radhika went on, 'I asked Duniya, these Sanghaali women need to ask themselves what do they really want? How fair is it to put their babies' lives at risk or commit suicides? Who knows why they are killing themselves? Do you think that they would kill themselves just because they had a surgery that their culture supposedly prohibits? Or is it because they are looking for the government's support dole? You know what Duniya said?' We both patiently listened. She had the frenzy of a schoolgirl who had just found the answer to a math problem that she was working on for a long time.

'Duniya said, just wait. Everything will make sense.' Radhika waited for me to respond.

I was confused even more. 'What do you mean? If you speak in riddles like this, what can we understand? How would anything make sense?'

Radhika said softly, 'According to Duniya, the Sanghaali women have rebelled against their husbands!'

'Against their husbands? I thought it was against us?'

'I thought so too. Truth has many layers to it. Duniya was talking mysteriously that what can't be achieved in life can be accomplished in death. Suicides can be an opiate for the masses, and stuff like that... I didn't get a whole bunch of what she was talking. I did not talk much. In a nutshell, this is what I understood: Our surgeries were not the sole reason for their deaths. We are partly off the hook.'

I stayed quiet.

I could not sleep that night. Rebels? What kind of rebellion is this? Deserting your children and committing suicides—can this be called rebellion? Are the wives of Hassan, Abdhi, Ali really rebelling against their husbands by committing suicides? If that is so, then why the timing? Radhika's Cesarean sections are just an excuse? Or her misfortune? Why did this Mohammad Mohammad give us a lecture on Sanghaali women and the Sanghaali community? Does he have no role to play in these deaths?

What does Duniya know about all these events? Did Rukhiya and Fadhuma talk to her before dying? Of course, Radhika is so gullible at this moment, she would be receptive to any comments that would absolve her of any guilt. Duniya might have mentioned to her, 'These women killed themselves because of bad marriages and abusive husbands not because of C-sections' and she believed her. Radhika had held on to Duniya's words. Rebellion didn't make any sense to me.

It is said that a person navigates across five phases when confronted with bad news—denial, anger, compromise or negotiation, depression and then acceptance. Radhika has crossed the first three phases. Now she is trying to pin the blame on others. I didn't get if this was compromise or denial. I thought she may be rationalizing.

The light in her room was switched on all night.

7. The Churn

One bright morning, just a week after this incident, Giri showed up in Amoka. I was already late for work, I greeted him with a quick 'Hi' and went to the hospital. Srikantha had already left, ahead of me. Radhika had taken the day off.

When I came home that night, I could sense the tension in the place. The whole place had a funereal ambience.

Radhika and Giri were eating supper quietly. Srikantha had settled down in his room. I apologized to Giri for not being able to talk to him in the morning. I grabbed the tomato lentil curry from the fridge, heated it in the microwave, mixed it with rice and sat down with the two of them to eat.

'Guru, I've been telling Radhika since morning. Quit this fucking job and come with me right away. We can look for a job in Austin. But when has she listened to me?' The tone of this conversation-opener took me by surprise.

Radhika was wearing a cotton churidar and had her dupatta wrapped around her neck like a shawl. She was wearing her thick glasses. That she was not wearing her contacts meant only one thing: she had cried without a break since morning.

She said softly, something that they had discussed all day, 'Giri, please watch your language. None of us have done anything wrong, that requires us to leave this town. Hear me out. I'm not going to quit this job.' It was awkward for me to be with them in the middle of what seemed to be a big fight. I couldn't help thinking that I stood there destined to be a witness to a verdict that might emerge from this argument. I did not say anything.

'Guru, you are her boss, right? What the fuck is all this? I can't make any sense of it. She did the surgery, and they died. But apparently there is no connection between the two? Listen to this shit, this is supposed to be a fucking Sanghaali rebellion! Who will believe this kind of a cock and bull story? Radhika says that the media folks have not mentioned anything on air or print. Until they do, we should not assume anything, it seems. This is basic common sense, man. She operated on two Sanghaali women and both fucking killed themselves. This is a no-brainer. It is nothing but stupid if we naively believe that there is no connection between the two and do nothing now. Stupidity? Huh, it is a fucking understatement!'

Boy, was he furious!. I hadn't heard so many F-bombers with an Indian accent ever before. But I could not disagree with him. Yet, I said, 'Giri, it is not as simple as you think. I am not sure whether at this time Radhika can quit, even if she wants to. Let us assume, like you said, that their deaths are connected. Do we know what the connection is?'

'What kind of a foolish question is this? Radhika did both these Cesarean sections, right? If there is an investigation, wouldn't she be questioned? Don't think you are safe. They are going to come after you too, my friend. Such naiveté on your part is utter foolishness.'

Radhika asked, 'Nobody has questioned us so far, right?'

I added, 'Yes, we may be questioned for all we know. But then, if we quit now, wouldn't we be declaring ourselves guilty? And wouldn't that be implying that there is a connection between us and these tragic incidents?'

Radhika said, 'Giri, let's be patient for some time. If I work for another two years, I can apply for my green card. If not, all the time we served in this cesspool will be a waste—precious time down the drain.'

I thought she brought up a wrong topic at this time.

'To hell with your green card! I'm tired of listening to this shit. So, what if we don't get our green cards? We go back to Bengaluru, right? What's wrong with that? People living there ... are they not human beings? Living here in this lousy fucking town, you talk about Bengaluru's traffic and pollution, what are you guys doing here?' His voice was loud and trembled with rage.

Radhika said, 'Giri, there is a logical end to everything. The question here is not of going back to Bengaluru. If I go back now, would it not mean that I've lost. I'm not prepared to lose for any reason!'

'What the hell are you talking about? What battle are you fighting to lose?' Radhika didn't answer. Frustrated, Giri asked, 'No use talking to you. What are you planning to do?'

'I will keep doing my job.'

'What if more people kill themselves because you did C-sections on them?'

'God! Giri, how can you speak like that? I will watch myself. I will behave. I will try not to do any Cesarean sections as much as possible.'

Giri did not respond. He was probably tired from arguing all day. He said, resignedly, 'It's always about you and your job, right? Do whatever it is that you want to do. But don't ever call me crying. It is not easy to get to this fucking place. I don't know why you guys land in places like these and suffer. It's your karma.'

The next morning Giri had left for Austin. Radhika's good mood and the glow on her face puzzled me. I wondered if I'll ever comprehend this couple's dynamics—their fights, their little make up love acts and who knows what. If they can settle their differences after one night of togetherness, I prayed: 'God, let there be many such nights.'

I thought that Radhika was coming back to being her old self. However, I couldn't say if this image of her was something that she wanted to project to the world or whether it was genuine. She would suddenly lock herself in her room alone for hours. She kept to herself and her work at the hospital. She didn't talk to us much at home either. When she talked on her phone to Giri, her conversations were insipid, rehearsed and mechanical. She flicked through the local TV channels every hour and searched the internet for random things. Once she came up to me and said, 'Apparently someone in Columbus, Ohio is working on a PhD thesis paper about cultural reasons behind these Sanghaali women's opposition to Cesarean sections. The person doing this research is from Karnataka. She has agreed to share her research papers with me.' Three days later, she came yelling, 'Damn woman! She says she can't share it. Apparently, she has signed some non-disclosure agreement. If we don't help each other, then who will?' Many nights, we could see the lights turned on in her room till dawn. She would get up in the mornings and go to work with swollen eyes and sagging eye sacks. Of late, I had not seen her wear any makeup at all.

I was most surprised by the fact that the media buzz about these suicides did not last for more than a couple of days.

This solace did not last long. The news that was supposed to have gone cold sparked back to life. It didn't take us long to realize that this short-lived peace was the lull before the storm.

Meanwhile, the local radio and TV channels started broadcasting two new developments as 'Breaking News'. There is a small town called Chapel about twenty miles north of Amoka. This town has a population of three thousand. There was a company called Chapel Meats here that was in the business of packing processed meat. It was an all-white town, and in the past six years about fifteen Sanghaali families had moved in there. The men from each of those fifteen families were all working at Chapel Meats through a New York based contracting company.

In the past eight weeks, two young Sanghaali women had killed themselves at Chapel.

According to the news on TV, both had infants less than six months old. There were no suicide notes here too, just like Fadhuma and Rukhiya's cases. One woman hanged herself from the ceiling fan in her room using her Hijab—a death that was eerily similar to Rukhiya's. The other woman had chosen a rather different and novel approach. She sat in her car with its engine running and closed the garage door and died of carbon monoxide poisoning. When her husband came home, he thought she was asleep in the car. It was reported that he had no idea that someone could die in this way.

I had no clue where this Chapel town was located. To tell the truth, we ourselves were unaware of what was happening here, let alone convincing others into believing our story.

8. Interrogation, Courtesy Visit

The incidents that followed, unfolded quicker than what we could imagine. The media, which appeared to be asleep, suddenly woke up to the happenings following the incidents at Chapel. The local TV channels started beaming the news on the deaths of Rukhiya and Fadhuma and the girls at Chapel all day. Headlines screamed, 'Serial deaths of Minnesota Sanghaali mothers', 'Are these suicides or murders?', 'Do patients have no rights?', 'Newborn infant, Dead mother'. Tickers flashed across television screens. What we learnt subsequently was that the girls from Chapel were also young mothers who had delivered their babies about six months back at a local Minneapolis hospital. Both had come to America from Sanghaala last year.

Media vehicles were parked all the time around the hospital. What was weird was that there had been no statement whatsoever from any representative of the Sanghaali community. A couple of reporters from one of the local channels had accosted me with questions at the parking lot, while I was making my way into the hospital. The incessant broadcast of the video clips of me running in and out of hospital with reporters chasing frankly had scared me.

Radhika's mood wavered a lot. Soon after Rukhiya's death, she had panicked as if she was going to lose everything that she had worked for. But, after Fadhuma's death, she appeared quite composed, thanks to Duniya's theory of 'Sanghaali women's rebellion or revolution'. Now, watching the news on TV she started panicking again. For someone who was very confident about her work and her skills, she appeared overwhelmed. She seemed convinced that this whole series of incidents had started with Rukhiya. She confided in me about her fears and the self-doubts she was grappling with and said, 'I should have listened to you, Guru. I should have referred her to some other hospital and washed my hands off this thing. Duniya tells me stuff like, revolt against their husbands and all. How does she know? How can I trust her? If God averts this crisis for me, I will never do a Cesarean section on any Sanghaali woman so long as I'm here. What shall I do, Guru? Shall I quit and go away with Giri? If I quit this job, my visa will expire in two weeks. It is not easy to get a job in Austin that can renew this visa. I may have to return to India.' I listened without having much to say. I had no words to console her. She was also accosted by the media for interviews. The clip that showed her running away from the reporter who was chasing her in the parking lot was quite dramatic. A passerby had recorded that incident on his phone. That too was broadcast by the media. She watched it multiple times, no matter how terrified she was after watching each time. The long and short of it was that everyone was clueless as to what was happening and scared of what might happen.

Jack Powell, the CEO of the hospital, overwhelmed by the menace of the media was trying to push me into giving a press statement. There was a gag order from the board of directors to all of us about talking to the media. Powell had reluctantly agreed. He had come up to me and said, 'Guru, we can't be quiet for too long. If we don't talk now, these media folks will put words in our mouth and you know how that will be distorted and exaggerated. I don't have to tell you the mess that we will have on our hands. These board members don't get it. Media has almost passed the verdict that the series of events originated from 'the Rukhiya delivery' in our hospital. For some reason, none of these Sanghaalis has given a statement. In this situation, don't you think that we must be better prepared? If anyone from the media stops us on the road and asks some random questions, and if we ramble something nonsensical in response, wouldn't that put us in a lot of trouble?'

Obviously I had no answers.

Radhika and I were sitting in the office when Srikantha walked in with a large cup of coffee in hand. He said as he was taking a seat, 'Officials from the Minnesota State Health Department and the local police had paid a visit to the hospital and met with Powell.' I had wondered sometimes, how he could get all this information. He loved these gossips more than his work. Neither Radhika nor I had any clue about this new development. Powell had not sought us out for this supposed meeting either. I was a bit surprised and said, 'Radhika, do you know about this?' She did not answer but sat there in a corner sniffling.

I looked at Srikantha and said, 'I think Powell is hiding something from us. He might be planning to fire us. You have read our contract clause, right? We are "at will" employees. They can fire us without giving any reason. The management might use this mess to roll some heads and who do you think that they will fire? Razak has always kept himself away from this chaos. He still minds his own business. He is angry at Radhika for dragging him into this shitty mess. We are in America only because of this job. If we lose this job, we lose our visa. We can kiss goodbye to our green cards. I think we are screwed'.

Radhika's face reflected almost everything that I said, and it appeared as if she would lose her sanity at any moment. She started sobbing loudly, 'Guru, stop it. Young women are dying here. I thought my job was to save lives but I don't think that I am doing anything remotely close. In fact, I might have triggered these events. Why are we not sensitive about this fact? We are only thinking about our jobs. I do not want a job that kills people!'

'You guys will be fine. Nobody will fire you.' Srikantha pitched in like some hotshot lawyer. I got a sense that he may be saying so to comfort Radhika. He looked at me and said, 'Guru, think about it. There's not a single complaint from anyone, anywhere. Why would the hospital fire you guys and make a tacit admission that it's their fault? Powell is a smart guy. He will wait till anyone from the Sanghaali community talks to the press which could incriminate us or the hospital. At that time, he will have to act. You guys are the perfect first line of defense. Letting go of all three doctors is a highly visible response. If he lets you guys go now, who will he fire when it is really the time to fire people? Do you think that he will answer the press? He cannot get you guys back to talk to the media at that time even if he wants to. By then you would have forfeited your visas and you'll be back in India.' It was not clear if he was trying to console or scare us.

I tried to cheer up Radhika. We decided that it was best to meet Powell and ask him what the hell was going on. At this point Radhika was so vulnerable that she was ready to listen to anybody's advice. She just followed me.

Once we reached Powell's office, we were not so sure whether we did the right thing. Sitting in his office was Amoka's chief of police. Powell did not speak. I squinted my eyes at the police chief and looked at Powell suggestively asking what he was doing there.

Powell laughed and said, 'Nothing much. Just a courtesy visit... heh heh heh.' I almost had a fit, seeing a police officer in Powell's office. 'Look,' I said, 'if you want to keep us fully out of this mess, we will be happy to stay out. Don't drag us into running your errands like giving press statements and attending meetings. We are not stupid enough to not know what's happening in Amoka. I expect complete transparency from you. Keep us in the loop. I'm not a fool. I know that this is not the time to huddle in the office over free coffee.' Powell looked at the police officer seated across.

The police officer asked Radhika and me to take our seats and, cleared his throat and said, 'The issue here is so very complicated, you know. Until now, neither the police nor the Health Department has received a single complaint. So, no one is clear on where to start an official investigation. This whole business of mass suicides is a media buzz, complete bullshit.' He looked at us to make sure that we were still with him. 'The whole shebang makes no sense. All the four deaths have occurred at homes, not at any hospital. The cause of death in every case has been officially declared as suicide after a detailed analysis and autopsy. But, have you guys observed? There is no common thread that connects them. But, no one will buy the argument that these are mere coincidences. Who knows why none of the Sanghaalis has filed an official complaint? Are they planning something big? Something more devious? No idea. Nada. We cannot keep quiet, doc. So, we arrested the husbands of the dead women on domestic abuse charges and questioned them. We had to let them go as we didn't have diddly squat on anyone. We cannot arrest anyone at random. All we need is one complaint, just one. It does not matter on whom. If any relative of any dead person files a complaint that her husband was abusing her, we can swing into action. You can then see how things will unravel and skeletons come tumbling out.'

Radhika asked, 'Have you given any thought about this Dr Mohammad fellow? This whole series of deaths started since this Minneapolis doctor came to our hospital and had a meeting with us. Do you think that this is just a coincidence?'

'Doc, you speak like a detective. Yes, he did come to your

hospital for a meeting. Does that mean we can link him with the suicides? He is a respected person in their community. We cannot bring him to the police station at our whim for questioning. We can only ask his opinion. Our detectives have tried to contact him. He is not reachable over the phone.'

His constant references of 'we' and 'them' made me wonder if there are two parties now—us and them. I was somewhat surprised that Dr Mohammad Mohammad was not reachable over the phone.

Radhika said, 'Did anyone from their side leave a note or something stating that they were taking their lives because C-sections were done against their wishes or against their religious beliefs?'

'Doc, you are opening a Pandora's box. Don't you even go there. Don't put words in anyone's mouth. The media is on an overdrive on this news. They have nothing better to do other than talking about this topic, days on end. You've got to be happy that this is still on local channels, not on cable yet. Let it be that way for some time. This is the age of the internet and social media. We can never know when you guys will be "world famous".' He gestured the quotes with his fingers. 'However, Dr Radhika, you do have a point though. I'll try to answer your question. Let's say if someone did file a complaint against you guys. That will only give us a possible cause. This is not strong enough to arrest you. Anyway, who are we going to arrest here, doc? Who should be arrested? If someone died directly as a result of complications of your surgery, then you could be guilty. My advice—clean up. Go over your medical records. I'm guessing that you have accurately documented your discussions with these two patients. Ensure that there are no mistakes from your side.'

Radhika replied, 'What is that supposed to mean? The medical records are medical records. They are clearly documented. How can we change them now? There is nothing to be changed anyway.'

He got up, 'I did not tell you to doctor those documents, doctor' then laughed at his own pun. 'I asked you to clean up. No loose ends. Nice meeting you both. Jack, I will see you later. I've got to go to Chapel, you know. They have given those cases to someone else since it is not Fair Blue County. Just because something is not in our jurisdiction, is it right to squabble over which case goes to whom, like they do in the movies? I've asked the higher-ups for some latitude. Let us wait. I hope no Sanghaali chick blows her brains out. Speaking for myself doc, I hope this affair ends here. I'm tired of it. By the way, I forgot to mention, there will be a squad car stationed outside your home from tomorrow. You guys, don't leave this town. Just some due diligence, you know.' He shook our hands and left.

Radhika and I stood there, silently watching the spectacle taking place before us. It was, however, not clear as to what we were supposed to do. The events had overwhelmed us, and we stood there in the eye of a storm, too surreal for us to comprehend.

A car from the Amoka County Police Department was parked about a hundred yards away when we went home.

Srikantha advised, 'Oh my goodness! Are they guarding you or watching you? It may be good for you both to talk to an attorney.'

I said I'll think about it. Radhika made no comment.

9. Board Meeting with Rick H.H. Jackson

The hospital's board had called for an emergency meeting. The hospital board in Amoka always reminded me of the Panchayat—a grouping of village chieftains—back in small-town India. It was a random group of Amoka's finest—the school principal, the insurance agent, the lawyer, the car dealer and the plumber—who had not even an iota of knowledge about medicine. This board was elected by the town folk and was specifically tasked to oversee our work. A big brother to all doctors! If a doctor gets invited to a board meeting, that was always bad news. No board member ever congratulated any doctor for saving a life. There were no pats on the back, no trophies, no appreciation of any sort. On the contrary, if there were any complaints from patients about the quality of our care, we would almost surely be summoned to one of these meetings. Therefore, an invite for a board meeting always foretold trouble and meant that there was nothing to cheer about.

As the chief of medical staff, I was the only person invited to the board meeting today. I had sent an email to all the board members requesting that Radhika be invited to the meeting too. Her input would be more crucial than mine in this case. The board had approved my request. On hindsight, I always felt that this request was more for self-preservation, to save my own ass.

The meeting started with civility contrary to what I had expected. There were no critical comments about our work. Instead, there was a run-down of all possible ways that the hospital board could react and respond. It was an anticipated lumping of questions; like preparations for a future apocalypse.

Once the Board President Rick Jackson joined the meeting, the tone of the meeting changed completely. Rick, who was born and raised in Amoka, was the president of the town's Rotary Club, the Chamber of Commerce, the school board and Amoka Golf Club as well as a well-known attorney in this part of the state. An imposing man with a pinkish complexion and a prominent red moustache, trousers held in place with suspenders over a protruding belly, he was the quintessential mid-westerner. Everything about him fit this archetype. His typical Minnesota accent punctuated with constant refrains of 'You betcha', his annoying demeanor of slurping coffee and speaking with half the brew in his mouth. I didn't know the man well as I didn't attend the board meetings that often. The letters HH tattooed on his forearm caught my attention. My sketchy Hollywood knowledge suggested that the letters meant *Heil Hitler*. I suspected that he might be a member of some white supremacist group. The thought had also made me wonder if we could expect any help from him at all. I could feel a shudder down my leg. He noticed me looking at his tattoo and tried to cover it with his hand and said in an awkward loud voice, 'Hubert Humphrey. Minneapolis airport is named after him. A proud citizen of our state. He served as America's vice president after the Kennedy assassination. My dad golfed with him.' If this tattoo was indeed Hubert Humphrey as he claimed, then why did he try to hide it? I wondered.

After a brief exchange of greetings, he addressed me directly, as if to put an end to my Aryan line of thinking, 'Doctor, in both these cases related to our hospital, are you convinced that your colleague Dr Radhika is not at fault? Are you happy with your investigation?'

I laughed nervously, 'In the first place if Dr Radhika had

done anything wrong, these women would not have committed suicides, but instead, they would have sued our hospital.'

'Doctor, please, let us discuss keeping in mind only the matter on hand. This is no time to joke.' Jackson's gaze conveyed the caveat, not to expect any kind of sympathy from his side.

I reeled off everything that I knew about these two cases. I said, looking at Radhika, 'In both the cases it is apparent from going over the records that there was no option but to perform the Cesarean sections.'

Radhika did not say anything.

I continued, 'In the first instance, when Rukhiya's husband Abdhi Abu-Bakr wrote a formal complaint to us, I had sent all her records to Razak and Dr Smith for a review. Both gave the same opinion that what Radhika had done here was right. In Fadhuma's case, I was present right there witnessing the procedure. In fact, I was the one who had sedated Fadhuma.'

'Are you an anesthesiologist?' the conversation took a different turn.

'No; but I have the license to sedate people for minor procedures. We call this moderate sedation. This is not anesthesia.'

'What was the medicine given to Fadhuma?'

'It's called Propofol.'

'Didn't Michael Jackson die from the same medicine?'

I was furious. What's on his mind? What was wrong with giving this medicine? I glared at him.

'Just checking. Sorry doctor. I speak my mind directly. In this situation here, you, Dr Radhika and Razak are on the same side. Nobody on their side will believe that they can expect an impartial review from any of you. We need to protect ourselves better.'

I couldn't hold myself back and said, 'Mr. Jackson, none of us here have done anything wrong. If you show these records to any professional, you will get the same opinion.'

'Dr Guru, there is no reason to get agitated. It serves no purpose. There is one thing clear here. Two young women have taken their lives after your colleague operated on them. Please keep that in mind when you speak. Can I ask a question? Well, I will ask anyway. Why this stubbornness to handle these cases in our hospital? We could have transferred these patients to the University, right? This is a small town. Ours is a small hospital.'

'Mr Jackson! Please. This is not a court. Sure, you are a lawyer, but you are also the president of the hospital board. You should represent us. Instead, if we knew that you were going to court martial us, we would have come prepared too. Feel free to send the medical records to anyone. We couldn't care less! Let us see where that leads to.' My voice was quivering.

Radhika squeezed my hands. They were cold. She was also sweating.

Jackson perhaps noticed this. 'Dr Guru, Dr Radhika, are you two related?'

Radhika and I looked at each other.

Radhika said, 'We have been friends for a long time. We are here for our work.'

'Do you live in the same house?'

'That is nobody's business here.' I thought she might start crying any second!

'Oh!' Jackson exclaimed sipping his coffee.

'What is that supposed to mean? We are just friends. And I have a boyfriend who loves me more than his own life.'

And no sooner did she utter these words, she could not hold back her tears any more. The restraint she had shown till then collapsed and tears started running down her cheeks. She ran out of the meeting room sobbing loudly. A hush fell on the meeting amidst sympathetic sighs and a verbal chorus of pity. I followed Radhika. I saw her standing alone, by the restroom, crying. I went up to her. I did not know what to say and I took her hand and led her out. We walked to my car which was parked at the back side of the hospital to evade the media. Radhika continued to hold on to my hand.

It was dark when we came out. I opened my car door. She hugged me suddenly, 'Guru, please help me out of this mess. I don't know what I did wrong!' and then started crying loudly. Tears flowed abundantly down her cheeks. She stood there holding me close for almost five minutes. A breeze brushed her curls against my cheeks. Her breath warmed my neck. I gently rubbed her back to console her. I lifted her chin up and held her face against mine. Her eyes were open. I raised my hands to wipe the tears from her eyes, when she raised her head and kissed me on my lips.

It's hard for me to say what was going through my mind at that moment. In there, everyone—Giri, Mohammad, Fadhuma, and Abdhi—drifted as images between Radhika and I like a slideshow. Just moments ago, Rick was alluding to a relationship between us. It looks like we are trying to prove him right. Is it normal to feel this way when kissing a girl? And after all, who is this girl? It's Radhika. I've known her and Giri for a long time and I can recollect every facet of their relationship; as well as Radhika's assertion of, 'I've a loving boyfriend', in the meeting.

I felt dizzy for a moment and held her afar. Radhika came close to me again and held my arms. 'Guru, can you help me out of this mess? I just want to get my green card and get out of here.' She was gazing into my eyes. Her eyes were filled with tears and seemed to seek some assurance from me.

I was shaken, as if someone had kicked me on my crotch. None of what was happening felt real. I'm the boss. Radhika works for me. That obviously makes me more powerful. She thinks I can help her out of this mess and pull her out of this trouble. This kiss is a Thank you Card even before the favors were dished out!

I was overwhelmed with shyness. I felt like I was stripped naked—a full Monty—in an open field. I regained my senses and seated Radhika in the car and ran straight to the restroom.

My head was throbbing. What do I make of all this? That Radhika who lives under the same roof as me, suddenly had developed some tender feelings towards me? How do I face Giri? I was swept in a mix of emotions: anger at Radhika and disgust at myself.

My car stood alone in the parking lot outside, as a mute witness to the incident. I started my car quietly.

On the way home, Radhika sat next to me, silently with her head down all the way. We didn't speak with each other till we came home. After parking the car in the garage, I said without looking at her, 'Radhika, I don't know if I've made some mistakes in all this mess. But the incidents here are rather upsetting. I get it. However, I'll handle my mistakes and responsibilities personally as much as possible. And you should do so too. Please let us not drag ourselves into each other's problems.' She went inside without uttering a word.

I couldn't help but feel that, maybe, I was unnecessarily blunt with her.

10. Amoka on the World's Stage

Surprisingly, after the parking lot incident, Radhika and I had gone on with our business-as-usual life and acted as if nothing had happened. That night I could not sleep well and reflected on what I had remarked to Radhika. In the spur of the moment, I had told her that it was better for us to handle our responsibilities individually. But then we do this? When we were home, we must consciously desist from speaking about this incident. In fact, we should forget about it. Was this possible? Could a kiss be exchanged only in moments of vulnerability?

I had decided that just for a few days I needed to forget everything and live like nothing had happened. If that turned out to be awkward, then I would have to talk with her about one of us moving out.

The next day when I finished brushing my teeth, Radhika handed me a cup of coffee. I stared at her in surprise. She said, 'What are you looking at? Do you want more sugar in your coffee?'

At that moment, I understood what her decision was.

Life is strange. We aspire to live in a certain way, but life finds for us its own ways. The events at Amoka had led to a feeble spark between us albeit in a weak moment. For reasons clear and for reasons vague, we had taken the responsibility for the origin of all these events at Amoka. Did we feel secure being together, in case things turned worse? It was not clear.

In a nutshell, we could see our relationship in an altogether different light. And it seemed to us that we were also realizing that the spark between us was so weak that Giri and Srikantha and banal things like living in the same house were enough to put this out.

I really didn't know how she felt. I did not try hard to understand. I thought she could not move out without giving Srikantha or Giri a reason, or so I thought.

Only six weeks had gone by. There were no new deaths in Amoka. However, there was a suicide in a nearby town of Bombay. I had no clue that Minnesota had a town called Bombay. I looked it up on the internet. The town was named after a 15th Century English immigrant by the name William Bombay. He had killed the local native American chief, married his daughter and gave this small town its name; similar to other eponymous towns like Alexandria from Alexander and Hyderabad from Hyder Ali.

The mystery behind all the deaths so far was that no one had indicated the reason for their death. There wasn't a single suicide note. Nobody had filed even a single complaint. No local Sanghaali community leader had given any statement.

A Sanghaali professor from a small private university in Seattle had given an interview for a local TV channel, 'It is important for the law enforcement to ensure that the events at Minnesota don't spread all over the country. Ours is a small community but we have a strict code of beliefs. No doctor has the right to override our beliefs and force their decisions on us. The doctors in Minnesota should realize this,' This interview had drawn responses in the form of some articles and more interviews online.

Amoka's Sanghaali community also had not reacted. Apparently, there were Sanghaali gangs in Minneapolis. However, there was not a single instance of a riot or disturbance reported from there either. The police took no chances and had beefed up all kinds of security in Amoka, anticipating disturbances. But nothing, none whatsoever, happened here. Yet, there was a stunned, mournful ambience everywhere. As for me, I could not so much as look a Sanghaali in the eye if one crossed my path.

The news of six deaths in four months was pretty much relegated to local news channels as if they were mostly local incidents and had very little news value elsewhere in the country. National channels like CNN and FOX News had broadcast the interview with the Seattle professor. Other than that, these channels had covered the news about these deaths only for a couple of days. After that, they were just ticker news... The public television crew had come to Amoka and shot some video footage, but none of that was broadcast. Srikantha suspected that they may have done the shooting for a documentary. Of all the media, the Minneapolis radio channels seemed to be more active and pugnacious about these issues. A left of center news channel acted as a mouthpiece for women's lib organizations and was proclaiming that women's rights in Amoka are in a tenuous situation, the right leaning channels blamed this on America's liberal immigration policy: 'Every immigrant brings his/her own baggage. Culture is a part of this baggage. Cultural entitlement will destroy what is ours. Nobody knows who is a real American anymore,' they screamed.

The local channels had invited experts and aired discussions on a host of topics: Sanghaala, the country's internal conflict, female genital mutilation, their pregnancies, their childbirths, their indigenous medical systems, their beliefs on Cesarean sections, their folklore, the recent rise of terrorist groups in the country and their relationship with the ISIS.

I made a surprising observation that in all this information overload, there was no news of Dr Mohammad Mohammad anywhere. *Amoka Daily Herald* had tried to contact him. His visit to our hospital had made the newspaper's front page. It was not clear how they had got hold of this news. Let alone the news, the newspaper also had a picture of Dr Mohammad Mohammad with Fadhuma and Hassan posing in front of the Amoka General Hospital. I looked for the photographer's name in the small print beneath the picture but could not find anything. On a hunch, I called the office of *Amoka Daily Herald* and asked them where they got the picture from. The guy answered, without even a moment's pause, that it is in the public domain and is circulating on the internet. Surprisingly, when I googled the name, Mohammad Mohammad, I found out that this picture was his Facebook profile picture for a short while. It was titled 'My brother Hassan and Family' and it had 2K likes to it.

I looked at Mohammad Mohammad's Facebook status messages. He had shared links to all articles and news reports in *Amoka Daily Herald* related to the Sanghaali deaths. He had also listed links to YouTube interviews related to this topic. This was shared by many people. When I searched their profiles, I could see that this news was shared in many parts of the world like Dahir-Bar, Ethiopia, Nairobi, Seattle, London, Delhi and many more. There were hundreds of comments: 'Your fight has our Support. *Insha Allah.*' 'Come what may, don't stop your fight.' 'What are you doing? Al Tewagi?' And so on. Al Tewagi had recently claimed responsibility for the London city bombing. It had its major terror network in eastern and northern Africa. Dahir-Bar, was one of the major cities out of which this organization operated.

There were numerous places that had references to Radhika and my names. And, in fact, Radhika's Facebook profile picture was used by many in their comments!

I typed Sanghaali suicide on the Google homepage and searched. Some had condemned the suicides of young women at Amoka in their blogs. The blogs carried the usual local newspaper reports, video clips. I googled Radhika's and my names. I could see our names listed along with the hospital name and Rick Jackson's name, all with pictures. The news link redirected to the online editions of *Amoka Daily Herald* and some local Minneapolis newspapers. Since we had not given any press statement, a lot of liberty was taken with the truth and people had written according to their whims. *Amoka Daily Herald* had questioned the absence of any statement from the hospital in response to Fadhuma and Rukhiya's suicides.

I don't follow social media that often. I don't frequently post comments or update my statuses on Facebook. The last time I was on Facebook was two weeks ago. After the Bombay suicides, I'd noticed that I was tagged to many posts which had provided links to the news bytes and video links on these suicides. Each post was flooded with comments. I was not sure if Radhika was also tagged. Srikantha was on Facebook too, although his interests were different. When I looked at these news items carefully, I could see that they were mostly posted by Mohammad Mohammad on his wall or by people with whom he had shared them. Since I was his friend and he had tagged me on almost every one of these I could see all his posts. I suddenly remembered that he had sent me a friend request the day he visited the hospital and I had accepted it almost immediately.

I looked for our mutual friends. Razak and Srikantha's names came up. Radhika's name was conspicuously missing. Mohammad's statuses were all public. So, these were visible to everyone. He had tagged several of his friends on many of his posts. Since these messages were shared randomly across Facebook, I guessed they had come to the attention of many. He had also tagged all his status updates to Srikantha and Razak. Thankfully neither of them had approved or shared them. It was therefore possible that Radhika had not seen any of them unless she went specifically looking for Dr Mohammad's posts. If she had, she would have told me by now.

Radhika and I did not have much of a presence on the internet in general other than our profiles on LinkedIn or WebMD. However, I now realized both of us were very popular on Facebook.

I shut down my laptop for a while and switched on the TV. According to the reports on TV nobody knew about Mohammad Mohammad's whereabouts. Hassan, Abdhi, The Chapel husbands and now, Bombay—nobody had said a single word. They were all summoned to the police station and interrogated. There were no charges against them other than domestic abuse. And there was no evidence to support these charges either. The newspapers carried no additional information.

I looked out of the window. It was quiet and desolate. There was nothing around except for a small press vehicle. Five minutes back, looking online on the computer, the world seemed to be in the grip of a massive churn with disturbances all around. Here I am in this small town and in the hospital where the series of suicides were supposed to have originated. Looking through the window, the world seemed to be at peace with itself. Even while the local TV channels were broadcasting the news, my friends who lived just about six hours away in Chicago, were blissfully unaware of the news here. But when my Facebook friends read and responded to the interviews posted there, it felt as if Amoka was at the center of the world and every news that was, and that could be, was about it.

In this social networking era where news can also be personalized, what is important news? What is breaking news?

The news I read tomorrow is determined by what I had read yesterday. Its magnitude and intensity depended on one's network.

I checked out the list of my Facebook friends. There were only seventy-two. Mohammad Mohammad had maxed out on the number of his friends.

Was the real news at Amoka where the suicides had occurred or was it on the internet?

Those who were following the news on the local channels and the newspapers could possibly conclude this news was insignificant, as something that was local to Amoka. However, when those interested looked online, the scale of this news came across as something huge.

11. Breaking News, Fake News

The hospital board seemed a bit friendlier as things became more chaotic in Amoka. Rick Jackson who was abrasive and rude in the last meeting, had called me for the second time today. Since the last meeting when Radhika had walked out crying, he had called me a few times and had enquired about her. He appeared genuine in his concerns. He'd apologized to me for what happened at the meeting. I was not sure if he had spoken to Radhika.

'Hello Guru, are you following social media?'

I suspected that he may also have seen the *shared* news, 'Yes,' I said. I knew this would open up a long conversation.

'Looks like we have become very popular. We are all over Facebook…'

'Are you a friend of Mohammad Mohammad on Facebook?' I asked him. For some reason, I was reminded of the tattoo HH on his arm.

'No. But I think he follows the hospital Facebook page. All his messages are public, and anyone can see them.'

I realized that my friendship with Mohammad Mohammad was after all not that big of a deal. I could see his posts even if I was not his friend on Facebook. I guessed he may have befriended me to keep tabs on me. I felt I should close my account.

'But there is no news on the national TV. Whatever chaos we see, everything's on social media.' I said.

'That surprises me too. After all, how long does it take for the news to find its way from Facebook to TV? Anyway, that's not the reason I called you. We have got a letter from the State Health Department. They have not received any complaints either. Apparently, the word on the street is that everyone who gets a Cesarean section done at our hospital, goes home and commits suicide.'

'Not everyone. Only those two Sanghaalis. We do ten Cesarean sections a day at our hospital and for god's sake, the state doesn't have to respond to the word on the street.'

'Guru, I am aware of that. But go on the internet once. There seems to be a near consensus that we started this mess. These inspectors from the Health Department have mentioned in that letter that they will only review Rukhiya and Fadhuma's records. Nobody has called for an official enquiry yet.'

'How can anyone ask for an enquiry? Radhika has performed a medical procedure and it is called Cesarean section! The hospital experts have reviewed the cases and concluded that everything was done right and there were no complications. The state's inspectors have not got a single complaint alleging any sort of negligence. What business do they have here? Moreover, according to the patient privacy laws, the patient's health records cannot be shared with any unrelated parties.'

'Look, I'm just the president of the hospital board. I am trying to do damage control here. Looks like we are becoming popular among folks in Africa, Indonesia, and Asia—almost down to the southern tip of India. I can tell you for sure that these people have no idea where Amoka is. I'm a bit baffled as to why this Mohammad Mohammad guy is giving so much publicity to this news. Sanghaalis with no knowledge of English have Facebook accounts. And they are sharing all his posts. I sometimes wonder which Sheikh had these two, Rukhiya and

Fadhuma, in his *harem*. What if a lunatic armed with a bomb blows himself up in our hospital? Currently, our safety is more important than patient privacy.'

I couldn't help but smile even in that situation. I thought Rick may be into Facebook a little too much.

I asked him, 'Rick, where are you going with this? Are you implying that some terrorist Sheikh in Dahir-Bar impregnated Rukhiya and Fadhuma and sent them to small towns like Amoka with explicit instructions to commit suicides once they deliver their babies, and this would give them a reason to attack hospitals like ours and blow them up?'

'Guru, it may not be that dramatic. For all we know these two suicides may not be related. We might have done nothing wrong. But when you look at the news going around, it is scary. No one may blow up the hospital, but we may have our license revoked if the State believes that people die after getting surgeries done at our hospital. We should be cautious.'

'People who have had Cesarean sections done at other hospitals have also died.'

'Of course, I know that. When there is an epidemic, people try to locate the source of the epidemic—the place where the first case was reported. They call it as the index site. We are an index site. Our internal review means nothing if someone from the state doesn't approve and puts his or her John Hancock on it. Don't worry. You or your friends aren't going anywhere. If we fire you guys, we will be in more trouble than you. The smart thing is to fire you at the right time. You are in admin. Don't you know when people get fired? Strategic firing, that's what I am talking about,' he laughed at his own joke. 'Well, I can't help you if there is a government order to fire you or some immigration court decides to deport you. One thing is for sure, if we are all here, we need to handle the media a bit more carefully. I am talking about the news media. Screw social media! News on social media is something you manufacture. If someone is making news about these Sanghaali deaths today, tomorrow you and Radhika can be the toasts of the town for saving the same Sanghaali chicks who wanted to kill themselves. Or, we can create such news ourselves! We are updating our hospital's website. In fact, we have uploaded a CCTV clipping of the CPR you did in the hospital's parking lot and saved that old guy's life last month. We have also uploaded video clippings of many of our success stories. You should share them on your Facebook page. And there is one important task that we need to do.'

'What?'

'We have to leverage this media to our benefit. We should change the narrative in a way that people should believe in Amoka General Hospital and our staff again. We need to create an impression that there is no chance of people dying here no matter what. Think about it, if Sanghaali suicide is bad news, voluntary Sanghaali Cesarean section is good news, in fact very good news. We can use this spin to inform our narrative. And merely asserting that Cesareans are safe is not enough. We need to demonstrate that with enough evidence. Let us record a Cesarean section and upload the video onto YouTube. We can then share the link on Facebook. Once we get forty to fifty thousand hits, which I'm confident we will, then watch how our reputation will be restored. People here should not be scared to get a Cesarean done for any reason. I need to discuss with you in detail. This is not a topic for a phone conversation. When are you available?'

I wondered if Rick Jackson was off his rocker. I was not sure if he was serious about this business of uploading the Sanghaali Cesarean section video onto YouTube or if he was joking. I could not detect any hint of humour in his words. Nevertheless, he continued talking 'Search on YouTube or on Google Images for Sanghaali female circumcision, you will get all kinds of graphic images and videos. Why are these Sanghaali women, who do not fear such inhumane gory acts, afraid of the Cesarean sections? Nobody has any idea. This problem started in our hospital, right? Let us find the solution ourselves.'

'Rick, do you really think that uploading a video on YouTube can solve this problem? What credibility does a video from a small hospital like ours have? If it was the national media then ...'

He cut me mid-sentence and said, 'Fuck the media. Let's make the news that we want. By some god's grace this disgusting news has not made it to the national headlines! I suppose that is for our own good.'

I did not know what to say, 'I can meet you next week.'

He asked, 'Have you spoken to your friend Razak recently?'

I was surprised that Razak's name popped up suddenly. I said, 'Not outside the hospital. Why? What's the matter?'

As though he caught the fear in my voice, 'My god! Guru. Nothing, really. I casually asked. That's all. After all who is there in this town to check on your team's well-being? We are all like a family. Aren't we? I have to take care of you guys.'

I laughed without uttering a word.

'Ok. You and Powell must call an emergency press meet now. I was planning on attending too but it may not be appropriate for the board president to be in that meeting. It will be good for the hospital's public relations if we issue a press statement. For the hospital to stay in business, our relationship with the people and community needs to be really good and you probably know that already. In the past two months, Amoka General Hospital has seen a decline of 10 per cent in the number of childbirths. This is an upsetting fact.'

The stink was apparent. Rick Jackson's idea of uploading the YouTube videos did not come from a place of compassion to help the Sanghaali community. He was trying to get more business. This was another marketing strategy. I felt disgusted. I should have known better. All he cared for was the bottom-line. As long as people came to deliver babies, that's all that mattered!

'Don't forget to call me next week. Let's meet at my place. I've something important to discuss with you.'

I said 'Yes' and hung up. And before I did so, he remarked, 'Guru, don't worry about the government enquiry. It is a necessary evil. It is just a procedure.' I nodded.

12. Pregnant Zeba

I called Radhika on her cellphone. She did not answer. Radhika and Srikantha had the day off and were at the temple in Minneapolis. I tried calling Srikantha. He didn't answer either. Srikantha's phone was switched off. He never kept his phone on while driving. Of late, it appeared that Radhika was going to the temple a lot. Last Friday she had not eaten anything all day. When I enquired with her, she had mentioned that she was fasting. It was apparently for *Sankashta Chaturthi.* I did not wish to talk to her about this subject anymore.

I called Radhika again. I got her voicemail but did not bother to leave any message. For some reason, it occurred to me that I should call Razak and give him a heads-up about Rick Jackson's enquiry. As soon as the phone rang, he answered as if he was waiting for my call. 'Guru, I was about to call you. I was browsing Facebook. Boy, oh boy! The chaos out there. I did not have a good feeling about this right from the start. First, it was Amoka, then Chapel, now a couple of other small towns. What do you think is going on? Zeba is very upset. I'm clueless as to how to console her. We have been trying to call Radhika for a long time. Is she there with you by any chance?'

I told him about Radhika and Srikantha visiting Minneapolis.

'Are you guys free in the evening? If you are home, we would like to visit you.'

It was interesting that Razak and Zeba wanted to visit us.

And Rick Jackson who had never ever mentioned Razak's name, had enquired about him today.

'Razak, what did you and Zeba see on Facebook?'

'What else? All the news about Amoka. Facebook is full of these Sanghaali suicides and all the sordid details.'

'Where did you see them? On Mohammad Mohammad's wall? Or someone he had tagged?'

He thought for a moment and said, 'Yes.'

I felt comforted, 'Anyway, what's the matter? Why did you want to meet us at home?' I did not tell him about Rick Jackson asking about him.

Razak said hesitatingly, 'Guru, I need to tell you something. Zeba is pregnant. She is four months into her pregnancy. I did the ultrasound by myself at the hospital. The baby is doing well.' I could sense fear in his voice.

I did not know what to say. Oh god! These pregnancies… children… all these are supposed to be joyous moments, but the word pregnant is making Razak tremble. Words failed me. I did not know how to respond.

This was Razak and Zeba's second pregnancy. They have Reshma, who is two years old. He was sharing this news with guilt and fear as if he had done something wrong. He hadn't even made a mention of this till Zeba was four months into her pregnancy.

I tried to cheer him up and said, 'Hey, congrats man, Razak! You need to cheer up, dude. These are happy times. You sound like you are about to cry.'

'Not sure whether to feel happy or sad. Young moms are dying here. Every time you turn the TV on, there is news of suicides of mothers in Minnesota. Facebook is flooded with these posts and comments. Zeba has no idea what to do. She has been crying all along.'

'Razak, get a grip. How is Zeba's pregnancy related to anyone's suicide here?'

'Guru, who the heck knows. Nothing makes sense. There's so much confusion and chaos everywhere. I deliver babies all the time, but lately the very word pregnancy makes me nervous. Now my wife is pregnant. I'm not sure whether this is an irony or a coincidence Guru, I think this is not the time to get pregnant or have a baby in this cursed town.'

I was overwhelmed, 'Hey, what are you saying? Relax. I'll tell Radhika to give you a call as soon as she is back. Let us talk about it. Ok? Get out of your room. Stop spending so much time on Facebook. May I ask you a question?'

'What?'

'Do you know Mohammad Mohammad outside of Facebook?'

'What do you mean, Guru?'

'Don't get me wrong. There are no mosques in Amoka. You go to Minneapolis every week to pray. Have you met Mohammad Mohammad there under any other circumstances?'

'Guru, what are you talking about? Is it because both of us pray in the same mosque?'

'It was a general question. Don't read too much into it.' As an afterthought, I felt that I should not have asked the question, given the circumstances.

'Guru, if Zeba and I had any other friends, why would we call you first with the news of her pregnancy? Trust me, we have no one else in this country. You guys are our only friends.' I thought he may break down at any moment.

I felt like someone slapped my face. I said, 'Sorry Razak. I made a mistake. Say what, unfriend Mohammad Mohammad on Facebook right away. Or at least stop his notifications. Don't go to his wall and post messages. You are aware that all his messages are public. Now give the phone to Zeba. I will talk to her. Again, I'm sorry.'

I could sense Zeba holding the phone. She was quiet. There was no voice on the other side. I said, 'Congrats Zeba.'

She replied, 'Thanks.' Her voice was a little mellow.

'Come on. Cheer up. You are going to have a baby!'

'Guru…'

I did not speak.

It is surprising how people on the phone can understand each other's emotions without saying a single word.

She asked, 'Do you think that I will die if I have this baby?'

I was stunned. I was speechless for a moment. After getting my wits together, I asked, 'Zeba what are you talking about!'

'Guru, I don't want to die,' and then she started sobbing loudly.

I tried to console her, 'Zeba, keep the phone down. Radhika, Srikantha and I will come over to your house. Your husband is an OBGYN doctor. Nothing is going to happen to you.'

'Let me ask you something. I'm not a doctor myself. Do you honestly believe that all these young mothers who died around here committed suicide?'

'What does that mean?' I found it difficult to understand her.

'I don't know, Guru. Can you all doctors here say for sure that all these deaths are not due to any pregnancy related complications?'

That these kinds of doubts can even arise surprised me. There are doctors all around her, including Razak. Despite that if she asks such questions, what can I say?

'Look Zeba, Please. You are intelligent and educated. You should not be asking such questions. Don't you watch TV? All of them killed themselves. No pregnancy related complications or any bull like that, ok? I promise. Nothing is going to happen to you.'

'Are you sure? What if I commit suicide too? I saw a program on TV which talked about how suicides can be contagious, how they can be a community phenomenon, how they can turn into an epidemic.'

'Zeba, you need to rest a bit. You are blabbering. I want you to understand one thing. We will get to the root of the problem. These are not mass suicides. And for God's sake, this is certainly not any kind of community phenomenon. Don't worry. As soon as Radhika returns, we will come to your place. Let us have a talk.'

'No, not now. We are going out. After we are back, I'll talk to Radhika myself.'

I called Radhika again. This time she picked up the phone. I gave her the news of Zeba's pregnancy. She and Srikantha were on their way back home after having their dinner at the temple. Radhika wanted to go to Zeba's house and meet her. I gave her a subtle hint of my earlier conversation with Zeba and suggested that this may not be an appropriate time for that. Radhika agreed and sent a 'Congrats' message to Zeba and Razak. I could hear the 'swoosh' of the sent message.

'Radhika, Is Mohammad Mohammad your Facebook friend?'

She paused for a while. The fact that I suddenly raised Mohammad Mohammad's name must have surprised her.

'No. After our meeting, he had sent me a friend request. Who in their right mind wants to be friends with him? I declined it.'

'I'm friends with him on Facebook.' I could hear Srikantha's loud voice in the background. It was obvious that Srikantha had not told her about all the chaos on Facebook . I thanked God for putting some sense into Srikantha's mind. More than anything, I was relieved by the fact that Radhika is not friends with Mohammad Mohammad. At least one of us is prudent enough to stay out of the internet. Ignorance appeared blissfully peaceful.

After I became the chief of staff of this hospital, I have attended several leadership seminars. Suddenly, I remembered one such lecture series on risk management. Some management expert had talked about how any event that occurs in the world is not an accident and each event is related to some other—something he called a Butterfly Effect. He had talked about how any potentially harmful or dangerous situation can be harnessed to our advantage. And how well someone does that, indicates how good a leader he can be.

It was somewhat perplexing that these lines from a lecture, that I attended quite a while back, came to mind as soon as I heard the news of Zeba's pregnancy.

How can one believe that these mothers' deaths and Zeba's pregnancy are in anyway related? That Rick Jackson, behaving completely unlike himself, had enquired about Razak today. Does it mean that Rick knew about Zeba's pregnancy?

I logged onto hospital medical records from home and browsed through Zeba's chart. I was aware that it is illegal to read someone else's medical record but that did not stop me.

I was basically looking to know if Zeba's first delivery was a natural delivery or a Cesarean section. Reshma was born by Cesarean section. Once I got this information, I logged out of the computer.

13. No Comments

Powell had called for a press meet a couple of days later. He had requested me to sit in with him. In the press meet, he read from a prepared statement, something he had drafted much before.

> We would like to bring some important facts to the attention of the residents of Amoka and make a fervent request. Amoka General Hospital is the best hospital amongst the towns around. Our hospital has the distinction of having an excellent facility, state of the art gadgets and a highly competent medical staff. Your health, safety, and security are our primary concerns. We offer our sincerest regrets for the incidents that have occurred in the town in the recent past. You can be rest assured that we support Sanghaali interests wholeheartedly. You have my assurance that our doctors will cater to the needs of patients of all communities and all cultures. We shall commit ourselves to the highest standard of care with zero tolerance for errors. We pledge to go by the 'First Do No Harm' dictum regardless of the patient demographic, complexity of the procedure or the urgency of treatment needed. The obstetrics department is our hospital's bedrock. This was the only department we had when we started this hospital. After all, our life's journey starts in this department! Thus, there is a special relationship between this department, our hospital and our town. Ninety per cent of the women in this town deliver their babies in our hospital. Last year we delivered two thousand and two hundred babies. We are happy to inform you that all these

> babies are very healthy and doing well. I would like to thank Dr Guru and his staff for this accomplishment. Without them, this hospital would not be in business.

Then he shook my hands.

A reporter asked, 'Mothers?'

Powell looked at him inquisitively. I was under strict instructions from the hospital's board to not say anything other than the two magic words: 'No comments.'

The reporter explained, 'The babies are fine, but what about the mothers?'

Powell was speechless for a moment and looked at me. I whispered in his ears, 'Shall I respond with "No comments"?'

'For god's sake, not now!'

I grabbed the water bottle in front of me and took a sip from it. 'Same with the mothers too. As per our hospital's statistics, not even a single complication has been reported so far.' I remembered something that I had heard in a seminar, that drinking water frequently while speaking to the press conveys nervousness or anxiety. I kept the bottle down. He said, 'It may not have been reported to you, but they go home and commit suicides.'

I replied: 'No comments.'

Murmurs, hushed remarks, and whispers started filling up the room. Since the press conference was being held in the hospital's premises, visitors of the patients were also present. There were about twenty Sanghaali women in the crowd. I thought that we should have held the press conference behind closed doors, with only the press reporters in the room.

Powell remarked looking at the Sanghaali women, 'There is absolutely no connection whatsoever between these events and us. We have no comments to make as we have no information on this topic nor do we have anything meaningful to say. I believe there is an inquiry in progress. If the inquiry results show any wrongdoing from any of our staff members, we shall take suitable action.' Duniya was also present in the room. He said, 'Duniya' and gestured with his eyes summoning her to the podium. She walked over to the podium and delivered a long monologue in Sanghaali.

I did not understand why Duniya was invited to this press meet. Powell sensed my question and said, 'There are so many Sanghaalis here. They need to understand what we are sharing with the press.' I agreed.

Duniya spoke for about five minutes. Powell and I could not discern much of what she was talking. I could make out that she was translating Powell's assurance, that there has been no direct adverse impact due to our doctors performing Cesarean sections. But there was no way I could have a clear understanding of what else she said. Since I heard words like 'Sanghaali' and 'operation', I thought she was translating at least some of Powell's remarks.

Once Duniya stopped talking, people started getting up from their seats and got ready to leave. Four reporters stood there with microphones and video cameras in their hands. Duniya's talk sent the reporters there in a tizzy. It was not clear if they understood that Duniya was an interpreter. A reporter asked as if he was interviewing her, 'What is your community's opinion on these Sanghaali suicides?'

She responded, rather curtly, 'I'm just an interpreter who works for the hospital. I'm not here to give any statement.'

He persisted, 'Were you the interpreter for Rukhiya and Fadhuma also?'

'I cannot publicly discuss my work. The conversations that I've had with my patients are strictly confidential. Please excuse me.' She stepped down from the podium and joined the other Sanghaali women who were leaving.

Powell had no choice. He led me inside. I expected that

the reporters and the media personnel would come chasing us with microphones in hand. Nothing like that happened. Our press conference ended rather abruptly.

While we were walking into the hospital, the hospital's only General Surgeon, O'Reilly, was walking toward us, having a loud conversation with a Sanghaali woman. She seemed to be crying. He stopped upon seeing us. Pointing his finger at me, he addressed the woman, 'Look, this doctor is our boss. You can ask him any questions you might have,' and stood there with his hands crossed, looking at me, implying that his job was done, and I needed to answer any question the woman might have. I gave them a blank look being totally unaware of what was happening. Powell stood there too, sensing that something had gone wrong and he might have to answer a few questions.

It was hard to say if the woman was angry or was crying with sorrow writ large on her face. She complained in her broken English, 'Four hours. My son inside operation room. Just appendix... simple surgery... Dr Mohammad tells. Why so late? Why long cut on belly? Dr Mohammad tells appendix keyhole surgery.' Her voice displayed less interrogation but more of anxiety, expectation, fear, sincerity and honesty. She appeared genuinely concerned.

O'Reilly looked at me and said, 'How can I answer such questions? It was already late when they came to the hospital. His appendix had already ruptured, and his abdomen was filled with pus. This woman does not understand. It was a miracle that this boy even survived! Even before the surgery, she was asking me how long would the incision be and how many stitches her boy would get. She didn't get it when I tried to explain that I couldn't answer those questions before the surgery. With all the complications he had, it was impossible to operate in forty-five minutes.'

'Mohammad Mohammad do that.'

'You should have taken your son to him. Why did you bring him here?'

She started wailing loudly, 'Kid. Too much sick.'

Powell tried to scoot away from there sensing that there was nothing for him to do. I asked him to stay for a moment and went near the woman. 'Look here ma'am, the kid is alive now, right? He was going to die, and this doctor has saved your son. You should be happy about that. Operations like these take more time. Dr O'Reilly is a good doctor. There is absolutely no doubt about it. Moreover, where is Dr Mohammad Mohammad now? If you would like, you can call him. Dr O'Reilly or I will talk to him. He is also a doctor. He will understand.'

She seemed shaken and said, 'Don't know phone number.'

Nobody seemed to know the whereabouts of Dr Mohammad Mohammad. That being so, the fear she displayed at my simple question surprised me. I understood the futility of digging any deeper and said, 'Okay, what can we do to make you feel better?'

'CT scan,' she replied with no hesitation.

O'Reilly looked at me.

I asked her, 'The kid just had the surgery, why do you want a CT scan? Do you want to see if there is any more pus inside?'

'No, no,' she hesitated a bit.

I looked at O'Reilly, frustrated.

'I know why she is asking for a CT scan. She suspects that I may have removed her son's kidney or any such useful organ when I had opened his abdomen. Is it not so ma'am? Now I must show that the boy's organs are safe, and none are missing.'

She nodded her head crying, 'Yes.'

'O'Reilly, what kind of madness is this? Is this something new? '

'Welcome to my world. Whether I remove an appendix or a gallbladder, I must swear before these people that I'll remove the appendix, the whole appendix and nothing but the appendi. And after the operation, I've to show them the proof that I've done so!'

'Entitlement?'

'Guru, it cannot be called an entitlement. Can she really think on those lines? Don't you think that someone else is feeding into her head?'

I didn't even know the woman's name. She understood only a smattering of English. It made me uncomfortable that O'Reilly was speaking about her right in her presence.

'I know it all. First son...kidney stone. They take him surgery. One kidney gone!' the woman started sobbing.

O'Reilly said, 'I've heard such stories many times over. Where was this surgery done? In America or in Sanghaala?'

'Sanghaala.'

'I rest my case. Look, I can't do a CT scan of your son's belly. I think you know that too many CT scans can cause cancer. If you do not know, go ask your Mohammad Mohammad. I've done my job here. If you have any complaints against me, then these two standing here, are my bosses. You can complain to either of them.' Almost immediately, he left.

That woman stood there crying.

I spoke to her, 'Look ma'am. You may have had a bad experience in Sanghaala. But here in America, nobody can remove kidneys or other body parts that easily. Let the boy rest for a while now. We can watch him. You talk to him when he is more awake. If you continue to have your doubts, let us talk again.'

It was not clear if my words consoled her or made her feel that any further discussion was futile. She went inside crying.

Powell walked in, 'I don't know if these people fear

Cesarean sections or if they are simply ignorant of any surgery in general? Just get a CT scan done. We can show them that everything looks fine and be done with it. If needed, I will ask our accounts department to waive the charges.'

'Seriously? You are a typical Administrator. It is wrong to get a CT scan for no reason. What O'Reilly said is right.'

'You know quite well that everything cannot be done by the book. So far, only those who underwent Cesarean sections have committed suicides. Tomorrow if the kids who were operated by O'Reilly start killing themselves, what do I do?'

This line of thought by itself was scary. But still, this is O'Reilly's patient. It would be wrong on my part to get a CT scan done. There was no option but to wait.

'Powell, we have no choice other than praying that no such thing happens. '

'Even if these people have no faith in us or in our work, I cannot for the life of me understand why they are killing themselves?'

'We are physicians. We do our work. You are an MBA and you manage this hospital. The police are there to investigate this mystery and get to the bottom of it. Right?'

'I don't think they have any clue at all so far as to what is going on. I believe we should do our part and try to help as much as we possibly can. Guru, has Rick Jackson spoken with you?'

'He wants to. Has he told you anything?'

'No. But he made a subtle suggestion. He wants us to prove publicly that Cesarean sections are harmless. I think it would be good to start to come up with ways of doing that.'

It occurred to me that Rick had talked to him about his pet project of the Cesarean section video.

I asked, 'What exactly did Rick tell you?'

'Not much. Anyway, he said he will speak to me in detail.

By the way, is it true that Razak's wife Zeba is pregnant? How is she doing?'

'She is doing fine.' I ended our conversation.

I was surprised that Razak had shared the news of Zeba's pregnancy with the management even before he did so with us!

14. Assad Delmar Abdhikarim AKA 'Kuki'

I had first met 'Kuki' under a strange circumstance. Amoka's police had arrested him. In fact, the police had tased him and brought him to the emergency department. Apparently, they had found three marijuana plants in his car. But 'Kuki' tried to flee and had to be tased. Taser use by the police had got a bad rap as there were at least two deaths in Minnesota after police tasing. Amoka County had a strict policy about the use of tasers on unruly offenders. Each time someone got tased, the police had to bring the offender to the emergency department and have the doctor certify that the person was in sound physical and mental state to go to jail, meaning I needed to reassure the cops that the guy wouldn't die on them in jail. In the absence of such certification, the arrested person could not be detained.

Kuki's real name is Assad Delmar Abdhikarim. He is thirty-seven years old now. He was a twelve-year-old boy when he came with his uncle to America from Sanghaala as a refugee. His parents had not accompanied him. His uncle had him schooled in Amoka. He had graduated from high school in Amoka and then got a nursing degree from Minneapolis' Franklin University. Apparently, he had worked as a Registered Nurse at the Amoka General Hospital for a couple of years. He had enlisted himself in the military to get tuition waiver and was posted to Afghanistan as an army nurse. It was said that he had his own misgivings of being able to get into America's military. However, since he had literally walked into America with his green card, he didn't have any problems getting recruited to the military.

After serving the American government for about two years in Afghanistan, he had returned to America as a completely changed person. Nobody seemed to know the cause of his metamorphosis. Each time this question was raised, people came up with different stories, most of them probably apocryphal. According to one of these stories, he had visited Sanghaala a few times during his posting in Afghanistan for reasons that were not clear. It was not known whether it was on official work or to visit his parents. If asked as to why he had been to Sanghaala, the conversation would in turn spawn another sub-story.

According to that story, when he was in Afghanistan, he had developed contacts with a terrorist organization. This organization had its operations spread across Sudan, Sanghaala, Ethiopia and other African countries with Al Qaida's help. American passport holders like Assad working in the military, who could travel from one country to another with no hassles, were a gold mine to such groups. Such groups were ready to pay resources like Kuki any amount of money. And moreover, Assad's family lived in Sanghaala. There was very little information on their whereabouts. One of these terror groups apparently had persuaded Assad to go to Sanghaala.

All said and done they were all stories with no proof. It was hard to differentiate truth from fiction in these stories. Most of them were gleaned from a few bored cops sipping coffee and tattling with the nurses when they waited for the test results of some unruly inmates suspected of trafficking cocaine into jail.

It was said that Assad had returned to Amoka after spending nearly a year in Sanghaala. Upon his return, he was posted to Iraq almost immediately. Nobody knew what happened to Kuki in Iraq, but it appeared like he had got into some serious trouble. Within three months of his posting, he was dishonorably discharged from the military. According to police gossip, when he was in Iraq, a soldier had stepped on a land mine and injured his leg. They had brought him to Fleet Hospital 6 where Kuki was serving as Combat Medic/Nurse. Kuki was taking vitals and the doctor had not examined the soldier yet. He apparently was in a lot of pain and asked Kuki for morphine. Assad had apparently given him 1000 mg paracetamol telling him that he had only suffered a toe injury and did not need stronger pain medications like morphine and that he was saving those for some real injuries. Being in a lot of pain, the soldier had retorted, 'Would you withhold morphine if I were a Muslim?' This had infuriated Assad, and unable to contain his anger, he had tried to punch him in the face. That was the end of his military career. Everyone had their suspicion if this was enough ground for a dishonorable discharge. Since there were no alternate narratives, this story had stuck. I was able to garner this much of information during Asad's numerous emergency department visits in the last two years.

Kuki's another unique accomplishment was that he was instrumental in starting Amoka's first Sanghaali gang. After he was fired from the military, he was roaming around the streets of Amoka in search of a decent means of livelihood. However, life had other designs for him. He wanted to get back to work at the Amoka General Hospital, but Powell did not hire him again. It was not clear to me as to why he had not gone to Minneapolis or other big cities that could offer many opportunities. According to the police he had then organized gangs of Sanghaali youth and had turned into a peddler of methamphetamines, marijuana and other recreational drugs. In fact, he was one of the main distributors in this part of the country. The name, Assad Delmar Abdhikarim didn't go well with his newfound profession, so the moniker Kuki stuck to him. Nobody knew if it was the police that gave him this name or if it was his customers. Anyway, whatever that might be, each time the police called to alert us that Kuki was being brought to the ER for 'medical clearance', it would cause a flutter of excitement in everyone. The reason was simple: behind his every visit there was an interesting story!

When I first met Assad, he had already transitioned to 'Kuki'. I remember quite clearly the very first time I met him. The police officer had brought him to the emergency department—profusely bleeding from a scalp laceration. He was arrested for causing a ruckus at Amoka's infamous bar, Grandpa Bob. The story goes that he had continued drinking up to the bar's closing and demanded more whisky. The bouncers had to forcibly kick him out. An enraged Kuki apparently had urinated right there at the bar's entrance. When the bar owner admonished him, Kuki had cursed him and pulled a knife. The terrified owner then had to call the police. The police had picked Kuki up, ostensibly to file a misdemeanor charge. As he was being driven in the police car, he had banged his head all over and started bleeding profusely. The scared police officer had to bring him directly to the hospital instead of jail.

'C'mon arrest me, you racist motherfuckers. You serve scotch to that white son-of-a-bitch but not to me, huh? I'm a veteran. I worked in the army, you fucktards! Do you really want to mess with me?'

I had given 2 mg of Haloperidol to calm him down. I had introduced myself politely, 'Hello sir, Mr Abdhikarim.'

He'd looked at me and said, 'You are not white. Call me Kuki, brother. Where from? Pakistan?' The Haloperidol was starting to do its job.

'No, no. India.' By then he had already gone off to sleep.

After he woke up, mellowed, the police had taken him to jail.

Kuki had a special affection for me. He would calm down the moment he saw me no matter how much of a violent brawl he had gotten into. Apparently, he had not seen any other non-white doctors in Amoka. He could not have possibly known or even seen Razak or Radhika since his business was mostly with the police and the emergency department.

Once, he had visited the hospital before going to jail. He didn't appear drunk. According to the police he was under the influence of some drug. But his blood and urine results were negative for any trace of alcohol or any street drugs. I thought that this was such a pain; why couldn't they take him straight to jail? I sat near Kuki and had warned him, 'Kuki, if you have drunk or smoked some crap, that's your problem. I can sign off telling that there were no traces of any drugs in your urine or blood and send you to jail. If you have taken some drugs that cannot be detected by routine tests, then you are inviting trouble for yourself.'

'Doc, you have to trust me. I am on no drugs. None of us are. I will get all my boys here and ask them to pee, right in front of you, supervised piss, ok. Isn't that what these motherfuckers call that? Test them for whatever you want. If anyone is positive for anything other than pot, I will cut their dicks off.'

Talk about solving the root of the problem. I didn't want to talk about it anymore. 'Kuki, why this gang business? Why can't you live a decent life? You are not only messing up your life but also that of these kids!'

He had retorted, 'I'm protecting our boys, doc.'

'From what?'

'From these drugs that I sell and from the great United States of America.'

I didn't get what he was talking about. He'd looked at my blank stare and continued, 'Doc, you don't get it. Do you? You people come here with all the education and stuff. Even after these many years, there are no Indian gangs. Why do you think so? We didn't come here to be gangsters, either. Why do you think there are Sanghaali gangs?'

I was quiet and had no real answer to his question. Kuki had continued, 'Poverty, doc. We are all poor. No education, no job. America got us here. They welcome us and take care of us for what, six months? Then we are on the streets trying to get a job. Our boys have no education. Back in Sanghaala, getting two meals a day was tough. But poverty in America is different, doc. Nobody is hungry, but a lot of us are poor. Back home, if you are poor, you are hungry. Here it is poverty without hunger. America gives us food stamps but no decent jobs. What do you do when you are not hungry but have no job? You hang out on streets and smoke ganja, hash, marijuana, pot, whatever you call it. When you get a chance, you sell the stuff. Control doc, if I control my supply then I control my distribution and customers. I put my boys to work and show them the money. There is no other way to keep my boys away from pot or coke. It was tough at first but check them out now. I can say for sure that none of my boys do any drugs.' Kuki had no dearth of stories. Each story had the same strange narratives, the same strange logic.

Kuki was in the emergency department charged with possession of marijuana in his car. I had to examine him and certify that he was medically fit to go to jail.

I had not examined Kuki yet. I was going over his records when Powell came in.

'Guru, I would like to talk to you for a bit.'

'Powell, I have to go now to see a patient.'

'He is the one that I have to talk to you about. This is very important.'

I closed my office door and looked at Powell inquisitively.

'Guru, I don't have to tell you how to do your job. But no

matter what, do not admit Kuki to our hospital. Let him go to jail. If in case, you think he needs to be hospitalized, send him elsewhere on the pretext that we do not have specialists in this hospital.'

This was funny. I had not yet examined Kuki. I did not think he had anything that needed hospital admission. Even if he did, the decision was mine. Powell was not a doctor, but he was telling me not to admit him.

I smiled, 'Powell isn't that supposed to be my decision?'

'I agree, Guru. Please work with me here. I think this is a high profile case. The real reason that Kuki has been arrested is to enquire about the Sanghaali girls' suicides. All this marijuana business is just an excuse. The police needed a reason to arrest him. It is suspected that Kuki also has links with a Sanghaali terrorist organization, just like Dr Mohammad Mohammad.'

I did not know what to say. The Sanghaali mothers are committing suicides for apparently no reason. No one was sure if Radhika's C-sections had anything to do with these suicides. How were Sanghaali terrorists responsible for these suicides? Can a small felon like Kuki engaged in petty crimes be a terrorist?

I asked Powell, 'Who told you?'

Powell said, 'Amoka is not a big town. The police chief here is my brother-in-law. He is the one who arrested Kuki. The higher-ups of his department have asked him to send Kuki to Minneapolis somehow or the other. There is a warrant for arrest against Kuki in Hennepin County. But this guy is here. If we pack him off to Minneapolis, our job is done. Then the "higher higher-ups" will investigate. Even my brother-in-law does not know if it is the police, or someone even higher, who will be investigating Kuki.' He gestured with his fingers and wrote FBI in the air when he mentioned 'higher higher-ups', as if confiding a secret.

It was not clear if this was all cockamamie bullshit or if there was some truth to what he was saying. He sounded excited knowing that a person wanted by the FBI was in our hospital. He winked at me when he was writing those letters with his fingers. He appeared to be in a state of mysterious thrill.

'I'll do my job as a doctor. Moreover, I don't think Kuki has any serious illness. Let us see,' I slipped away from Powell and his questions. For a moment I was not sure if I was practicing medicine.

I went to Kuki's room to talk to him. Kuki was busy, continuously texting on his phone. The police officer who had brought him said with unconcealed petulance, 'Doc, it looks like he is sending messages to all his friends. And our legal system will not allow us to seize his phone either! I am trying to get hold of my chief. No success there. When asked to stop texting, his excuse is that he is texting all his family members to inform them that he is in the hospital. Sometimes I can't help but wonder if our criminals have more rights than us.'

I asked him, 'What's happening, Kuki?'

'My chest hurts, doc.' He did not even try to look at me. He continued furiously texting on his new Samsung phone. I was surprised at his texting speed.

I was not in the least convinced about Kuki's complaints much less its seriousness. Arrested criminals locked up in jail need a pretext to come to the hospital. A complaint such as chest pain usually warrants an ECG, blood test and other sundry tests. This can easily keep them away from jail for at least about three hours. Till I certify that they are healthy, the arresting police officers cannot take them back to jail. And in his case, they have tased him too, which adds an additional layer of entitlement. The police, therefore, were more careful. They were in no hurry to take him back to jail. The police officer pulled a chair and sat next to him.

I looked at Kuki and asked him, 'Kuki, how long have you had this chest pain?'

Kuki did not change his stare, 'Since these bastards tased me. The folks from Amnesty International say tasing is torture. I'll sue your ass till your last penny.' He looked up at the police officer.

I told him, 'Kuki you should not speak like that. They are doing their job. I heard that there was marijuana in your car?'

'Doc, they found two plants; for my own use. No big deal.'

I looked at the police officer. The officer gestured to me to step outside with him. Once we were out of the room, he told me, 'Doc, I'm not officially supposed to disclose all these to you. Yes, we did find only two plants; but each one was like a small Christmas tree. I wonder where he grows them. Why don't you okay him and release him? I'll take it from there.'

This police officer seemed to be ignorant of the plans of Amoka's police chief to banish Kuki to Minneapolis. Their way of working clearly showed that the left hand does not know what the right hand is up to. It made me clueless about what to do next.

I told the police officer, 'You stay here. I'll go in and talk to Kuki,' and went inside.

Kuki was still busy messaging. 'Kuki, if this messaging is that important to you I'll come and see you later. I have other work to do.'

'Just a minute, doc.' He pressed the send button one last time and switched off the phone.

'Ok. Where exactly is your chest hurting?'

'I have angina, doc. It starts in the left side of my chest and goes to the left side of my neck, left shoulder, and arm. It gets worse with exertion and becomes severe if I walk for some time. I also get shortness of breath. I can feel the heart thumping loudly. I start sweating a lot. I have both high blood pressure and diabetes.' It sounded like he was reading the lines from a medical textbook—as if he had memorized all the symptoms of the disease and blurted them out.

We were both aware that everything he said was a lie. Yet, this was a game between us. Kuki knew the right words to say to buy him an admission to the hospital. I knew exactly how to deal with people like Kuki. I looked at him and smiled.

He did not smile back. 'Doc, don't you laugh. You have to do an ECG and do some blood tests. One ECG isn't enough. Can't people having a heart attack have a normal ECG? Admit me to the hospital, doc. Check my enzymes. Don't you guys do that enzyme test several times? If that doesn't do it, then I need to have that stress test. If I can run on that damn treadmill, then I get to go home, right?

'By then you would have got hold of a lawyer who will have you released from the hospital. Are twenty-four hours enough for your lawyer to do his job?'

'Doc, are you going to admit me to the hospital or not?'

'No. There is nothing wrong with you. I'm going to discharge you. Go with the police directly to the big house.'

Kuki said immediately, 'Doc, my pain is getting worse.'

'Oh, is that so? Let's do one thing. I'll send you to a cardiologist in Minneapolis right away. If they determine there is nothing wrong with you, they'll discharge you.'

Kuki's expression changed. His face paled with fear. 'Oh No! You can't send me to Minneapolis.' I immediately remembered Powell's words: 'The marijuana was just an excuse for his arrest. He was, in fact, arrested for investigating the Sanghaali suicides. Send him to Minneapolis for some medical reason. The higher-ups will take care of him.'

In fact, the thought of transferring him to another hospital had never occurred to me, but seeing his fear of going to Minneapolis, I couldn't help thinking that what Powell said may have some truth to it.

I sat next to him and said, 'Kuki, let's do another ECG after an hour. Then once we get your blood report, let's think about what to do next.' I entered some orders in the computer and looked at him, 'Would you like to watch TV?' He said yes, and I switched on the TV. Channel 12 was airing a program on the Sanghaali suicides. I had not expected Channel 12 to come on air when I switched on the TV. It was weird to both of us. I stood there watching without switching off the TV. Kuki did not speak at all. He sat there watching the program wide-eyed without batting an eyelid.

After about five minutes, I could not keep quiet anymore. 'Kuki, what is your opinion on all these incidents at Amoka, Minneapolis and all of Minnesota?'

Kuki did not speak.

Sometimes, in my profession, the treatment of a patient goes beyond the conventional pills and shots approach. There is a popular saying with a ring of truth to it that some light banter can cure half the disease. In fact, even in places like the emergency department where we are supposed to 'treat and street' the patients, physicians 'small talk' them out of their ailment. For instance, I throw in a comment like, 'The weather in this town sucks' to a patient who has come in for flu in the middle of winter. Or I say 'Sometimes this damn black ice can be tough to deal with' to a patient who has broken his leg after rolling his car into a ditch. I listen with practiced patience, dripping love story of a patient with gonorrhea, or a lecture on economy by an alcoholic stockbroker. These conversations veer around the relevant and the irrelevant topics of both the patient and the disease. I indulge in these conversations motivated by my imagination that my words can be enablers for their cure.

'Isn't the act of suicide considered haram in Islam?' I asked not knowing why I did so. That was only an attempt to keep the conversation going.

Kuki glared at me for a minute. I was a little terrified and looked towards the closed door. The thought of the police officer outside comforted me.

'Doc, are you a Muslim?' He looked at me with his sharp eyes. Kuki had a strongly built imposing physique.

'No.'

'Yet you know that suicides are haram in Islam?'

I did not speak.

'Doc, can we have a chat? You got no patients, right? Who the fuck comes to this hospital anyway?'

I looked at his face passively.

'Sorry doc, scratch that. Do you have any idea why we Sanghaalis came to America, to Minnesota? Any idea how we live?'

'There is a civil war in your country and many of you have come here as refugees. Right?'

'Yes, doc. There is a war, alright. Who the hell are we fighting? I was very young when I came to Minnesota. I have no idea how my mom and dad look like. They used to write letters sometimes. I am from a small village near Dahir-Bar. It was a hellhole, doc. Bullets whizzing through our windows from who knows where, bombs from above—we were right in the middle of this war. For some reason everything stopped one day. No bullets, No bombs. People started to get out of Sanghaala. Some came to America. Some went to Germany, England and France. But my folks decided to stay back. I came to Amoka with my uncle. I went to school here. I worked here, right in this fucking hospital. Then as you are aware, I served in the military. I went to Afghanistan, doc—Afghanistan, when all these little white boys stayed here all cozied up with their families. I didn't stay there long. When I came back, my uncle told me that he hadn't heard from my parents. I will tell you one thing, doc, when shit hits the fan, our people know how to get out and live out in the desert. I assumed that something like that has happened; but when I didn't hear from them for one year, I decided to go there and check them out.

'I don't know how much you know about Sanghaala. There is no government there. Everyone carries an AK-47. There are some folks whom America calls Warlords. When you give guns to some gangbanger, how hard is it for him to become the lord, doc? Only god knows where the hell they get these guns from. They always blew up food trucks and planes of America, the United Nations, the Red Cross and what not. They would bring down planes carrying food to our hungry people. They would attack trucks and steal all food packets, milk powder bags and drinking water. These motherfuckers kept my people hungry and terrified. America started bombing them and called it the war on terror. There were bombs everywhere, dropped randomly from the sky. Cities and towns were gone, poof, just like that. The bomb doesn't know who you are. It kills you no matter. You could be a killer or you could be a baby. Yes sir! You could be an imam or a hooker. Everybody was gone. Those who lived got a free ticket and a visa to America, Italy or England as refugees. They were told that they can start new lives. Those who were left behind started their own gangs. When "war on terror" killed one gang, another looting gang in the next street called themselves terrorists. They name themselves, Al Tewagi. They are no terrorists. Bunch of gangbangers, I would say.'

I couldn't help but smile at Kuki's hypothesis of how Al Tewagi, the notorious terror organization of Sanghaala was born. But his argument had some meat in it. 'Kuki, if refugees are brought here and given jobs, isn't that better than being in the middle of a war in your country?'

'That's how it looks for you, sir. Look at our people. They don't know English, they got no skills. Do you know where they work? Have you seen the jobs they do? They work in paper mills, on chicken farms, at fucking McDonalds, doc; almost half the janitors in the Minneapolis airport are from Sanghaala.'

According to his logic, America starts internal strife and civil war in Sanghaala, gets the survivors here on a visa and puts them on menial jobs like slaves for its own benefit.

'Kuki, you are not making any sense at all. Think about the difference between how it would have been there and how it is here. Your people get green cards more easily than any of us. Think about your next generation. Do they have a better future here or in Sanghaala?'

'Agreed. Yay to us, considering what kind of a shithole Sanghaala is now. But do you know why this happened? Let me tell you another story. You seem to be in the mood today. As I told you earlier, I had visited my town in Sanghaala, a few days after I came back from Afghanistan. When I went there, I noticed that my town, my house, my father, and my mother were all gone. Fucking rubbles, sir. Everything was wiped out clean by bombs and grenades. In that garbage, I found Pepsi bottles and "Made in America" grenades, doc. They said that was the work of a gang in Dahir Bar. How the fuck could a gang get a grenade? Now, nobody knew who the enemy was and who the friend was. The people who were fighting America were doing that using grenades made in America. If they used them, it was terror, if America used them it was war. Nobody knew if America was helping us. Doc, let me tell you, when I was still in the country, the war started and it was hell again. I'm an American citizen, right? When I went to the American Embassy for protection, they opened gunfire on me. I was in full military uniform. But the motherfuckers at the embassy didn't let me in. I escaped to Kenya in a small coracle. The embassy there also did not let me in. They gave an excuse that Sanghaalis tried to sneak in by wearing a military uniform. I was shocked. I had no idea who I should I be angry with. My entire town was destroyed, and no one knew who did this. I worked for the American military but when I tried to seek help, our embassies tried to kill me. Imagine if I had died, I would just be another number. May be not even that.'

'Kuki, I agree that you have been wronged. But then so are many others. However, what is the relationship between that and the events in Amoka?'

'There is a relationship, doc.'

I looked at him.

'Doc, are you a vegetarian?'

'Kuki, what has that got to do with what we are discussing here?'

It seemed this way of going around the topic is the characteristic of these Sanghaalis. I was reminded of Mohammad Mohammad who also had a story for everything.

'Are you or are you not?' He wanted an answer.

'Yes, I am.'

'Do you get your Indian spices in Amoka?'

'No, I get them delivered'

'How does it make you feel if the government tried to force you to eat a hamburger every day?'

'The government cannot do any such thing.'

'You have come here on a visa, so it should not be a problem. Our people are here as fucking refugees, can they force us to live in a certain way?'

'Who is doing that now, Kuki?'

'If we are brought to this country and are made to feel grateful for everything America did for us, or if such conditions are created back in Sanghaala which would make it impossible for us to go back, could they force us to live in a certain way?'

'How can that happen? It is our fundamental right to lead our life the way we want.'

'Hah, is it your right or does your religion tell you to do that?'

'My religion?'

'Yes, doc. Like, does your religion ask you to be a vegetarian?'

'I do not know anything about that, but I have been a vegetarian since childhood and I'm one to this day.'

'That's fine, doc. If eating a fucking hamburger is considered haram in your religion, isn't it easy to refuse to eat it by saying your religion has forbidden it? No one can force you. Not even the government.'

I found it hard to follow Kuki and where he was going with his reasoning. I just said, 'Possibly Kuki.'

'Doc, if we follow our beliefs even in little things like what we eat or what we drink, there is nothing wrong with expecting our children to be born in a certain way. And especially if that is what our religion says.'

'What is that supposed to mean? Is it wrong if children are born by Cesarean sections?'

'What if it is beyond fucking wrong? What if it is haram?'

'Meaning?'

'Meaning, if these women are unable to deliver babies normally and they have to get their tummies cut to deliver their babies, it could mean haram to them. Isn't it possible that many religious minded women may have thought of choosing death over doing any such thing?'

'Are they thinking like that?'

'I don't know, doc. I was only saying that if you are a believer, you would know if it isn't worth dying for, it isn't worth living.'

I couldn't believe what I was hearing. I was scared for a moment. Is this a religious war of clashing faiths?

Kuki continued, 'If more and more Sanghaalis are born here, who would suffer more? Sanghaalis or Americans?'

'What does that mean?'

'When we were growing up in Sanghaala, it was common for a family to have ten to fifteen children, doc. So, if our Sanghaalis here in America wish to have many children, then that cannot be wrong according to our faith. Right doc?'

'If women go on killing themselves, how can you have more children, Kuki?'

'To keep a mother who can have ten kids alive, mothers who can only bear two kids must make some sacrifices, doc.'

'Do you also believe that if women deliver by Cesarean sections, they cannot have ten kids?'

'Can you or your friends guarantee that they can?'

I could not continue this conversation any longer. Is Kuki trying to bullshit his way into generating a public outcry if Fadhuma and Rukhiya's deaths are given this spin, whatever may have been the actual reason behind their deaths? If these women really wanted the media's attention why would they die such anonymous deaths?

Why in Amoka of all places? There are larger cities like New York and Chicago. They would get way more publicity there. Or, just because they are dying in Amoka and no Sanghaali is talking to the media, is there any dearth of publicity?

Kuki's blood results were back. As I had anticipated, everything looked normal. Kuki hadn't had a heart attack.

I asked Kuki, 'In all of these events, what is your role?'

Kuki looked at me and laughed, 'Doc, our women are good mothers. All they do is get pregnant and raise kids. Don't try to teach them how to deliver their own babies. If you say that they do not know how to make babies and pop them out, they can even give their lives to prove you wrong. Nobody knows if there is such a thing as religion. Nobody knows if there isn't. But they think you are directly challenging their motherhood.'

I told Kuki, 'Your blood reports look alright. However,

since there is some risk, we must send you to Minneapolis. It is not safe to discharge you without a cardiology evaluation.'

Kuki replied, 'Please don't doc. I will not go to Minneapolis. Please ... let me go.' He started shouting.

I stepped away to inform the police officer sitting outside and get an ambulance ready while Kuki kept yelling.

15. Movie-Making

Kuki's words bothered me for a long time. An ordinary drug dealer had thrown some light on incidents unravelling in Amoka. In fact, in all of Minnesota. None of us had thought that a routine medical procedure widely accepted and practiced by the healthcare community could be offensive to a faith. No text book had taught us that Cesarean section is a taboo to certain religions and culture. I had thought that we learnt a lot about the Sanghaali culture after that meeting with Dr Mohammad Mohammad. However, after my conversation with Kuki, I was more confused as to what I needed to know and more importantly, what I didn't need to know. Or as Kuki put it, does faith succeed in exerting the right kind of pressure where the law of the land fails?

Were things really happening the way Kuki claimed? Had the religious leaders of the Sanghaali community ruled that bearing children by 'cutting the belly open' goes against their beliefs? Had these women resorted to suicides fearing excommunication from their religion? Or had elements like Kuki exploited this fear to their advantage by resorting to every dirty trick of the trade—jihad, religious war, the call to sacrifice lives for the greater service of god, etc.?

And after all, it is not as if I'm some big shot that Kuki must explain and clarify these questions to.

What do I do with this information? I had not shared it with anyone except Srikantha. Not even with Radhika. However, the thought that I knew something about these suicides that no one else did was kind of suffocating. I thought that I should share it with someone, and get the weight off my chest.

It was at this time that Rick Jackson had called Radhika and me for another meeting. I had asked Radhika if she had any prior knowledge of such a meeting. And she said that she had none.

There were not many attendees in the meeting. There was Radhika, Powell, Amoka's police chief, a couple of strangers and me. Radhika sat next to me and took my hand in hers. Her hand was sweating. I squeezed her hand and gestured to her not to worry.

Since Rick Jackson was the president of the hospital board, he called the meeting to order. 'I want to say this is an informal meeting. I think we all know each other. But our higher ups want to make it as formal as possible. So, I think it would be appropriate to have a formal introduction. Let us start with me. My name is Rick Jackson. I'm the owner of the law firm, Jackson Associates. I'm also the president of the hospital board.'

Radhika and I introduced ourselves. The strangers that were present there apparently worked for the State Health Department as contractors. They had inscrutable titles like chief liaison officer, director of performance excellence and media consultant. For a moment I couldn't help wonder why the government would outsource these positions. Then I realized that this may not be the time to delve into such thoughts.

Jackson continued, 'We all know Katie Couric, right? She was working at America's NBC channel a few years back. She was happily married to a very handsome man and had two children. She made good money and was quite comfortable with her life. Unfortunately, her husband was diagnosed with colon cancer at forty-two and died within six months of the diagnosis. It was a life changing event for Katie. She had lived a life of privilege and celebrity all along and this was a big blow to her. She was clueless about what to do with her life and she quit her job and stayed home for the next six months. She was clinically depressed. Then her psychiatrist had advised her, "Look Katie, you can either stay home brooding over your husband's death or you can tell the world about what can be done to avert such untimely deaths. Use your fame for the greater good of the world. And you all know what Katie did, right?"'

It was not clear to me why Jackson was parroting this story, which the world knew by now. I replied, 'Yes. She had a colonoscopy performed on herself on national TV in front of the whole world.'

Jackson added for the benefit of the police chief, 'I think we are all familiar with colonoscopy, right? It is a procedure that involves the inserting of a tube, with a camera at its tip, from the anus up to the intestine to check if there is any cancer inside. This test saves about ten thousand lives every year in America.'

'Did she really get a colonoscopy done on national TV?' The police chief asked.

I had a feeling that the chief may be feigning ignorance. How can he not know anything about this incident! This had made big news all over America.

'After Katie Couric's colonoscopy, there was increased awareness about colon cancer and colonoscopy among all Americans, and the number of people getting colonoscopies doubled the very next year.'

I started to get the drift of where he was going with all this talk, but nothing was clear yet. I was aware that he was setting a precedence to his plan of the YouTube video of a Cesarean section but when he mentioned network TV, I suspected that he was gearing up for something much bigger. I did not utter a word.

The police chief said, 'Wow! Look at the strength of the media.'

Radhika asked, 'Strength of the media or Katie's popularity?'

'Both. If Katie had her colonoscopy done in a regular hospital, it would not have made such big news, or if some average Joe had his colonoscopy done on national television, it would still have made news, maybe not on this scale.'

Radhika said, 'Ok. Why is this incident important to us now? Why are we discussing it?'

Rick Jackson looked at the police chief's face.

The police chief said, 'Look, six women have committed suicides in this state. What do you think is the common factor? Cesarean sections and Sanghaali women. Hence, we have racked our brains trying to get to the bottom of this mystery and the role of these C-sections in these suicides. Experts have gone over the medical records of every patient. They have tried to contact their family members. But no one has got any real lead. All tracks have gone cold. We are unable to come up with any explanation for these suicides. Someone might have brainwashed these women that they may die or may not be able to bear children in the future if they underwent this surgery.'

For a moment I thought about sharing what Kuki had told me. The instant this thought occurred to me, I could feel a scary intuition of being sucked into a giant vortex. Words failed me, and I remained silent.

Rick continued, 'Our experts have studied this situation thoroughly and given us some suggestions. Let the investigation proceed as planned. On our part, we need to come up with ways in which we can effectively educate these Sanghaali women and show them that these are safe surgeries. However, we have to do this very strategically and need to be careful on how we communicate with them.'

I now understood why Rick Jackson had raised Katie Couric's case here.

'So, do we also need to telecast a Cesarean section on TV?' Radhika laughed.

Rick Jackson said, 'Exactly my point,' and looked at the officials from the state's health department. The woman who had the tag of 'Media Consultant' clipped on her, spoke. 'My name is Molly. I'm a media consultant with the Health Department. We have decided to shoot a short documentary on the Cesarean sections for our Sanghaali community. Our intention is to show them that the Cesarean sections you do at your hospital are safe. We need a local touch for this documentary. It will be shot right here in this hospital. The patient should be from this community. The commentary will be in Sanghaali with subtitles running in English.'

Radhika replied, 'Are you going to shoot this with real patients and real doctors?'

'Radhika, that's why it is called a documentary,' said Jackson.

Radhika and I fell silent again.

Jackson said, 'Both of you should speak up and participate in the discussion. Be team players. What good would it do if you don't participate?'

I said, 'The problem here is not that of Cesarean sections. Isn't it more about the "once a C-section, always a C-section" issue? They strongly believe that a C-section would curtail their chances of having more children.'

'May be so. But we need to start somewhere. Your guess is as good as mine on what we get out of this. We have no control over future deliveries. For now, we can show them that there is no danger from the present one,' chimed in the woman from the Department of Health.

Rick whispered in my ears, 'Guru, this is damage control. This nuisance started from our hospital. We must show the public that we are taking it seriously and not winging it. I know it looks like a sham, but as she said, *we must do something*. We must act on it. I have already alluded to this with you before.'

I assumed that Radhika may have overheard our conversation and wondered how that may have registered in her mind.

I addressed the whole group, 'Could you please clarify what you are talking about? Are you talking about recording the Cesarean sections that Radhika, Razak or Smith do at our hospital and broadcast them on TV?'

Molly said, 'Well, Rick, would you like to continue?'

'To tell you the truth, this Cesarean section must be performed by Radhika. She was the one who performed the C-sections on Rukhiya and Fadhuma. Hence it stands to reason that it is desirable to have Radhika do this one too. One more thing, Razak should not do this operation.'

'Why?' Radhika asked softly.

'Ok, let's come straight to the point. We would prefer to shoot this documentary with a pregnant Sanghaali woman. It lends credibility to this project. But no Sanghaali woman will consent to it. If we did succeed in convincing them, what if they kill themselves after this real time C-section on TV? That will prove their point with the much needed publicity they might be hoping for. So, we have decided to settle for the next best thing.'

'What is that?'

'A South Asian or an African American woman in this town.'

I said, 'Zeba?' I remembered going over Zeba's medical records as soon as I heard the news of her pregnancy. It was a reflex action then, driven more by circumstances. Today it meant something else. Am I thinking like a leader? Am I one of them?

Rick Jackson nodded in agreement.

Radhika was shaken. She shouted, 'What!'

'Guru. Stop this nonsense. No…no…' Her lips were quivering, and her eyes welled up.

Seeing this melodrama of screams and tears unfold, the media consultant was shaken for a moment and held her hand to her chest. 'My Goodness!' she said, as if she was invoking the benediction of her god for some sanity.

I couldn't be quiet any longer. 'Rick, I find it amusing that you don't seem to understand that these Sanghaalis are not the same as Zeba and Razak. There can be a thousand reasons for Sanghaalis not consenting to Cesarean sections. But, Zeba is a Pakistani. She would never say "Yes" to this surgery. In fact, if my memory serves me right, her first delivery was also by a Cesarean section. If you plan to fool the public by showing Zeba as a Sanghaali woman undergoing a Cesarean section on TV just because she is Muslim, you are making a grave mistake.'

Rick Jackson was quiet for a moment, and then said softly, 'Guru, you have to believe me here. This is not my idea. There is a lot of pressure from the higher-ups.'

I asked, 'To do what? Make a movie?'

'No, to have an unequivocal positive response from our side to these suicides.'

Radhika asked, 'Isn't firing us a better response?'

'Dr Radhika, we have discussed all our options. To tell you the truth, we did discuss firing you. That is not a positive response. This is somewhat like shadow boxing. Sanghaali women are trying to highlight some problem in our system by committing suicide. Their intent is perhaps to make us stop performing the Cesarean sections or ensure that no other Sanghaali woman gets it done. Apparently, this is some kind of jihad. Again, I have no basis for my claims other than the word on the street. It may be impossible to know their real intention. You tell us what it is that we can do. Several people have brainstormed the situation and come to this decision. We must demonstrate to all that this is a safe surgery and we are not at fault for what has been happening in Amoka. Since Zeba's first delivery was by Cesarean section, if we do a C-section for the second, it can at least prove what we are trying to say.'

I asked, 'Who has come to this decision?'

'Doctors, you guys have to understand something. I'm only a middleman doing what has been told to me by my higher-ups. I hope you do the same.'

'What if I do not agree to this proposal? Or if Razak and Zeba do not agree?'

'Dr Radhika, the higher-ups have decided not to fire you only to save the reputation of the hospital. It is true that the Sanghaali women whom you operated upon committed suicide. This can be a significant reason, but then there can be a million other reasons too.'

'Isn't this blackmail?'

'No. If there was another way of proving your indispensability, I would gladly do so. But then, what can I do? You are not giving me any options. We are desperate! You have to believe me.'

For some reason, my gut told me that we should trust him.

Radhika kept quiet. She must have sensed the futility of any further discussion.

I was unable to keep quiet and said, 'Ok, assuming Radhika agrees to do this surgery, how do you know that Zeba needs a Cesarean section? And if by chance she needs one, are you certain that she will get it done here?'

'Since she had her first baby by C-section, the probability of the second one also needing one is high.'

Radhika started blabbering, 'That's so not true. She can possibly have a normal delivery. Isn't she only four months into her pregnancy? Do we have her consent? What if she does not agree? What if she leaves town?'

'Dr Radhika, no one can compel anyone here. This is

America. This is a free country. Everyone works here for their own interest. As far as I know, Razak has also come to this country on a J-visa. Like all of you, this job is his existentialist gateway into this country. It determines his right to stay here or leave. And Zeba is five and a half months into her pregnancy; not four months as you think. We have three more months to convince all the parties involved. By then if we get a Sanghaali who is ready for this, then we can cross Zeba off our list.

'You son of a bitch...'—the words stayed in my mouth. Perhaps my facial expression mirrored my words. Dr Jackson smiled.

I did not speak.

'Guru, Radhika, I can understand your predicament. I'm not such a bad person as you guys perhaps take me to be. If Smith had agreed, I would have had no need to put pressure on you. He has been in this place for a long time now. He is in no mood to listen. Please help us. Trust me, I'm under no illusion that this TV documentary, this movie can change everything. We must do something. The higher-ups are looking at it as a first step.'

I told him, 'Whatever is happening here is because of someone's provocation. These Sanghaali women are not doing these things out of their own volition.'

Molly said, 'Is there any proof towards that? There's not a single complaint registered. The police files have registered them as suicides with no explicit motives.'

'Can we solve such cases based only on Minnesota police investigation? Where is the FBI?'

Molly laughed loudly, 'Doctor, do you watch a lot of these Hollywood crime thrillers? Do you even know how the FBI works? Do you think they will keep you informed on everything they do? Your perception of an FBI agent is someone in a dark suit who wears his Aviator glasses and sits in cars with tinted glasses taking pictures, right? Let's say that if there is a directive from Washington to make a movie like this one, would you agree then?' She drank water from a bottle placed in front of her.

I fell silent again.

Rick observed the drift of the conversation and tried to change the topic. 'It looks like there is a lot of yarn being weaved here. I'm confident that Razak will convince his wife. I can promise you that Zeba's privacy will not be compromised. Other details must be worked out. We shall give you everything you need.'

I didn't know what to say to Rick. Time and again when he kept reiterating that 'Guru and Radhika, you two must believe me,' I had no clue who to be angry at and whom to suspect. My silence was taken as my consent.

Did my little chat with Kuki a few days ago have any impact on my words or my silence today?—I reflected on that only later.

On my way back home with Radhika, I asked her, 'Radhika, do you think this Molly is really a press liaison?'

'What else? Do you think she is an FBI agent? You know what, I really don't care! Let me ask you something. This TV documentary or whatever, you did know about this drama right from the beginning, didn't you?'

I did not know how to respond to this question. It is true that Rick Jackson had raised an initial proposal with me to record a Cesarean section and post its YouTube link on the hospital's Facebook page. But I was not aware that this plan had been further repurposed to a documentary of a Cesarean section on a proxy Muslim woman since a Sanghaali was not available. Would Radhika believe me even if I tell her what I knew? For now, I had to give her an answer. 'A couple of months ago, Rick Jackson had brought this up at a very basic level without much details.'

'Yet, you did not share it with me. Heck, you did not even give a vague heads-up that this was coming. I thought you were a friend! And so did Zeba and Razak! But you turned out to be nothing but an administrator. A teacher's pet always looking for the management's approval.' She closed her eyes. It was hard to miss that she was furious at me.

16. Saanvi—New York, NY

Sometimes, when we are unsure of doing something, we end up acting on a random impulse. When I reflect years later, I'm not so sure whether it was a good idea to call Saanvi who was in New York. I had not yet shaken off the hangover from the Rick Jackson meeting. After the meeting, I was certain that Rick would convince Zeba, and Radhika herself might end up doing Zeba's Cesarean section. But Radhika was mad at me. She was even more convinced that I was siding with the hospital administration. She had neither looked me in the eye nor spoken with me. It was not clear whether she had agreed to perform the operation.

I felt that this plan of Rick Jackson was laughable to say the least. Was it fair, or even sensible for Radhika to operate on a Pakistani woman to demonstrate to Sanghaali women that Cesarean sections are safe? This whole affair of using a proxy Muslim woman was patently naïve. I couldn't help but question whether Rick Jackson and this media consultant Molly, had seen the world outside of Minnesota. But they were asserting that the directions to do so had come from Washington. The more I thought about it, the murkier it got.

Apparently, Srikantha had convinced Radhika to be a part of this documentary by promising her that Saanvi would produce and direct it. The moment Radhika agreed, Srikantha had swung into action. He had spoken to Saanvi twice in the past week and had cautioned her that I would be calling her to share the details of this Amoka Project. He had insisted that I call Saanvi right away before Radhika changed her mind. To be honest, I was also apprehensive that if there was any delay, Rick Jackson may end up giving this project to some other company. I decided to co-opt Saanvi first and then talk to Rick about her.

I called Saanvi. The moment she picked up the phone, she started. 'Guru, it has been a long time since you called. Srikantha had called a couple of times. And there is no news from Radhika! I had planned on calling you, but I got busy. Anyway, after Srikantha told me all about it, I looked at your hospital's Facebook page. I navigated through all the links and got at least some sense of what the heck was going on over there. How did you guys let the situation come to this? Boy, such a mess. No thanks to you, boss. Those women are losing their lives. What's with all of you guys? Why are you guys forcing procedures on them that they are totally against? And despite all these, why this hush hush in the national media? Why are they not talking about them?' It was the same old Saanvi with her trademark staccato, non-stop talk, totally oblivious to the other person.

Saanvi is a friend of Kristina who did her residency with us at New York. Kristina is a physician like all of us and Saanvi had done a cinematography course at NYU. She had produced a few documentaries. Some of her movies had been screened at local film festivals. The short film that she had done on honor killings was on PBS's *Frontline*. This had given her high visibility and her name had started coming up frequently on the national networks. She was originally from Mangaluru. Cinema was her life. Prior to coming to New York, she had briefly worked with filmmaker Dibakar Banerjee in Bollywood. She had met Kristina at a movie premiere in New York and was immediately attracted to her. They now live together.

It was not clear if Saanvi was able to make a living from making documentaries, but Kristina was well-off. She had helped her girlfriend set up a Whole Foods store that they named, 'Maya Good Food Store'. Everything sold in this store was organic—be it vegetables, dairy, wine or poultry. Kristina was a yoga pants-socks and sandals-Go Green enthusiast. Diminutive Saanvi was an extremely active liberal who made documentary films on subjects like war, LGBTQ in India, Mumbai Metro, Kamatipura, and more. It was natural that they were attracted to each other. It was tough to say how much Kristina liked being a doctor. After she started living with Saanvi, she took up a part-time job at a women's clinic in Queens and started spending most of her time at Saanvi's store. Saanvi's store was a non-profit co-op, and offered free access to everyone regardless of race, gender or sexual orientation. They had also formed a small NGO called Maya Co-Op and published a newsletter titled *Color Purple.*

Though Kristina was a doctor like the rest of us, we had grown closer to Saanvi, perhaps because she was an Indian and even more so because she was from Karnataka. While we, the qualified medical professionals, lived in towns like Amoka for the sake of our green cards and to find a bearing in this country, Saanvi had comfortably settled down with Kristina in New York extending her visa every year. Her laissez-faire approach to life on issues that we stressed about surprised us, like her response when we asked her what she would do if she gets called out by immigration: 'You guys are all here as witnesses. I will marry Kristina in a jiffy!'

I replied to her on the phone, 'Saanvi, we are not forcing anyone. They most certainly need these Cesarean sections. Talk to Kristina if she is there. She can explain everything to you.'

'I don't agree. Srikantha talked to me in detail. I agree with your boss, Rick Jackson to a large extent. You guys are not doing a good job at explaining to the Sanghaalis on why they need Cesarean sections or someone else is doing a better job at influencing and misleading them on why they should not get a Cesarean section done. Men in the Sanghaali community are typically very controlling. Has any one of you spoken to them? In fact, Kristina and I are planning on coming there with some other folks from our "Maya".'

The hits kept on coming! As if we were looking for more trouble. I was not sure what Srikantha had discussed with her. The prospect of a New York's women's rights organization coming here and protesting for the rights of Sanghaali women would complete the last missing piece of this messy puzzle. Frankly, the thought scared me.

I told her, 'Saanvi, we have already had a great deal of trouble. Please do not come here and start your hartals and picketing. I called you to discuss the documentary. Srikantha may have already briefed you about it.'

'He has given me some information. He said that you would explain in detail. Go ahead, I am listening.'

'Look, we need a short documentary to explain to the people here what these Cesarean sections are and why and when do we do them. It should be fine even if this documentary comes across as an ad film for the Amoka General Hospital. I do not have much money budgeted for this. The main objective of this exercise is to make the town's Sanghaalis understand that the Cesarean sections done at our hospital are safe. This needs an effective local touch. The documentary must be shot right here in our hospital. And the patient should be one of our own. I think we should be able to broadcast the documentary on our local channels. We can also post it on YouTube. The commentary should be in Sanghaali with subtitles in English.' I told her, as if by rote, whatever Molly had said in the meeting. I decided to bring up Zeba's name now. Srikantha had told me that he had already hinted to Saanvi about Zeba's possible role in this C-section.

'And another thing,' I said rather casually, 'Srikantha might have already told you. Zeba is now pregnant. She is five and a half months into her pregnancy. Her first delivery was by Cesarean section. Radhika has examined her thoroughly and confirmed that this delivery—her second—will also be a Cesarean section.'

'Even if it isn't, you guys will ensure that it shall be so.'

I did not react to her words but continued, 'If we can somehow convince her and shoot the whole surgical procedure and broadcast it in all its details, Sanghaalis may get convinced that this is a safe surgery. And, Zeba is from this town. They would be comforted by the fact that our own doctors are operating on our people. Apparently, this would convince them that the Cesarean sections are quite safe. This is how our leadership thinks.'

'Are Zeba and Razak going to agree to this plan?'

'I don't know. It's our management's task to convince them. They will pull out every trick in their book. I hate to get Razak and Zeba involved in this. But, if you can come and make the movie, it might be easier on them too. For you, this is a simple job. For Zeba and Razak, it depends on how you play the pitch. Dads take videos of their baby's birth with their camera phones anyway. Razak will do the same. Let him shoot the same video in high definition under your direction. You can edit it to fit your needs. If we interview Razak and Zeba before and after the surgery, and show their close-ups, it will lend authenticity to the whole process.'

'Guru, you talk like a true businessman, dude. You don't seem to have given a thought to whether Zeba will agree to this plan.'

Saanvi's words did not surprise me at all. I had not asked

either Zeba or Razak. I had believed that Rick Jackson will convince them and reached out to Saanvi. In my mind, I was only looking at this as a job to be done; a task that needed to be accomplished. As I was starting to introspect the right and the wrong, Saanvi interrupted, 'That's ok Guru. If you guys do not seem to be bothered, why should I? But is it enough if we make this documentary and release it only on your local cable? I've been thinking about this ever since Srikantha spoke to me. Instead of broadcasting a recorded Cesarean section, it would be cool to broadcast it live as that gets more publicity and a larger viewership. And more sponsorships too! We could even shoot for a national network. I've contacts at NBC. You are aware of the Katie Couric case. Aren't you?'

There it goes again. Katie Couric had her colonoscopy live on TV several years ago and now everyone still talks about it!

Ever since she heard about our plans, Saanvi had emphasized her interest in broadcasting the C-section over the national channels. It was not clear if this was the eagerness of a TV journalist for eye-popping headlines or the natural excitement of a women's rights activist trying to help Sanghaali women.

I said, 'Saanvi, I'm not looking to increase the ratings of the news channels. My interest is to communicate to the Sanghaali community that there are other people in Amoka who are getting C-sections done. And that our own doctors like Radhika are doing these operations which are safe.'

Saanvi retorted, 'Appropriate packaging of news is also an art.'

'Saanvi, there's something you should understand here. Both Fadhuma and Rukhiya who delivered at our hospital were new immigrants to America. I've gone over other cases of suicides also. They were all new immigrants too. Please understand my situation. The hospital's board is exerting pressure on us to address the situation. Somebody in Washington has decided on how to educate the Sanghaali community. I don't believe anyone is all that interested in turning this into headline news.'

'Ok, Guru, everything is very fuzzy here. Six Sanghaali women have died but, that has made news only on social media. There is hardly any coverage of it on the national network. And, not just that. Folks like Rick Jackson and Molly are asserting that they will fix everything if we can make a video that is more like a commercial and broadcast it on Amoka's local channels. But apparently, they have got instructions to do so from Washington? And, who is this Mohammad Mohammad? His Facebook page is flooded with posts about your hospital and these suicides. Why so? Don't you think he is giving as much publicity as possible to this news? But no one seems to be interested in taking things to the next logical level. The many links of these cases are not clicking into place.'

The moment she raised Mohammad Mohammad's name, I knew that she had done her research well.

'Hello ma'am, I've thought about this a lot and rubbed most people the wrong way. Now they have given me this task. I'm guessing there's one thing you are aware of. This is the age of social media. People don't get their headlines from the newspapers. They can make their own headlines. I believe our management is trying very hard to create our own headline news to avert this from turning into someone else's narrative. Folks like Rick and Powell may come across as vile people, but the fact of the matter is that they are just doing their jobs. Therefore, I'm seeking your assistance. Please let me know if you can help or not.' I ignored the Mohammad Mohammad part of the conversation on purpose.

'If we are doing it anyway, which would reach more people? Making a forty-minute documentary of the procedure or the news that a Muslim woman will undergo her Cesarean section live on TV?'

Everybody comes with their own agenda. This made my mind go mad with frustration. I asked her, 'Saanvi, by doing so aren't we giving it more visibility? The idea is to keep it local.'

'I hope you are not so naïve to believe that just because some news does not make the national headlines on CNN, it has remained local. You mentioned just a little while ago that this is the age of people making their own headlines.'

I remembered that Mohammad Mohammad's Facebook posts were shared even in Indonesia. I thought for a moment, 'Let's say we go by your plan, but then this is a Cesarean section. Can that be planned at all? Even if it can be, do you think Rick will consent to that? Will his superiors consent to that?'

'It is precisely because it is a Cesarean section, it can be planned. Today when people plan their baby's births for all kinds of reasons, for names, birth stars and what not, isn't it possible to plan a baby's birth for a good cause? Brief Rick on this plan. He is the hospital board president. He will always have the "bottom line" on his mind. He would never let go of this free publicity.' She did not soften her stand on Rick.

I did not know what to say. In fact, I had completely lost my thoughts on what I was planning on asking her to do.

Saanvi said, 'Zeba being a Muslim lends this whole exercise an authenticity, isn't it? And having her dressed traditionally and putting a hijab on her would enable the Sanghaalis to identify themselves with her.'

I told Saanvi that I would get back to her. I called Rick Jackson to give him a heads-up about my conversation with Saanvi. And to ask him to talk to Zeba and Razak as well. For all I knew, he may have already talked to them by now.

17. Hassan's Sister Amina

I was in the office going through my emails. I had received an email from Saanvi. She had mentioned that she was clearing her schedule to make time for Zeba's delivery. She had also offered to talk to Razak if I was hesitant to do so. I asked her to stay put and not do anything for now. I assured her that I would talk to Razak at the right time.

Kuki was discharged from the Minneapolis Heart Institute the very next day. The Minneapolis Police had arrested him since there was an arrest warrant against him in Minneapolis' Hennepin County. He was charged for possession. Surprisingly nobody had bailed him out. Each time I came across Amoka's police chief, I asked him if Kuki had been taken to Minneapolis' federal building. The chief would invariably give an evasive answer. In my mind, the fact that the FBI might be involved in the investigation made it a huge deal. I believed that so long as the investigation was done by the local police, everything would remain purely 'domestic'. It could never be so once the FBI gets involved.

It was almost as if we were witnessing a game in progress with a naiveté that made us believe the sport is being played for us to watch, cheer and gamble. But I had felt several times that the whole game was rigged. The players and the patrons were all, in fact, controlled by someone else. Zeba's live Cesarean section was the new addition to this puppeteering. What could be accomplished by this, if at all?

Trust?

Doctors and the Sanghaali mothers should develop a mutual trust. The mothers should trust that the Cesarean sections done by our doctors will cause them no harm and similarly doctors like Radhika and Razak should trust that the mothers will not end up committing suicides.

For a moment, I was shaken by my own thoughts. Things had come to such a pass in Amoka that if one Sanghaali kills herself, we would start guessing who might be the next. And under what circumstances? We almost believed that every time a Sanghaali delivers a baby, she could kill herself. Death literally followed birth in Amoka.

And to all this, as the chief of staff of the hospital, what was the solution I discovered for this problem? Zeba's live Cesarean! Would it be any better if this was done on a Sanghaali woman instead? Better optics? But who can I persuade at this time? I had raised this dilemma with Saanvi and she was very clear. 'Dude, in movies, we try to cast a specific actor for the lead role and look for a specific location to shoot. If that does not work out, what do we do? We look for the next best thing. A hijab, a name like Zeba and a little makeover will do the job for us. We can do it. Trust me, we can take advantage of her being a Muslim.'

She too was talking about 'the next best thing'. Am I a doctor? Am I rehearsing for an act or a show? Am I the lead actor in this absurd play? Or am I the casting director? I had morphed into someone else. The curtains on the ongoing play will come down with a movie shoot. The omissions of this burlesque should probably not even be introspected.

I got a call from the nurse at the labour ward, 'A twenty-year-old Sanghaali girl by the name Amina just checked in, complaining of abdominal pain. She is still four weeks shy of her due date. She is Dr Radhika's patient. We looked for

Dr Radhika. She is nowhere to be found. She is on call. Did she go home by any chance? Also, I think it is important to bring something to your attention. Do you remember Fadhuma? The woman who had her baby in our hospital and committed suicide right after? Remember her husband Hassan? Amina is his sister. Just to let you know.'

I remembered Amina. At the time when Radhika and I delivered Fadhuma's baby, Hassan had taken her name before going home and had, in fact, shouted that he would never get Amina's delivery done by Radhika. None of us knew who Amina's husband was. There used to be bubbler talk going around in the emergency department that she was pregnant outside of wedlock. God knows how such gossip starts but the moment Amina came to the emergency department the ambience turned fretfully pure and sanitized.

Now she had come to the hospital complaining of belly pain. It was not yet clear whether it was labour pain or something else. And Radhika could not be traced even after searching all over the hospital. I was surprised and called her on her mobile. She answered the call and without even waiting for my question and said, 'Guru, I have a severe headache. I've asked Razak to take my calls. If there is anything, contact him,' and hung up.

The OBGYN department did their own schedule. If one of them was sick, it was their responsibility to cover for that person. I had no clue where Razak was. What kind of irresponsibility is this that she assigns me the task of finding her coverage and goes home for a nap? I called Radhika again to say, 'Radhika if you cannot be here it is your responsibility to call Smith or Razak and ask them to cover for you. If you can't find someone to do that, I am sorry. I must ask you to come to the hospital immediately. Amina is sitting here, ready to deliver.'

'Both of them are not answering my calls. I'm in no position to come to the hospital today. Call them again. If they don't answer, somehow have her transferred to Minneapolis,' and she hung up again.

I looked in the call roster. It still had Radhika's name on it. I called the labour ward again and enquired if Radhika knew that the patient coming in for delivery was Amina. I got the reply that it was only after hearing about Amina's arrival that Radhika said she had a headache. I was furious. I called Radhika again. 'Look Radhika, your name is on the roster. You cannot excuse yourself from work today.'

'Did you check where Razak and Smith are?'

'That is not my job. It is yours. You have to come to the hospital, if not then you will be responsible for whatever happens next.'

'Ahh, Mr Boss, are you threatening me? What will you do? Go to the operating room and look for Smith. Razak may also be there. You know what? From now on, I'll not be doing any Cesarean sections. Are you going to fire me? Go ahead. I'm not coming. Period!' She hung up. When I tried to call her again, her phone was switched off.

I was running out of ideas. However, I had to get things squared up before I got the next call from the labour ward. I'm not that proficient in delivering babies. And this wasn't a garden variety delivery. It was Amina's and a premature one at that! Nobody can predict what could happen in such situations. People like me are the Men Friday in such small hospitals. I get called if no one is available. Something had to be terribly wrong, or else Radhika would not have been this stubborn. Whatever that may be, she needed to be in the hospital.

Left with no choices, I called the Amoka Police Department. I gave them my home address with the request that I'm concerned about Dr Radhika's health. 'There has been no response from her for all my phone calls. She is on call and there is a patient waiting for her. Could you please check her place? And if she is there, can you inform her that we have an emergency?' Then I went to the operating room looking for Smith and Razak.

18. Unbearable Lightness of the Womb

Five of Smith's children were seated outside the operating room. Smith had six kids in all. I knew the eldest daughter, Jacqueline. Jacqueline was a high school senior. Everyone fondly called her Jackie. It was rumoured that Jackie who was raised with strict catholic values had strayed a little in high school. Once, Smith had brought her to the emergency department. Apparently, she was found unconscious in her room. She was obviously drunk. Smith was concerned if she had any drugs on board. After all the tests, he had taken her home with the consolation she hasn't sinned by resorting to street drugs. A devil's bargain of sorts!

Jackie was recently found to be pregnant. The Smith family, like any orthodox catholic family was strictly against any kind of birth control. It was quite apparent looking at his six children that Smith had not so much as even sniffed at a condom. The devout catholic that he was, it made him happy that no matter how much Jackie had strayed, she had not veered so much off course as to use birth control devices. He had not kept Jackie's pregnancy a secret. In fact, he went around telling everyone that he will be a grandpa soon.

I did not see Jackie among his kids seated outside the OR. The other five kids sat there in solemn silence. None of them spoke or acknowledged me. I put on my scrubs and went into the OR. Jackie was lying on the operating table. She looked like she was under general anesthesia. Smith and his wife stood in a corner. It was hard to recognize everyone inside since they were all in scrubs and masks. I thought the surgeon was Razak. But to my surprise it was O'Reily.

I did not know what to do. I looked at Smith, said 'Sorry' and got ready to step out. He looked at me quizzically, seeming to ask the reason for my presence. I said, 'Radhika is sick. We need you or Razak. There is a patient waiting upstairs.' His face was fully covered except for the eyes. They suggested deep sorrow that could only come from grief and loss. It looked like they were pleading with me to understand his situation. I went near Smith and said, 'Sorry, I can understand your situation. I'm not asking you to come. I will look for Razak. Do you need anything from me? Is everything alright?' I had a hard time trying to get a handle on what was happening there. It was not even clear to me if the Smith family was ok with my presence there.

Smith told me softly, 'Jackie's pregnancy did not last. We could not save Henry. Henry was sixteen weeks old. Since yesterday, Jackie has had a lot of bleeding. I was checking him by ultrasound every hour all day yesterday. Even at ten pm last night, I could see and hear strong heartbeats. I went to bed thinking that everything would be alright. Come morning, around six, I couldn't hear any heartbeat. No movement on ultrasound. Henry had left us sometime in the middle of the night.' Smith was overcome with grief.

Jackie was four or five months pregnant. Unfortunately the pregnancy didn't last. But if this was an incomplete miscarriage, she needed a D&C (dilatation and curettage). In fact, I thought that O'Reily was doing a D&C. And I didn't really understand who this Henry was.

Smith had remarked as if he had read my thoughts, 'Henry cannot ascend to heaven if he does not have a proper funeral.'

It had just occurred to me then, Henry was Jackie's unborn child!

In the next five minutes, the surgeon had taken out a tiny Henry, small enough to be held on the palm of my hand. Jackie was asleep. I still didn't understand why O'Reilly is surgically taking out Henry with as much care as he would do if Henry were a living baby. There is really no difference between this procedure and a Cesarean section. The only difference being that the baby is neither living nor fully grown. The surgeon's scalpel is the same, but the purposes are different. One seeks to give an opportunity to live, the other seeks to grant a dignified farewell.

Henry was a sixteen-week-old fetus; no different in appearance than that of any species of birds or animals. Henry was laid down in a small bowl. Our surgeon O'Reilly gently examined Henry and handed a pair of scissors to the Smiths. Smith tried to cut at a place that O'Reilly pointed. I assumed that it was the ritual cutting of the umbilical cord.

I stood there stunned, unable to speak. Smith and his wife were crying. O'Reilly stepped out and brought Smith's other children inside. Henry was laid down in a beautiful Blackwood box as small as a jewelry box. Everyone stood holding hands around the box in a circle, closed their eyes, and started praying.

Smith's wife held onto my finger. I reckoned she may have mistaken me for someone else because our faces, hidden underneath our surgical masks, were not easily recognizable. I did not have the heart to withdraw my hand. Another finger on my other hand was held by his son. I too closed my eyes and said 'Amen'.

As we were coming out of the OR after five minutes, Jackie was slowly waking up. Smith said, 'Vigil is on Saturday and funeral on Sunday. Please attend if possible.'

I did not say anything.

'Guru, children sometimes do things that may or may not be right. We were eagerly awaiting the arrival of a new member to our family. Jackie was also very excited. Our fortunes did not favor us. God took Henry away very quickly.'

I said warily, 'I came here looking for Razak or you. Couldn't you get hold of Razak to do a D&C on Jackie? Was this surgery really necessary?'

I had not completed my sentence yet. Smith said, 'Guru, you did see for yourself, didn't you? She didn't have a real miscarriage. I had no other choice. The baby was alive till last night.'

I was in a quandary. 'You could have waited for some more time and then got a D&C done?'

'Guru, you are from India, right? I'm not aware of your beliefs. We believe that life begins as an embryo right after fertilization. In fact, it is wrong to call it an embryo. He has arms and legs like us, a heartbeat like us and has a life. When we come into this world, we should come as a whole and when we depart, we should leave as a whole.'

What could I say? I could not think for a while having witnessed something that I had never seen before in my life and something that was beyond my wildest imagination. I had not seen such a small fetus even at medical school. This guy is a gynecologist. He believes this is the only way to get the baby out with no harm. And for what? For its last rites!

Smith said, 'Thanks.'

I looked at him again.

'As it is, losing our loved ones is a tragic affair. And on top of it, it is a sin if we don't bid a proper adieu to those who pass. God's anger will be upon us. Everybody deserves a proper goodbye. Thank you for providing this opportunity today. This surgery is off the record. I don't want to get O'Reilly in trouble. Please understand my situation.' He squeezed my hands and begged me.

I freed my hands, went straight to my office and sat down.

There was a message from Razak: 'I got your message. There is no need for Radhika to come to the hospital. I've examined Amina. She will most likely have a normal delivery. Maybe today. Or it could be a false alarm. But I have to speak to you on a different topic.' Even as I was trying to respond, he came knocking and barging into my office. He held my hand and said, 'Guru, Smith is getting a Cesarean section done, I mean hysterotomy on his daughter.' I was afraid that he noticed a smile on my face.

'Why are you smiling? This is not a laughing matter. He is getting his daughter's uterus cut and taking out a twelve-week-old baby. This is against the law.'

'Smith said that the baby was sixteen to seventeen weeks old and there was heavy bleeding. Apparently, there was no other choice. One more thing, this surgery never happened as per hospital records.'

'That is not true!'

'Razak, these are all one's beliefs. Smith believes that if he did not do it this way, god's curse would be upon him. And he is also a physician.'

'I've no words to express. On the one hand, we've to struggle with the Sanghaalis for doing Cesarean sections to save babies. And they question our competence and our integrity and at the end commit suicides because we cut their bellies to deliver their children. Here, a doctor himself does a ludicrous operation on his daughter to take out a ball of flesh, an embryo, a fetus that is long dead—to give it a proper funeral! Guru, what kind of medieval medicine are we practicing? Since when did religion, culture and god come in the way of medicine?' He sat there brooding, with his head cupped in his hands.

I was in no position to answer his questions. Seeing him, I got a sense that Rick Jackson had not yet spoken to him on Zeba's Cesarean section. Just as I was starting to think about it, Radhika rammed the office door open and came inside. She stood right in front of me.

'You sent police home to get me! How dare you? What do you think of yourself?' Her eyes were glowing red and her voice was shaking.

'Radhika, this is the regular procedure. It is in the hospital's by-laws. I did not send the police to arrest you. They were sent to check if you are all right since you were not answering phone calls. In the hospital when doctors on call don't answer their phones or beepers, we have followed this procedure. Haven't we?'

'I did respond to the beeper. Didn't I? How much more clearly did I have to tell you that I have a bad headache?'

'Radhika, be honest. Do you really have a headache or were you giving it as an excuse to duck out of doing Amina's Cesarean section?'

'Look, you might be my boss, but you can't bully me. You have no authority to send the police to my house.'

'Radhika, I've already told you that I asked them to check on you since you were not answering your phone. I have written so in the call roster as well. If you did answer calls, then you are missing work on purpose. That will be considered negligence and disciplinary action can be taken against you.'

'Hello boss! Do whatever you want. I had anticipated something like this. I'm going to surrender my C-section privileges to the hospital. I was planning on discussing this with you, but I did not get a chance. Going forward, I'll only do normal deliveries. I shall completely stop doing Cesarean sections. Never mind who the patient is—Amina, Rosie, Lilly, Maya or Zeba—I shall only do normal deliveries. Get me the whole Sanghaali community. I will tell them. You deliver normally, I'm your doctor. Do you need Cesarean section? Then find someone else. It's rather I do no surgeries, and they commit no suicides.'

She did not notice that she had mentioned Zeba's name when she got carried away with her words. I looked at Razak. He did not say anything. I said to her, 'Radhika, get a hold of yourself. Think calmly. You are the only lady doctor in this town. We simply do not have the luxury to pick and choose. In entire Amoka, you have the busiest OB practice. If you drop the ball here, what should people do? Where should they go in this small town? Besides, Razak examined Amina and said that she could have a normal delivery.'

Razak nodded.

'Let that be so. I'm happy. I'll supervise it myself. But if there is no other lady doctor for future C-sections in this town, then that is not my problem. My only interest is to stay here somehow for another three years and leave. Now if you'll excuse me, I have a baby to deliver.'

'Radhika, personally I don't agree with you surrendering your privileges for C-section. I'll be the first to veto that at the board meeting.'

'Guru, please keep me out of this entire nuisance. I'm stressed to the point of my head exploding into a million pieces. This is already affecting my personal relationship with Giri. He is urging me to quit this job and join him. I cannot go there till I get my green card. I think of going back to India almost every day. Please, leave me alone. I do not want to be held responsible for more deaths.'

Razak was bewildered. He said, 'Radhika, though Zeba is my wife, she is your patient. We want you to deliver her baby. Don't abandon us this way. Her only source of confidence is you being here.'

She quickly understood that I had not told Razak about broadcasting Zeba's Cesarean section live. She regained her composure and said, 'Sorry Razak. Guru, it's not so easy for me to quit this job. I'm sure both of you understand. But then, what can I do? These days whenever a pregnant woman comes to see me, my whole body starts shivering. Can you imagine the irony here? An OBGYN afraid of pregnant women! It's like a surgeon with hemophobia. See what these events have done to me. I'm constantly under a fear psychosis of making a grave error. How can I work in such a state of mind?'

I suspected that this maybe what Kuki was alluding to. It was anybody's guess on how many doctors in Minnesota, like Radhika, were traumatized. They are just trying to do what in their informed professional opinion is the right thing for their patients.

Who stands to gain by all this?

Is it possible for a spark like this in a non-decrepit town like Amoka to spread like wildfire everywhere?

Duniya calls this a rebellion. Mohammad, a war. And according to Kuki, this is jihad. Whatever may be the name, the fact that all of us were in Amoka, could make us living witnesses to this emerging phenomenon. Was that good or bad? Honestly, I had no idea.

Left with no options I whispered in Radhika's ears just loud enough only for her to hear. 'Radhika, if you need to take some time to think this over, do so. Please rethink your decision, at least for Zeba's sake, for Razak's sake.'

'My god, are you guys blackmailing me? Let us think about it when Zeba's delivery date is close.'

I told Razak, 'Make yourself free when possible. I need to talk to you about Zeba's delivery.' We were at a point when I had to talk to Razak about Zeba's delivery. While Rick Jackson had mentioned that he would convince Razak and Zeba, I strongly believed that I had to be there at least as his comrade-in-arms.

Zeba was not due for her delivery for a while. Yet, it was important to convince these two as soon as possible. Saanvi had taken the responsibility to bring the hospital board and the TV channels on board. I was confident that when even something as grotesque as a live murder is being telecast on TV these days, getting permission to broadcast a live childbirth by Cesarean section should not be that difficult.

Razak's beeper rang. He looked at Radhika and said, 'Amina is ready.'

Radhika replied, 'Razak, I am warning you, if she needs a Cesarean section, you are it. I'll scrub out and walk out of the OR,' and went inside.

I felt that she really meant it.

19. A New Dawn

I received a message from Razak. Amina had a normal delivery just as Razak had predicted. Radhika who didn't even want to come to the hospital had delivered the baby. I reckoned that everything happens for a good reason.

Hassan was sitting outside. I tried to engage him in a casual conversation, 'How are you doing?'

He looked at me and smiled. He seemed somewhat pale and weak since the last time I had met him.

'How are the children doing? Who's taking care of them now?' It was a little too late when I realized that I should not have asked this question.

'Amina has to take care of them, doctor.'

'Does she have any children of her own? '

'This is her first.' His voice was weakened to the point where it sounded like a feeble cry from the bottom of a well. The fire in his eyes was conspicuously missing.

He looked so different and weak, I wondered if this was the same Hassan who had threatened us just a few months back that heads would roll if a Cesarean section was done on his wife.

'What about Amina's family?' I suddenly remembered and felt somewhat disturbed about the rumours floating in the hospital a few days back whether Amina had a husband at all. To be honest, I had completely forgotten about it.

He started sobbing uncontrollably. 'I'm Amina's family. She's all I got.'

I felt deeply sorry to have brought this up.

'I'm sorry Hassan. I apologize. I was only trying to be courteous. Trust me, I had no other intentions.'

He did not say anything and continued crying.

'Doctor, please ensure that this delivery is not a Cesarean section. I beg you.'

It then occurred to me that neither Razak nor Radhika had told him that Amina did not need a Cesarean section. I looked around and could not find either of them.

'Oh god, Hassan! Hasn't anyone told you? Amina has already delivered the baby, and it was a normal delivery!'

'Thank you, thank you, doctor.' He hugged me tightly and sobbed. My sleeves turned wet from his tears.

By then Razak and Radhika came out of the labour ward. It was not clear what they thought when they saw Hassan hugging me. They stood there, silently. I continued consoling Hassan, 'It's not me that you have to thank. You should thank these two doctors.'

Even as I was ending my sentence, he let go off me. He held Radhika and Razak's hands and started crying like a baby again. I felt it may well be impossible to console him. I stood there watching him sob. Radhika was somewhat lost. She probably did not expect this reaction from Hassan. None of us did.

Hassan said, 'Doctor, I knew that Amina would be alright and everything would be just fine, you know. Yet, somewhere in the corner of my mind there was this apprehension about her needing a Cesarean section. She was however very stubborn. She told me on my way here that she will get a Cesarean section done if she needs one, no matter what happens. She has no idea. She is much younger than me. She came to America much before I did and went to college here. Next year she is starting her job as a Pharmacy Technician in Minneapolis. Once they have some education, our girls develop enough confidence to challenge the world, you know! If she had had that Cesarean section today, I could have lost her too. What would happen to her child? How can I take care of all these children? You are my saviors.' He sobbed again.

Radhika said, 'Hassan, take it easy. She had signed a document giving consent at the time of admission to the hospital. It explicitly stated that in case she cannot have a normal vaginal delivery, we will have to perform a C-section. She signed without the least bit of hesitation. In fact, when I reminded her of what's happening in the town, she had replied, "Doctor, I'm twenty years old. I became pregnant on my own will and I would like the delivery to go according to my wish too. You do whatever you think is right. If you think that I need to have a C-section, then so be it. Let us see what happens."'

Hassan asked in shock, 'Oh, I hope you did not do a Cesarean section just because she signed the consent. Because as her elder brother, I get to decide what's right and what's not right for her.'

Radhika replied, 'Hassan, legally you have no right to stop her. Amina is twenty years old. Moreover, she is the mother of a baby. She can make her own choices.'

I had a hard time believing she is the same Radhika who had holed up inside her house, refusing to come out—like Duryodhana hiding in the Vaisampayana Lake.

'Doctor, now everything is ok, right? I just want to let you know that you have done her a great favor by not doing a Cesarean section. You have saved two lives. I knew that you are all good doctors.' Then he ran towards Amina's room. Razak, Radhika and I looked at each other. I didn't want to even imagine the consequences had Amina had a Cesarean.

On our way home, Radhika remarked, 'Guru, what do you think of Amina? Doesn't she portend a new dawn in their community? There should be more women like her. And this

Hassan, who was all noise and thunder earlier, threatening to make heads roll, is a squeaking puppy now. I think this problem in their community is way beyond folks like Amina and Hassan. They have got themselves into some mess and are struggling to get out.'

'Radhika, if Amina had a Cesarean section today and committed suicide, how would Hassan manage the three children?'

'Guru, you should have spoken to her. She didn't look like she was going to kill herself, no matter what. She is educated and intelligent. Look at how education transforms these girls. I wish she had a C-section today. She would not have killed herself. Certainly not! Now that I think about it, I'm convinced that even Rukhiya and Fadhuma didn't really commit suicide. Someone has exploited their innocence and helplessness.'

'What's your point? Did Amina say something to you?'

'Nothing specific. I asked her if any of her friends were pregnant. I handed her my business card and asked her to call if she ever needs me. She was also quite interested. I'll call Saanvi. We should line up a few Sanghaali women and do Cesarean sections on them. Let us call the police if needed. It will be even better if we can provide these women some security after the C-sections. This is the least that the police can do.' I was starting to get scared. In fact, I always had this fear that Saanvi would look at these series of events from her perspective and would drag Radhika into it. But I didn't expect that a weak spark like Amina would start the fire. If Saanvi, so much as gets a hint that Radhika will join her, I'll not be surprised if she brings a whole brigade of volunteers along with Kristina from New York, pitches a tent in front of the hospital and convinces Radhika to do a C-section in the parking lot!

I remembered what Kuki said about 'some people' manipulating these women into believing that C-sections could be considered 'haram', eventually ending in suicides. I have no evidence for any of this. How can anyone take the words of a drug dealer seriously?

'Radhika, didn't you mention just three hours back that we should not get into this mess but only plan on staying here for three years and then leave?'

'I didn't know Amina then. I could not even imagine that a Sanghaali woman like Amina exists.'

'Radhika, please. I beg you. Trust me. Let us perform the Cesarean section on Zeba as Rick suggested for the documentary or whatever and wash our hands off this whole mess. If another girl like Amina comes forward, Rick will certainly be happy, but how long can we provide security to these women after their surgeries? What if they kill themselves three months after their live surgeries? Who would be responsible for that?'

'So, the plan is to operate on Zeba, since no matter what happens, she will not kill herself. It's a kind of a safe bet. Is this right?'

'Yes, that is also a factor.'

'Guru, your interest is not so much as to solve this problem but to put up a show. Please do not say another word. I may start hating you too.' She turned away.

20. The Sacrificial Lamb

A week later, I got an email from Rick Jackson. He had written about his meeting with Razak and Zeba. He had called them to his office and discussed in detail about Zeba's Cesarean section. Apparently, they were both infuriated and stormed out of his office. Rick mentioned that, Razak's tone and manner of speaking indicated that if push came to shove, he might leave his job but at no cost would he agree to this C-section. I was not surprised. On the contrary, I would be astonished, if he had readily agreed.

I felt like we had no option other than to wait with the hope that Razak and Zeba would change their minds. I was clueless about the way forward if they did not agree. All along, I was convinced that performing a Cesarean section on a few willing Sanghaali women and broadcasting it live was the best option. If not, Saanvi's 'the next best thing' was our option. Our failure to make even this happen put me in a quandary. Frankly, I was in a brain freeze.

Or, will things get back to normalcy, with Amina's entry and Zeba's exit, in the last act of this play?

I saw Razak's car on the driveway when I reached home. It was not difficult to guess what could have transpired inside. As I had expected, Zeba's eyes were bloodshot and swollen. Radhika and Zeba were seated on the living room couch trying to watch TV. The ambience was nothing less than funereal. Razak and Srikantha were standing on the backyard deck holding Heineken bottles in their hands. I sat down with Zeba and Radhika in the living room. I did not have the courage to face Razak. I didn't even know how to start a conversation. Razak came inside and sat right across from me. He didn't waste any time and came straight to the point. 'Guru, if you were married and your wife and the unborn child were asked to participate in this ridiculous drama, this soap opera, would you have agreed? Radhika, if you were pregnant, would you get a Cesarean section done on live TV?'

I said without hesitation, 'Definitely.'

Radhika was quiet for a minute, and then said, 'I am only doing my job here. Guru is also doing his, but I'm not sure if you have noticed, his job is that of a boss.'

Razak looked at me with contempt and said, 'Guru, either you are an inveterate liar, or you are unaware of the limits of a boss' responsibility. You tend to do everyone's bidding. You are turning into a pathetic lackey. Rick Jackson has spent all his life in the Midwestern backwaters. He is a hillbilly. He hasn't seen anything outside Minnesota or read anything other than The King James Bible. He cannot differentiate between a Sanghaali, a Sudanese, or a Pakistani. He thinks that all Muslims are the same. You didn't even have the courtesy to talk to me before convincing Saanvi? How can you be so insensitive?'

'Razak, do not be hasty. Think for a moment that you are not an employee of this hospital but the boss. Put yourself in Rick's shoes. What would you do? He is the board president. His priority is to save the hospital—to keep it in business. Sanghaali women are dying everywhere. All cases are registered as suicides. At this time what can Rick do if he gets instructions from the higher authorities to make such an educational video? Even he does not know who these higher-ups are!'

'Why us? What are the other hospitals doing about it?'

'I'm not sure if this is a matter of pride or shame. But these series of events originated here in Amoka. According to the police, ours is the index site which is a fancy word that means we are the source, the epicenter of these troubles. Rick is also a pawn in this game just like you and me. Nobody knows who is spinning the wheels here.'

'Yes, of course. All are pawns. Some are kings, and some are queens.'

'Razak, I know who you are referring to. Rick and I are also pawns. There are no kings and queens here. '

'Bullshit.'

'Razak, I'm not saying this to scare you. You may lose this job if you and Zeba do not agree to this plan.'

'How? Zeba is pregnant. It is not easy to fire me in this situation. The government has laws against it.'

'Well, the law only says that a pregnant woman is always entitled to have health insurance. It is true that since Zeba does not work, she is dependent on you for her health insurance. Once you lose your job and visa, she will lose her visa too. It is a fact that a one way ticket to Karachi is much cheaper than Zeba having a baby here. If you are lucky to get hold of a competent immigration lawyer, then they will first send you to Pakistan. The government might pay for Zeba to have her baby and then send both to Karachi. Your sole consolation would be that your child will be an American citizen.'

'Did Rick say this or is this whole spiel coming from you?'

'Razak, please believe me. I know how he thinks.'

'Why in the hell would I be fired?'

'Razak, are you really this naïve or are you not trying to understand what's happening here? There can be many reasons to lose one's job. For instance, there are a few complaints from patients in your file. Apparently three of the patients that you operated on, were readmitted for surgical wound infections. O'Reilly or Smith can be asked to review these cases and you could be reported to the state. A couple of nurses have whined that you are painfully slow in the operating room. The management can come up with a whole truckload of shit, my friend—the whole enchilada. You know quite well that in our profession, the rights and wrongs are always on a slippery slope.'

Razak was stunned. 'Guru, I thought that you were my friend.'

'Razak, I am your friend. Therefore, I'm sharing this with you. What are you going to do in Karachi? You didn't want to live there in the first place. If you are a little flexible, you can get your green card in less than a year. Then let's leave this town. I'll help you get a job.'

'Guru, America is not the only place to make a good living. Yes, it is true that we came to America looking for a good life and pursue the American dream. Yes, it is also true that we were star-struck and looked forward to good things in life. A beach house in California in ten years, travel all over the world and own a new BMW every year. After all this nonsense, I have no interest in Amoka and certainly not in America. You can keep this Dreamland to yourself!!!' He and Zeba stomped out homeward.

Radhika glared at me.

The very next week, Razak resigned ignoring everyone's advice and went away to Karachi along with Zeba. Since he resigned from his job, his visa was not valid anymore and he had to leave the country. I tried convincing him to reconsider his decision and left no stone unturned in doing so.

Radhika tried her part in convincing them. She spoke to Zeba and pleaded repeatedly. She told her that there shall be no reason whatsoever to do anything against her will—that she has contacted other Sanghaali women with the help of Amina who are willing to get a Cesarean section done and that this problem will be resolved very soon. Nothing had worked. All our requests were stonewalled. Razak and Zeba had no trust in us, much less in our words. Razak was unwilling to even look me in the eye while talking. Zeba looked like she was crying all week. Her swollen eyes and moist cheeks said more than what she could ever do.

My words had dried up. There was nothing else to do other than bidding a silent farewell.

Rick Jackson and Powell had only said a 'Good luck' to Razak. I was furious at Rick. I didn't even know whom to get mad at. To a certain extent, it was plausible that there was guilt nestled in my conscience as someone who may have played a crucial role in this whole act. Whatever that might be, I decided to confront Rick and give him a dressing down. I messaged him saying I have something to discuss and will come over to his office. He replied asking me to come after work, in the evening.

His office was located about two miles from our hospital. I called him after work to ask if it was too late for him, since it was eight pm. He said that he was still in the office waiting for me. He was done with his supper and asked me to come over.

There was no one at the reception desk when I reached there. I went inside. There was no one there either. I said, 'Hello.' It was certain that he was in the office. There was a bucket of half-eaten Kentucky Fried Chicken on his desk. A big bottle of Pepsi with its cap open stood next to it. The room reeked of half-cooked chicken. His computer was switched on. The old flip phone of his came alive on his table with a green glow for a moment, and turned silent. There was a letter from the Pakistani embassy on his table. I was curious to read it. I heard somebody flushing the bathroom toilet.

Rick came out. He did not have his dentures in his mouth. When he moved his toothless mouth, it looked as if he was trying to swallow. He had no shirt on him but only a tee. His pants were rolled up to his knees. His swollen feet and the blue veins on his lower legs were conspicuous since he did not have his socks on.

He said, 'Sorry.'

Seeing him speaking without his dentures made me nauseous. He did not even try to look for his dentures. He unzipped his pant, inserted his t-shirt and said while fixing his belt, 'Guru, I know that you are angry with me. I am not as bad as you guys think. My hands are tied too. I had no other way out. I had no objection to Razak continuing in his job. In fact, I did not want to lose him.'

He saw me looking at the Pakistani embassy letter on his desk.

'Look, I had no idea whatsoever about stuff like your visa and green card. It was only ten years back that we came to know that there are government programs meant to invite and encourage foreign doctors to come to towns like ours and serve. We neither had any awareness nor comprehension of the details of any of these programs. Our only involvement was to sign the letters from the government and the immigration department. Our hospital's lawyers have tried to educate the board members on these matters. No matter how many times I hear them, there's only one thing that I have understood: The foreign doctors who come here for work cannot quit their jobs for five years. It is unfortunate that we had to take advantage of this law with Razak. Trust me, I could not sleep for four days after Razak left. I sought my hospital's lawyers for advice on how to get Razak back. They advised me to send a letter to the Pakistani Embassy and ask them. Accordingly, I wrote them a letter. Now I have got their reply, apparently, even they cannot get him back once he reaches Karachi.'

It was clear he knew next to nothing about immigration. And I was impressed that he had written a letter to the Pakistani embassy to get Razak back. Not bad, I thought. Even this guy has his heart in the right place. For the first time, I felt a little sorry looking at this toothless, half-sleeved man!

I spotted on his desk a picture of him with a group belonging to the Masai tribe from Africa. On the wall behind his desk was a big framed picture of him and Jimmy Carter.

I tried easing him up and said, 'Let go of it. At this point, it may not be the best thing for him to work here and more importantly for Zeba to have her baby at our hospital.'

He muttered, 'Ok, the next time you meet Razak tell him that I said hello.'

I looked at him quizzically.

'I know that Karachi and Bengaluru are in different countries, but the world is round. And take my word—Razak will definitely be back in America after living in Pakistan for a couple of years.'

I came back home. I thought it may well be impossible for me to understand if this man was an innocent Midwesterner or a shrewd guy beyond my intuition.

A week after Razak and Zeba's departure to Karachi, Radhika had said that she will be moving out of the house. I did not ask her the reason. She had firmly believed that had I spoken to the hospital's executives or had I put in some extra effort, I could have saved Zeba from all these troubles. In fact, she had openly said that my irresponsibility had led to Razak and Zeba's departure.

Barely two weeks after Radhika moved to her new house, Saanvi also arrived in Amoka and settled down with her. I assumed that she, being alone in her new house, had called Saanvi over to stay with her for some time. When Saanvi showed no signs of leaving Amoka even after two months, I suspected something was brewing, but I could not guess what it was.

21. Asset Recruitment

It was a beautiful August afternoon. Habiba Ahmed was working in her farm. Her farm is located about eight miles from Amoka, off Highway 35. This year she had a rich harvest of organic tomatoes, potatoes, watermelons, kale, corn and other vegetables. In a farm full of shoulder length corn plants, she was walking slowly in a pair of ill-fitting sneakers. She must be about four feet six inches tall. Her husband, Aden Ahmed, worked in one of Amoka's local mills. She was pregnant with her seventh baby and was due for delivery any day. The Hijab on her head was wet with her sweat from the afternoon heat. Holding four bunches of carrots and corn in her hand she was walking towards the fence.

Radhika, Saanvi and another pregnant Sanghaali woman, whom I had never seen before, were waiting there in front of the farm for Habiba's arrival. I was torn between feeling sorry and being scared for these two Sanghaali pregnant women struggling to walk in the punishing sun. Srikantha and I sat in my car parked about thirty feet away. We were cautioned by Radhika not to let Habiba see us. Srikantha was watching all the activities unfolding before us through his binoculars.

Citizens providing their country's secrets to the CIA are referred to as 'assets'. Our work on that day looked like a clandestine operation of a CIA asset recruitment. When I asked Srikantha for more information on what was going on and why we were there, he hushed me, held his finger against his lips and shrugged his shoulders.

Habiba farmed in that place for at least ten years. Apparently, all of Habiba's resources—the place, the seeds, the water supply, the equipment and an old Ford Van—came from an NGO working for the resettlement of Sanghaali refugees. These vegetables found their way to organic food stores and restaurants in Amoka and small towns around. In the restaurants, the same vegetables were chopped, mixed with cooked quinoa and sold as home-grown organic salads!

'Shall we leave?' Radhika asked Habiba.

Habiba was fairly conversant in English. 'I've to deliver some vegetables to the Caleb's wholefood store and restaurant. Is it alright if we talk there?'

Radhika said, 'Sure.'

Caleb's is Amoka's only organic grocery store and restaurant. Habiba was driving her Ford truck very slowly. I got a message on my mobile from Radhika asking us to join them. Srikantha and I reached there well ahead of them and parked our car about eighty feet from the store, as instructed. We went in, ordered sweet lime juice, and settled down at a corner table. There was a sign in front of Caleb's, proudly proclaiming that they only used locally grown vegetables. Even amid that tension, Srikantha being Srikantha, couldn't help asking the restaurant owner why the sign did not emphasize the word 'Sanghaali', when majority of the local farms belonged to Sanghaalis. 'We could get in trouble with the law if we tried to do something like that. The vegetables are sourced from different farms. And these farm owners are from different countries like Guatemala, Haiti, Mexico, Ecuador and many more. Yes, there are more Sanghaalis than the rest of them, but, it is practically impossible to tag these vegetables as coming from whom and where.'

Fifteen minutes had passed and there was no sign of Radhika, Saanvi, Habiba and the anonymous Sanghaali woman. Srikantha messaged Radhika to check where they were. The dots on Srikantha's phone started to dance. Radhika was typing her reply. She took a long time and her message came back after about five minutes with a smiley emoji. 'It looks like our job got easier than we expected. Habiba's husband Aden has gone to Sanghaala a couple of months back to visit his family. After we first spoke to Habiba, she too had tried to contact Aden but with no luck. There was no news from the other side. It looks like he may not come back soon.'

Srikantha and I looked at each other. He messaged his reply with a dumb emoji, 'Meaning?'

'I don't know. I don't want to know.'

Srikantha messaged back: 'Is Aden going to be a problem?'

'Going forward, Aden may not be a problem for anybody. I believe he has a second family in Sanghaala. Habiba is not being completely upfront.'

As the message flashed to life, Habiba, along with Radhika, Saanvi and the other Sanghaali woman, walked into the store. I did not know the name of the other woman. Possibly Srikantha did not know it either. It was apparent she was close to full term. She wore a hijab too, but unlike Habiba's, it was not soaked in sweat. Her face that had seen regular facials, glowed with thick makeup. A waitress at the restaurant looked at Habiba and asked, 'When are you due?'

Habiba responded, 'It's due now. It can happen anytime. Can I get a cup of water?'

'We have bottled water here. Three dollars per bottle.'

Habiba turned around not wanting to part with three dollars for a bottle of water. It was not clear what ran through the waitress' mind. She fetched a cup of iced water and gave it to Habiba and said, 'Is it a baby boy or girl?'

Habiba did not respond. The waitress looked at the other pregnant Sanghaali woman and laughed, 'Oh, double trouble! Two Sanghaali pregnant women in the store.' The Sanghaali woman wearing the makeup reacted, 'Why don't you leave us alone!' She had a perfect American accent.

The chastised waitress scooted from there. It was a small restaurant. Ever since Habiba and her entourage walked in, half the patrons stopped talking and were staring at these four women. After the outburst of the other Sanghaali woman with the thick makeup, the tapping sounds of the cutlery—the cling-clang of the forks and spoons—came to an immediate stop. The untouched salad plates and the glasses of kale juice stayed on the tables. Srikantha and I could clearly see the waitress say 'What the fuck' by reading her lip movement. I hoped that this was not visible from Radhika's table.

Someone muttered, 'How did these people end up here? Who gave them the permission to come to Amoka?' It was loud enough to be heard by others. Or maybe it was intended to be so. Then the woman with the heavy make-up got up and addressed everyone. 'I was raised here. I was in the Amoka High School band. This dress came in the way of my pursuing activities like cheerleading and dancing.' And she laughed loudly so everyone could hear.

Silence settled in again. I messaged Radhika: 'Shall we leave? Let us not create a big scene here.'

She didn't reply. They were whispering among themselves.

I sent her another message. 'What's her name?'

She replied, 'I'll tell you later.'

'Let us get out of here as soon as possible.' I messaged her again.

Radhika responded with another message. 'Amina was supposed to come. She did not make it.'

It was not clear if she was ignoring my message or if this was an answer to my message.

Later, Saanvi took out a form from her backpack and both the pregnant Sanghaali women signed the form at all the places that Saanvi seemed to indicate. Radhika looked at us and gestured with both thumbs up, implying that the job was accomplished. Radhika had not shared the other Sanghaali girl's name yet. When I checked with Srikantha, he dodged the question and suggested that we talk later. Everything happened in a feverish surreal manner.

Ever since Razak left, Saanvi had moved to Amoka and started living with Radhika. They would eat their lunch in the hospital cafeteria together. When I checked with her a couple of times, Saanvi had evasively replied that she was too bored to cook and was taking a break. She had given some flippant answers when I asked her if she had left New York for good, what was she doing at Amoka or what was going on with her store. She would say things like Kristina was looking after the store, since Radhika felt lonely and asked to join her, she had come to Amoka. Upon my asking her if they had made any plans for the Live Cesarean section, she had given a vague answer. 'You are the boss. Can we do anything without keeping you in the loop?'

I was convinced that something was afoot but had no knowledge of any details. I was the blind man from the parable here, feeling the elephant. Amina's visit had engendered a great deal of optimism in Radhika. It had made her aware that what she had dismissed as impossible was quite feasible. The series of events—Amina's willingness to get the Cesarean section done, her brother breaking down with the mortal fear of the consequences had she had the Cesarean section—had substantially reinforced Radhika's conviction that these Sanghaalis were victims of coercion and emotional blackmail.

The previous week Rick Jackson had called for another meeting. It was in that meeting that Rick had spoken about the live Cesarean section for the first time since Razak's departure. He had exhorted that this live Cesarean section initiative was still very much in play and needed to be executed soon. I had asked Radhika, that with Zeba no longer here, who would she be doing the Cesarean section on? She had told me, 'Next week, why don't you and Srikantha come with us? There's one woman already willing to get it done. With luck we might get another one along with her.' Looking at all these developments of Radhika moving into her new home and Saanvi living with her in Amoka, it became apparent that Rick and Powell, along with Radhika and Saanvi, were planning something big.

These were the details that I could uncover: two friends of Amina were due for delivery the following month. Those two were none other than Habiba and the other woman who had sat with Radhika and Saanvi at Caleb's. They were not sure if Habiba had agreed one hundred per cent for the surgery and hence the 'asset recruitment'. They had invited Srikantha and me for assistance.

Once I became aware of all the details, it was apparent to me that Rick and the hospital management had kept me out of these developments on purpose. I thought of asking Rick or Radhika about it. Then I realized that it was not my domain of expertise. My role as chief of medical staff was to sign and approve the decisions made by all the 'higher-ups'. Nobody was answerable to me and my opinions didn't matter. The job was a sinecure and it felt like a spineless title with neither any authority nor much influence worth writing home about!

Regardless of what other people thought of me, I had tried to dig a little deeper and asked Radhika if she could provide additional information. She had replied, 'I've told you everything I know. Trust me, I'm also not privy to all the details. It is true that we had invited only a few for preliminary meetings in view of patient privacy. I too do not know much.

I was present in only one meeting to introduce Amina to the hospital board. Once everything was in place, I was planning on taking Rick's permission for telling everything to you.' Then she had tried to console me by adding, 'We had taken you to Habiba's farm, hadn't we? You will be in all future meetings. Don't worry.' The question of since when did Saanvi turn into medical staff, almost popped out of my mouth but knowing that there would be an evasive response waiting for that too, I refrained from asking.

There was no dearth of pregnant Sanghaali women in Amoka. The fact that we suddenly got hold of two such women did not surprise me in the least. However, it made me a little suspicious that both these women had agreed to get the Cesarean sections simultaneously. Getting Habiba on board was done like an intelligence operation by Saanvi and Radhika. I did not know even the name of the other Sanghaali woman. Radhika, excited like a baby bunny, had disclosed that three more expectant mothers from Seattle, Columbus and Portland had shown interest to get their Cesarean sections done next month but their Health Insurance Companies refused to cover the surgeries if done at Amoka. Those women were ready to get their surgeries done at Amoka if done for free.

Did we bite more than what we could chew? Doing simultaneous Cesarean sections on five expectant mothers and broadcasting them live on television! Who would assist Radhika in these surgeries? The one person who could, Razak, was not there anymore. Smith wouldn't even get to a sniffing distance from them. But then, when we can bring patients from elsewhere, how difficult was it to get doctors? Saanvi was on a mission to turn what was hitherto a local news into a headline news. To magnify a spark in a small Midwestern town that needed legitimate attention into a flame that engaged the world. To set in motion things that were directly contrarian to what we thought Dr Mohammad Mohammad was planning on doing, much before any action that he might take. I thought Saanvi and Radhika were planning on a preemptive strike: countering the YouTube videos of Sanghaali women suicides, with a live broadcast of successful Cesarean sections on primetime television. These still begged the questions: can three or four doctors accomplish this? The stuff that we were doing here—did they really come under a physician's purview of work? What kind of medical practice was it for Srikantha and me to accompany Radhika to Habiba's farm? I still had no idea why we had gone there. When asked, Rick's response was that it would be disclosed on a need-to-know basis. Radhika's explanation was that Amina had said that a Sanghaali woman by the name of Habiba had agreed for a Cesarean section and it was imperative that Radhika met her as soon as possible. She had asked Srikantha and me to accompany them just to have some men around. She had laughed at my barrage of questions—'Do you suppose someone would have attacked you? Even if it were so, what kind of protection could we have provided? Does the hospital's insurance cover any of this? What if something had gone wrong... ?'

I was waiting for Rick's next move. He didn't want to get into any trouble with insurance companies and had asked that preparations be done for the surgeries on only these two Amoka women.

Radhika had studied thoroughly the case summaries of these two friends of Amina. According to her, Habiba was full term pregnant and showed no signs of having a normal delivery. The other woman's baby apparently was huge and weighed about four and a half kilograms. Their babies were due a week apart. Therefore, she was convinced that she could do C-sections on them any day next week. The earlier the better. Godspeed.

Saanvi had already obtained permission from NBC. Rick and Powell had paid another visit to Washington to get the nod from the higher-ups. Neither of them had ever spoken with me about these higher-ups. They were clearly the phantoms of *this* opera. Radhika did not speak more about any of these. According to Srikantha, she had planned on doing both the C-sections one after the other in close succession, but the hospital and the 'higher-ups' were not willing to take the risk. They were apparently trying to get O'Reilly on board as an additional surgeon. O'Reilly was expected to agree.

Radhika had shared with me a few days ago, 'Guru, had we got women like Habiba and Amina sooner, we would not have pulled Zeba and Razak into this mess. Poor guys, they left America for Karachi for no good reason. In fact, I had hinted to Razak the other day when Amina came to the hospital, but then things were not clear. Timing is everything, I guess.'

'Radhika, whatever was bound to happen has happened. True, now we have Amina, Habiba and the other woman. Still, there is not much clarity yet on why we are doing this. You and Saanvi seem to be very excited. Live Cesarean sections on TV and what not... and not just one, but two. I'm happy for you guys. Have you spoken with Giri? What does he have to say?'

'Leave that to me. I'll handle it.' She said half-heartedly.

Something didn't seem right. 'What does that mean, Radhika? Is everything alright?'

'Guru, if you really want to help me, please leave me alone.'

I ignored the remark, went over and sat across from her and said to her, 'What do you mean? How long has it been since you spoke with Giri? Trust me, this job is not worth more than a guy like Giri. Please don't mess up your life.'

She got up and said, 'Guru, there is absolutely no need for you to feel guilty. It was not working anyway. I have thought a lot about it.'

'Please, tell me. Did you break up with him?'

'Guru, nothing like that has happened yet, but I can assure you one thing. Giri will not be a stumbling block in my professional life going forward. To tell you the truth, Giri as a factor will be totally irrelevant to my work. Only time can decide what happens to our relationship. Please, let us not discuss this anymore. We have lots of other things to do now.' She brought the conversation to a hard stop.

22. The Curtain Raiser

The 'Sanghaali Cesarean—Live' had received enough publicity. All the newspapers carried lead articles on it. There was a big billboard right next to the town's highway. On it, there was a picture of a pregnant Sanghaali woman with huge letters next to it saying, 'Cesarean section saves both the mother and the baby. Let us keep it that way.' Right next to it was an NBC logo and the announcement: 'Watch Live Cesarean section this Sunday morning at 10'.

Apparently, the PR section had decided that Sunday morning was the best time for a 'Live Cesarean' after consulting with a focus group. On weekdays, the primetime slot of nine in the evening would be the ideal time but not a good time for performing elective surgeries. That leaves just the weekend. Fridays were ruled out. Saturdays and Sundays seemed to be good alternatives. Finally, the focus group had decided that between those two days, Sunday morning is the right time. The TV channels had not revealed the names of the patients undergoing the surgery. And even in YouTube teasers, the faces of these two Sanghaali women were blurred.

NBC had interviewed Radhika. She had not shared any information about this with me. Srikantha and I watched the recorded interview at home on Friday evening.

She had started the interview by briefly describing the objective of this live Cesarean section, its safety, the beliefs associated with this surgery in the Sanghaali culture and opinions of cultural scholars about them and the relevance of doing this C-section at our hospital. We couldn't help but get a sense of déjà vu listening to Radhika saying the same things that Dr Mohammad Mohammad had spoken about in our hospital on the Sanghaali culture. The interview went like this.

Interviewer: Do you think that you will address whatever problem that you think there is by this live Cesarean? Aren't there more effective methods? For example, community education or raising awareness at the grassroots level. Isn't this really a public health project to be done by deploying local resources like social workers, volunteers and effective interpreters? Shouldn't this be the responsibility of the whole community? Don't you think what you are doing is a bit too dramatic, like in the movies?

Radhika: Our making of this video live will, at the very least, shoot up your channel's ratings, wouldn't it? (Both laughed loudly.) Don't you have the confidence in your channel's reach? (Laughter again.) No, your question is a serious one. Not a laughing matter. We have tried everything that you mentioned. This is one more approach.

Interviewer: Dr Radhika, don't the Sanghaali women know that the Cesarean section is safe? Have you not done Cesareans on any of them till now?

Radhika: Yes, I have. But after quite a bit of a struggle. I have had to explain every little step and implore them to get the Cesarean sections done. Despite that, many women have flat out refused.

Interviewer: What happened to them eventually?

Radhika: Delayed labour, fetal distress, uterus contracting to the point of rupture. Some of these women who declined to get the procedure done have never returned to the hospital.

I have no clue what happened to them, where and how did they deliver? What befell them? It's almost as if they showed up and faded away into a black hole.

Interviewer: About fifteen days back, a Sanghaali woman in Peoria, Illinois had declined to get a Cesarean section done that her doctor had recommended but came back and got herself admitted to the same hospital yesterday and delivered a stillborn baby.

Radhika: I was about to mention this case. Isn't this foolishness? I can say with one hundred per cent confidence that had she had a Cesarean section, the baby would have lived. We believe that our program could change the minds of such people.

Interviewer: Ok. I will cut to the chase. Sanghaali women who have had their Cesarean sections done have killed themselves. Does your program help stop that too?

Radhika: That is beyond my expertise.

Interviewer: You can't duck this question. In fact, the very women on whom you have performed the Cesarean sections have committed suicides. Haven't they? Did they do so on their own volition or were they provoked?

Radhika: I don't know. You must ask this to the police officials handling this issue.

Interviewer: On your hospital's Facebook page, there have been constant updates on your 'Cesarean section Live' program. Have you seen them?

Radhika: No.

Interviewer: Have you at least seen the comments?

Radhika: No, I have not.

Interviewer: Let me read out a few comments for you. Most

of these are from anonymous troll accounts. Yet, let me read them out.

This comment is from a group called, Protect Sanghaalis, and says: 'One C-section birth now. Ten deaths soon.'

Next one is from someone called, Jihadi Mom: 'C-section is for pussies not for Pussies with a capital "P".'

Radhika: Yes, I got it. This is a network channel, not HBO or Showtime. Can you show such comments here?

Interviewer: Let us worry about it. We will handle it. Is this 'Jihadi Mom', a Sanghaali mother?

Radhika: I don't know.

Interviewer: Is the only agenda of this live Cesarean section to educate the Sanghaali mothers about the safety of the Cesarean section? Who is this Jihadi Mom?

Radhika: Please ask this question to whoever has posted it. This is the hospital's Facebook page, not mine.

Interviewer: These suicides started about eight months ago in this small town. None of these women has given any indication about their reason for these acts. There was not a single note, there was not even a whisper of disapproval from their community. Honestly, to tell you the truth, this was not even a piece of big news till last month. In this situation you have set out to perform not one, but two Cesarean sections on national television. Have these women consented to these surgeries?

Radhika: Is it possible to perform a surgery like Cesarean section without a consent?

Interviewer: In my opinion, you are not being truthful about your intention to our viewers. I believe these mothers have been brainwashed and threatened to commit suicides. You are doing the live Cesarean sections on these Sanghaali women as a veiled challenge to the women and their community—you almost seem to be daring them for future suicides or those in the community who seek to threaten them.

Radhika: Who would I ever challenge?

Interviewer: Those who are trying to lure these women into committing suicides.

Radhika: Your fantasy is quite compelling. This is our hospital's initiative. I'm participating in the project merely as its employee.

Interviewer: Can you guarantee the safety of these women?

Radhika: You are asking the same question again. I'm only trying to demonstrate to these women that Cesarean sections are safe.

Interviewer: Will these women be under police protection after the surgeries?

Radhika: I don't know.

Interviewer: The Pakistani doctor, Razak, who was working with you, apparently returned to Karachi. Did he resign or was he fired?

Radhika: His mother was sick and Razak is her only son. Hence, he had to go back.

I felt that Radhika handled the interview well. The interviewer had come well prepared too. The hypothesis that she alluded to—that this live Cesarean section could possibly be a classified government intelligence operation that used these Sanghaali women as bait to catch a bigger fish, made it an anxious albeit a thrilling thought.

23. Gulab Gang

The day of the Live Broadcast was soon upon us, faster than we realized. Both the women were hospitalized under Radhika's care two days prior to their scheduled surgery. The name of the other woman that we had seen at Caleb's caught my attention—Asha Scott. Asha was undoubtedly a Sanghaali name, but Scott? I had never heard of such a name in their community. I wondered if Radhika had not disclosed her name to me on purpose.

A tent was pitched outside the hospital. The resistance that was so far confined to social media had now come out in the open. There were more than four hundred men, women and children of the Sanghaali community gathered there. A middle-aged Sanghaali woman was shouting at the top of her voice. The channels had brought along interpreters. The interpreters were shouting too. 'Please do not operate on these women. Who told you that these women need C-sections? Let these women go.'

Even as that woman was shouting, someone else thrust his face to the TV camera and screamed, 'Everything that this hospital is telling us is a lie. They are not operating on any Sanghaalis. They are doing this on some other women after making them wear hijabs. No Sanghaali woman would consent to such an operation. Would they?'

'No,' the crowd roared. The vocal power of the response didn't leave any doubt about the Sanghaali community's thoughts on the planned event.

I sat inside and was witnessing all the shenanigans. I remarked to Radhika who was right next to me: 'The television folks don't hesitate to cover any news if it shoots up their ratings. I hope you have not misdirected them for your fifteen minutes of fame. If there is even an iota of truth to what he is yelling about, every one of us will be in big trouble.'

'Guru, I know whatever I'm doing, I have done under the board's supervision. I've not jumped any hoops here.'

'Have you spoken to those women?'

'Haven't you seen me do that? At Caleb's, the other day?'

'Her name is listed as Asha Scott. Who is this Scott? She is a Sanghaali, right?'

'Of course, she is. You saw her yourself. Scott is her maiden name.'

'That is not a Sanghaali name'

'Her father's name is Henry Scott.'

'What about her husband?'

'She is not married.'

'Is she a minor?'

'Guru, would you like to talk to her? As the chief of medical staff, you have the right to do so.'

'Ah, is there any other right that I still have?'

'Guru, please! We had no intention to keep you out of any of these. After Razak left, Rick and Jack may have thought that it is easier to get things done through me rather than getting you involved in something which is not your domain. They started communicating with me directly. I went along with them.'

'I have no issues with that, Radhika. If you are convinced that what you are doing is the right thing, please go ahead. Who has done the preoperative evaluation on those women? Before the surgery, don't we need a doctor to clear them medically?'

'This is a Cesarean section, Guru. Many women get this done. It does not need clearance or any of that stuff. If you are curious about Asha Scott, go and talk to her. Feel free to evaluate both and write your medical opinion. They are all yours. It's always safe to have as many physicians' names on the chart as possible, in case of a lawsuit. They are in adjacent rooms on the first floor. It shouldn't be hard for you to find them.'

I went looking for them. A festive spirit permeated across the hospital. There was excitement all around. The busy sounds of shoes and sandals rubbing against the floor invested a sense of urgency everywhere. It was not tough for me to locate Asha Scott.

There were six or seven Sanghaali girls sitting with Asha. None of them looked more than twenty to twenty-two years of age. Each one had a phone in hand. They all had well made-up faces, groomed eyebrows, dark mascaraed eyes and wore a hijab on their heads. When I stepped inside the room, they looked at me inquisitively. I asked the girl on the bed, 'Are you Asha Scott?'

She said, 'Yes, I am.' She was the girl that I had seen at Caleb's. There was no doubt about it.

One of the girls in the group asked, 'Are you from the press? Do you want to interview her?'

'I am Dr Guru. I have to examine her and certify that she is medically fit for this surgery.'

'Fuck, I thought you were from the press!' The girl exclaimed.

I was a bit shaken.

Another girl asked, 'I would like to ask a question. May I?'

'Certainly. I'm here only to examine her. If you ask me about the live Cesarean section or anything else, I may not have the answers.'

'Hey, I know you. I have seen your pictures on the hospital Facebook page and your picture was on TV too. Aren't you like the boss dude?'

'Not really a boss, but somewhat like a supervisor to all the doctors.'

Then another girl remarked, 'Fuck man! You guys have come to this town and made this hospital famous. Aren't you all from India? I like India. I love Shah Rukh Khan. You guys rock. Keep the fuck up.'

I wondered for a moment if I'm in a high school girls' locker room.

Asha said, 'Farida, watch your language. This is a hospital. I'm sorry, doctor.'

'Screw it girl. You are going to be on TV. You are going to be famous. Let us have some fun. Doc, the other doctor who was interviewed by NBC, is she your friend? She is from India too, right? There's not a single picture of Asha shown on TV. The press has come nowhere near her. We were the ones who found Habiba for you. She is the mother of our friend Labaan. Who do you think we are? We are the Young Sanghaali American Women's Association. Do you have any idea of how much time and effort it took us to convince Habiba? They have told Asha that they can't show her on TV to protect patient privacy. Asha should get credit in some way.'

I had never heard about or seen this 'Sanghaali America' before. Let alone seeing them, I did not have even the wildest imagination that they could have the temperament and the swagger of typical high school cheerleaders with a generous smattering of words like 'fuck', 'dude', 'screw' in their speech.

I asked them, 'Are you all locals?'

'Fuck, no! Who will live in this dump? We are from Minneapolis,' came the answer.

Asha said, 'Doc, may I ask you a question? Dr Radhika has already said that I cannot have a normal delivery. What if we run into complications from this surgery?'

'Yes doc, what other choices does she have?' The girl Asha addressed as Farida, asked.

'That's not my specialty. I'm here only to examine you. I'm guessing Dr Radhika has already gone over the details like the kind of surgery you are having and the type of anesthesia you will be given and so on,' I said looking at Asha.

'Ok. Let us talk some serious shit. What if Asha does not agree to get a Cesarean section done? Asha, you know what, let us go fucking nuclear on them. You refuse the surgery, girl. Doc, would you guys then do a normal delivery and show it live on TV? Then you will have to show it on HBO. With a "For Mature Audiences Only" rating.' The two girls high-fived each other rather pleased with their act.

Do these girls even know why this live Cesarean section is being done and the effort and the struggle that has gone behind making this happen? It was not clear whether it was childishness, ignorance or sheer stupidity.

Or was this what we wanted? This total high-school-girl-like nonchalance towards everything. They were bound by no ideology or religion or jihad. Indeed, if all of them were pregnant and if all had to go through Cesarean sections, none of them would even remotely think about committing suicide. If anything, they might have a good laugh at the doctor's expense for little things that weren't planned well during the procedure. They were the other extreme of the Sanghaali rainbow.

They were not Sanghaalis nor Sanghaali Americans. They were Americans, pure and simple.

I didn't know if I must be relieved at this free-spirited fresh blood or worried about the chutzpah, they brought with them. I decided to finish up my work and leave. I told them, 'I need to examine Asha a bit, could we have some privacy?'

'We are Asha's best friends. If need be, we can die for her. If she commits suicide after this surgery, we will kill those mother-fuckers. If she dies from a complication during the surgery, we will bomb the hospital.' She looked at my face.

She started guffawing loudly at my confused foolish stare. 'I was kidding, doc. were you scared? No one will die. Look at Asha. Does she seem like someone who will commit suicide? Ask her. If she wants to stay alone in the room, we have no issues with that. We will leave now.' She turned towards Asha.

Asha asked, 'Can Farida stay with me?'

Not having much choice, I agreed.

'We will not come in the way of your live Cesarean program and wish you all success. Peace, come what may, let there be peace.' They made the peace sign holding their index and middle fingers across, in front of their right eye and left the room.

I did not speak for about five minutes. It was nothing but my naiveté' that I had painted all Sanghaali women with a broad brush as one group of the likes of Rukhiya and Fadhuma. Asha and her group had debunked my perception in no time. Saanvi and Radhika were somehow able to reach out to this demographic. Or was this also the handiwork of the higher-ups?

Radhika and I lived in the same house for a long time. Only a wall separated us. I was the one who had suggested Saanvi as the ideal person for this job and got her here. That these two had kept everything away from me till now made me feel very insulted.

I messaged Srikantha to meet me in ten minutes and read through Asha's records quickly.

Seeing me quiet for some time, Asha enquired, 'Dr Radhika has already examined me and said that there is no problem?'

'Maybe so. This is a simple but an essential checkup. I'll ask you a few questions. Your answers will help us determine your individual risk for this surgery and measures that we can take to reduce them, like for example: will there be any complications when we administer the anesthesia or how you would react to some of those medicines.'

'I have no health problems whatsoever.'

'Yes, but this is only a protocol.'

I read Asha's records. She had no physical problems of any kind. She had not had a circumcision either.

I asked her, 'Have you experienced problems related to stress, excessive anger or anxiety in large open spaces?' I was making up questions for this faux checkup. It was apparent that none of what I was asking was remotely related to the surgery.

'Meaning?'

'For instance, when you are on the operating table, you will be naked, there will be a camera zoomed in on you, and you will be under anesthesia. The whole world will be witnessing your surgery. Are you nervous about it?'

'A little.'

'I'll ask you a few questions from this questionnaire. All I need is a "Yes" or "No" answers to them.'

She looked at me in apparent agreement.

'Do you smoke? Do you drink alcohol or do drugs?'

'No, no and no.'

'Does anyone in your family suffer from heart-related diseases or have had side effects to anesthesia or related drugs?'

'Not that I know of. I don't know much about my parents. I'm adopted.' She smiled mischievously.

'Oh ... ok.' I paused and asked again, cautiously, not certain if this was another attempt to pull my leg, 'Do you know anything about the health of your biological parents?'

'I was told that I was born in Sanghaala. My adopted parents are from here and when they had been to Dahir-Bar on some missionary work on behalf of an Amoka church, they adopted me. I was an orphan. They officially consummated the adoption here in Amoka once they were back. I grew up in this town.'

Her religion was listed as Islam on the demographic section. I looked at her again.

I had not known the history of this woman. She seemed quite unlike any of the other Sanghaali women I had come across. It was obvious right from the day I saw this woman at Caleb's that she was an outlier, and an oddball to the whole notion of a Sanghaali woman we had had till then. Asha was born in Sanghaala, grew up in Amoka and listed Islam as her religion. And now she was ready to get a Cesarean section on live TV as a Sanghaali. Or did she transform into a Sanghaali only for getting this Cesarean section done?

'My parents subscribe to the Lutheran Christian denomination. However, they have never, even once, compelled me to go to church with them. I don't know if it was luck but when I was growing up in Amoka, I had hordes of Sanghaali friends. I would listen to their stories. My best friend Amina used to tell interesting stories—stories of the forest, camel adventures and desert fables. I read quite a few books on Sanghaala. I started wearing a hijab once I got into high school. My parents did not object to it. One year ago, I converted to Islam. Rather than calling it a conversion, one could refer to it as going back to my religion.'

There were many questions hungry for answers buzzing inside my head. Then my gaze fell on her protruding belly involuntarily.

'Then this guy entered my life.' She touched her belly, raised her hand and kissed it. 'He is all American, I can tell you that. I have made some significant changes and taken some important decisions because of him coming into my life. He is at present, non-denominational; does not subscribe to any religion.' She wiped her eyes. Her tears welled up and rolled down, darkening her cheeks from her mascara.

Farida got up from her place, 'Oh my baby, don't cry. How are all these related to today's surgery, doc? Why are you asking these questions?'

'Asha, please pardon me. I had no intention of hurting you with these questions. All these questions are from this questionnaire.'

'You people come up with these questionnaires for extracting your patients' most private information. Please stop this. If you have any additional queries, ask only those that are relevant to the surgery.'

'Ok,' I sat on a chair next to her to complete her chart. She is a Sanghaali by birth and then came to Amoka. Fadhuma and Rukhiya are also Sanghaalis by birth and immigrated to Amoka. The difference, however, is huge. They came here as refugees whereas she came to Amoka and was raised here as the adopted daughter of a Lutheran pastor. She grew up the same way as Amoka's Amina or Minneapolis' Farida or Smith's daughter Jackie. She had the full embrace of America and its opportunities and in addition its profligate freedom too! She is twenty, may not be in a relationship but is pregnant.

Habiba, who is getting her Cesarean section done along with her, has six children. Her first son Labaan is about the same age as Asha. It is probable that he may have convinced his mother to get this surgery done. He may have likely gone to high school with Asha. Asha's affluence is by adoption whereas for people like Farida and Amina, it could be just geography. Asha and Jackie's America is different from the America of Radhika or me which is entirely different from the America of Fadhuma or Rukhiya.

This group had leapt three generations ahead of Rukhiya and Fadhuma. Glory to America, the melting pot! Asha claims that she turned towards Islam after listening to Sanghaali folk tales and being inspired by them. How can one believe this? Did she want to be a Muslim, or did she want to be a Sanghaali? Does she even know the difference between the two?

Who is the father of her baby?

Amina also had gotten pregnant out of wedlock. When Radhika or I were in our early twenties, did we think like these women? Did I display the same hubris, the same conviction of choice? They come across as a lot different from Mohammad Mohammad or Kuki, people who are part educated, part informed about the happenings around them and always developing a self-serving perspective of them.

Or…

Are Radhika, Rick Jackson and Saanvi exploiting Asha's Sanghaali heritage for the live Cesarean section? Other than the fact that she has taken to wearing a hijab, what kind of a Sanghaali is she?

Sometimes one is better off not knowing much. Ignorance is not just bliss, but it can be therapeutic to the fear of the unknown and the helplessness of ill-defined responsibility.

'I like Indian culture a lot. I watch Bollywood movies regularly. Those colours, those dresses. Wow! I wish I can be an Indian just for those dresses. Are you married, doc? Do you have children?' She asked wiping her tears.

'No. Not yet.'

'Why not? You look like a handsome and successful man. Do they still have arranged marriages in India?'

As someone who wants to be an Indian for colourful dresses or a Sanghaali for stories, who does she really represent? The reformed Sanghaali mom of Radhika and Saanvi? Or the jihadi mother of Mohammad Mohammad and Kuki?

Only time will decide.

I turned around and stood there facing the wall. I flipped out my wallet and the picture of the Brindavana—holy tomb of Raghavendra Swami at Mantralaya and prayed in silence. Swami Raghavendra, please keep her safe and happy. Let her have a safe surgery and let her have the same good sense for a long time and no matter how stressed she feels, let her not take her own life. I wrote that there are no apparent medical reasons for her to not get the proposed surgery and signed my note. I did not go to evaluate Habiba.

24. Cesarean Section—Live

I saw Srikantha sitting in the cafeteria drinking coffee. The cafeteria was packed with people. The live telecast was to begin soon, and the TV was on. Rick Jackson and Jack Powell were standing in line to get some breakfast. The cafeteria in our hospital was usually closed on Sundays. The day being a special one, it was open. I went over to Srikantha and sat across from him. He was watching the TV broadcast without flinching an eyelid, oblivious to everything around him.

Minnesota's local channels were busy. One channel was broadcasting the stock shots of the suicides of Rukhiya, Fadhuma and the Bombay women. A live interview with a Stanford Professor was in progress on another channel.

The surprising thing was that—I had observed this some time back—there was not so much as even a mention of Mohammad Mohammad's name on any channel. He had come to our hospital advocating his support for Fadhuma. Other than the fact that he had shared all the news related to the Sanghaali suicides on his Facebook page, what role did he play exactly? Only Radhika, Razak and I attended that meeting. There was not even a single representation from the hospital's administration. Our hospital is in the news all over the country now; the movie that started as a staid documentary in our hospital garnered sponsorships from companies like Pepsi and McDonald's. The interest in its content had gone beyond the targeted Sanghaali community and its appeal was co-opted by the larger masses. If Mohammad Mohammad had any real intention of garnering publicity, could there be a better time?

'Srikantha, may I ask you a question?'

He looked at me affirmatively.

'The other day when we went to Habiba's farm, Radhika had mentioned to us that they were able to get one woman who was ready for the Cesarean section. She had also said that Rick and Jack were on board and it would be better if the two of us accompanied her.'

He looked puzzled.

'Were you aware of more details?'

'What do you mean?'

'Srikantha, when we were sitting at Caleb's, we saw another girl, remember? Do you know her name?'

'Must be something like Asha, right?'

'She grew up here as an adopted daughter of a Lutheran pastor. She is a Minnesotan for all practical purposes. American. Single mom.'

'But apparently, she has converted to a Sanghaali Muslim, hasn't she?'

Even Srikantha is better informed than me! 'It is possible to convert to Islam but how can she *convert* into a Sanghaali? Is she a Sanghaali citizen? As far as I know, she is still an American.'

'Guru, weren't Rukhiya and Fadhuma also US citizens?'

'Who shared Asha's information with you? Isn't this a violation of patient confidentiality? Unless you are directly involved with Asha's treatment, you are not supposed to know any of this.'

'Guru, I only know that her name is Asha. Radhika gave me her name at Caleb's when I saw her there. Think about it, does it make any sense to not disclose the name of the person going under the scalpel for a live Cesarean on TV? Wouldn't it defeat the whole purpose of this program?

As an answer to our question, the TV came to life with the program. The TV voiceover started with the introduction: 'Welcome to the very first broadcast ever of a live Cesarean section. Only on NBC!' The graphic on screen transformed into the NBC logo. 'It all started in this little town of Amoka, situated about seventy-five miles north of Minneapolis. This town is but a blip on the map of Minnesota. A town only slightly larger than a hamlet and like thousands of towns dotted across America. A town that one can miss in a moment's doze off while driving on the highway. The events leading up to today's program started about eight months back when a physician of this Amoka General hospital, Dr Radhika, performed a Cesarean section on a Sanghaali woman by the name of Rukhiya Abu-Bakr.'

A popup screen within the larger screen showed a stock shot of Radhika giving her statement in front of the hospital. 'In spite of my repeated attempts at explaining the safety of the Cesarean sections, all these women opposed it. No matter what we did, and how much we tried, our attempts were futile.' It was clear that the stock shot was taken a day or two ago, Radhika's hairdo gave that away.

The voice-over continued with newspaper clippings, carrying the news of Rukhiya and Fadhuma's suicides in the foreground, 'Rukhiya Abu-Bakr committed suicide just two months after Dr Radhika performed a Cesarean section on her. The same thing happened with another Sanghaali woman, Fadhuma Hassan.'

'These mothers never heeded any of our warnings that they were putting theirs and their children's lives in danger. Our medical staff and I tried every trick in the book and spared no efforts to convince them. I thank our chief of staff and my friend, Dr Guru, and my friend and colleague, Dr Razak, for their help and support,' Radhika said directly looking at the camera. This was also an old clip.

Srikantha squeezed my hand. At the farther end Rick raised his coffee cup and toasted the occasion, 'Cheers!'

'But when all of this proved futile, it was the Young Sanghaali Women's Association that came to our rescue. We were totally unaware that an organization like that existed. When a small production company from NBC and I contacted them, seeking help in the production of this program, they readily agreed to help us.'

Once again pictures of Rukhiya and Fadhuma as well as the newspaper clippings carrying their news flashed on the screen.

I was paying close attention to the telecast and noticed that not even once had Radhika referred to Rukhiya and Fadhuma or the suicides of the Sanghaali women, whereas the voiceover was always mentioning these suicides. Since the old clips of Radhika's comments had been juxtaposed with the statements of the voiceover, the result was a hotchpotch. It was not clear if this was intended. What was clear was that this Good Samaritan Live Program that only sought to dispel the myth of the relationship between Cesarean section and the Sanghaali deaths had turned into a reality show.

It had been decided beforehand that one of the women would be operated on by Radhika and the other one by O'Reilly. It was well-nigh impossible for Radhika to watch the telecast at that moment. She was probably busy inside, preparing herself for the surgery.

The TV voice said, 'Let's meet Dr Radhika who will be performing the Cesarean section,' and the camera zoned inside up to the entrance to the operating room. A silk curtain was hanging at the door of the operating room. Radhika entered from the left side of the frame. The camera zoomed in on her. She was in her scrubs. The operating room gleamed in the background, decorated with helium balloons and streamers which reminded me of Ayudha Pooja celebrations, back home. Radhika was well-groomed with generous makeup and looked more like someone attending a wedding with her fancy dangling earrings and an elegant chain around her neck. Her hair was not visible because of the sterile head cover. She really looked like one of those TV doctors from an episode of *Grey's Anatomy*.

'Dr Radhika, this looks like a set on TV. Oh, I forgot. This is a TV program, isn't it?' The anchor laughed loudly and looking at Radhika said,'You look somewhat nervous?'

'A little,' Radhika sipped some coffee from the coffee mug she held in her hand.

Srikantha remarked, 'Man, this should not give people the impression that she will be drinking coffee while she performs a surgery.' I was quietly watching the TV.

The TV girl said, 'Don't worry, you will be ok.'

'Thank you.'

'Till now you have not disclosed the identity of the women you will be operating upon. Isn't the whole purpose of doing this Cesarean section on TV to get publicity? To grab everyone's attention? What are you trying to achieve by hiding them from the world? Would it not defeat its very purpose?'

Radhika smiled, 'No, no. We didn't want to divulge their names and get into trouble. Besides, we wanted to surprise you all. She laughed nervously. 'Now, I'll certainly share those names with you. But before that, can I say a few words?'

'Sure, please do. This is your day.'

Radhika continued: 'I will not take much of your time. Come September, it will be three years since I came to Amoka. Ever since then I've had lots of trouble convincing the Sanghaali community to get Cesarean sections done. As everyone is aware, we cannot operate on any patient without their consent. In the Sanghaali community however, in addition to the patient's consent, we need consent from her family, mainly her husband and her father-in-law, if any. I grew up in India, and so I can understand the aspect of getting the husband's approval in this patriarchal system. However, this is fundamentally a woman's problem, so we women must find a solution ourselves. In the past two months I've met Sanghaali women of different backgrounds. My perception from these meetings is that the Cesarean sections are not the only problems of these Sanghaalis. They have many more pressing issues to deal with and these call for nothing short of a big revolution. I'm getting this revolution going in my own small way in my domain of expertise by performing these Cesarean sections. Cesarean section is not wrong. It is not haram. *Once a C-section, always a C-section* is a myth. A woman's uterus is quite strong. A cut made by my small knife cannot make it weak. The live Cesarean section organized today is to show the strength of the uterus, literally.' She sounded like a politician delivering a stump speech. I couldn't believe this was our Radhika.

'Radhika is now playing the woman card keeping the Sanghaali women's uterus upfront. Can there be any better cause than a uterus for a women's revolution?'

Srikantha did not say anything. I continued, 'Have you met the members of the young Sanghaali American Women's Association that Radhika was referring to?'

'No.'

'Cheerleaders, it was like meeting the Sanghaali cast for *Mean Girls*. I met them when I had gone to evaluate Asha Scott. I do not think they understand any of this movement, revolution, etc.—its objectives or the issues it is seeking to address. They don't know, and they don't care. They are kids—barely eighteen to twenty years old. Their main interest today is neither this Cesarean section nor the fate of Sanghaalis like Rukhiya and Fadhuma but, believe it or not Srikantha, their only concern is Asha not getting her fifteen minutes of fame!

No matter how we look at them, Rukhiya and Fadhuma can no way square up to Asha. They cannot be compared. Asha is every inch an American. Doing a Cesarean on her is no different from doing a Cesarean on any white woman from Amoka. Neither of them will take their lives.'

Srikantha stared at me, placed his index finger on his lips and hushed me. He then whispered in my ears, 'Habiba is also getting a Cesarean section done. In what way is she an American?'

I thought that Habiba has been living in America for sixteen years. She has agreed to this surgery upon her son Labaan's insistence. With a young Sanghaali like Labaan influencing her actions, how is she same as Rukhiya and Fadhuma? I felt that all my thoughts were more of a shout in the wilderness.

Radhika continued, 'This is something very bold, very strong. Our women should be proud of themselves for getting these Cesarean sections done without any fear. They should proclaim to the world all that they have done so, and yet they didn't kill themselves later. They should be our ambassadors of change—a gentle breeze that rustles the bushes before it uproots the trees with the ferocity of a tornado. To accomplish this, two women from our town have come forward to get the Cesarean section done on this program today. The first woman is Habiba Ahmed. This shall be her seventh baby. The second woman is Asha Scott. This is her first baby. By agreeing to get their live Cesarean done today, they are doing a great service to the Women community. They are celebrating womanhood. God bless them. We need your blessings. Please bless us.' She started clapping. Habiba and Asha emerged from the red silk curtain in the background, as if they were on the set of *American Idol,* waving their hands. The foundation on their faces and the lipstick on their lips, shone prominently.

Radhika asked them, 'On this profoundly important day,

how does it feel to be a part of this significant game changing event?'

Habiba smiled and said something in Sanghaali. Duniya wasn't around to translate. Offering her apologies, Radhika turned towards Asha.

Asha said, 'I'm feeling very happy. And very proud too. I'm fully confident that this operation will be successful. It would be great if this program leads to our community starting to consider our doctors' advice on what is good for their health.' She smiled. Her metal braces were visible.

'Ok, then let's continue with no further formalities. Shall we?' Radhika asked facing the camera and then there was a commercial break.

Later the whole series of programs on Sanghaali Culture, their beliefs on Cesarean sections and so on, were replayed on TV.

A half hour later, the cameras inside the operating room were switched on. Radhika was prepping Asha and O'Reilly prepped Habiba. Both the patients were given spinal anesthesia that immobilized them only from the waist downwards. They were still able to speak even while the surgery was in progress. A sterile sheet was hanging across their torso between the surgeon and the anesthesiologist who was standing by Asha's head monitoring her. While the camera focused on Asha and Habiba's faces, its wide angle lens included Radhika in the frame. Asha gestured that everything was fine holding both her thumbs up. She was in it for the ride and made no attempt to conceal it.

Only Radhika's forehead could be seen on the screen. Beads of sweat on it stood out as if to convey the tension of the drama and its importance to her.

The TV girl continued her commentary. 'Dr Miller and Dr Wilson from this hospital have already given spinal anesthesia to Asha and Habiba.' She addressed Dr Wilson, 'Doctor, is everything going as planned?'

Dr Wilson raised his thumbs again indicating that everything was.

'Now Dr Radhika will be making an incision on the skin. O'Reilly is already a step ahead. Since both the pregnancies are full term, there will not be many organs coming in the way between the skin and the uterus. All doctors agree unanimously that this will be technically an easy surgery. This is Habiba's seventh baby. How is her surgery different from Asha's?'

'You should be asking that question to Dr O'Reilly. I'm operating on Asha.' Radhika answered without looking at the camera, trying to focus on what she was doing. She appeared to be taking enough caution to not flutter the press.

O'Reilly did not say anything. He looked at Radhika and continued with his surgery. Radhika, somewhat chastised, answered, 'Technically there is not much difference between the two. Since this is Habiba's seventh pregnancy and her previous three babies were delivered by Cesarean sections, we did not wait long for a normal delivery to avert unnecessary complications.'

She was yet to finish when her eyes widened. There was fear in her eyes. She glanced at O'Reilly once and then looked at the camera and attempted to smile. Since she had her mask on, her eyes were the only windows to her emotions. She looked at the anesthesiologist and said, 'Is her BP ok?' She was intensely self-conscious about the fact that the camera was beaming the action taking place inside that operating room to millions of people. She tried to smile in an attempt to cover it. Her fake gestures and awkward body language unmistakably conveyed that something had gone wrong. A couple of minutes later she screamed looking at Asha's belly, 'Oh my god!'

Suddenly the lights in the cafeteria went out and it was pitch dark inside. The power supply of the entire hospital was gone and the emergency lights came to life. The emergency Exit signs turned on and the TV screen went blank. The operator announced on the intercom, which was audible to the entire hospital: 'Code Blue in operating room two... Code Blue in operating room two'. And just a minute or so later came another announcement: 'Code Red in operating room two... Code Red in operating room two'. The intercom was obviously working.

Hospitals have designated codes for all emergencies. Code Blue signifies a medical emergency which conveys that a patient's life is in immediate danger. A button by the patient's bedside when pressed triggers this Code Blue announcement from the hospital operator. Medical personnel in the hospital rush to the patient's bedside whenever this code is called. And Code Red is called when there is an operational failure in the hospital like fire or even if smoke is detected somewhere.

Now with the power outage in the entire hospital, it seemed that there was a short circuit and noticing smoke coming out of the operating room, someone had called Code Red. It felt a little excessive, but then at this time, it was clearly an appropriate response. I was also a bit puzzled about why the emergency power generators were not on.

Why this Code Blue though? Everything was going on well and the broadcast progressed until Radhika exclaimed 'Oh my god'. Then there were these perplexing Code Blue and Code Red calls successively. And the TV broadcast had completely stopped.

Srikantha started running towards the operating room.

I ran after him and glanced sideways to see if the TV was on. I couldn't see anything.

There was a big bustling crowd upstairs near the operating room. The Sanghaali community was present in full strength. Since these hospital hallways do not have any windows, only the battery-operated wall-mounted emergency lights glow regardless of day or night. Security outside the operating room was tight, and it had turned into a virtual fortress. People were trying to see what was happening inside using their phone flashlights. Srikantha and I had to struggle a lot to get inside even with our identity badges!

When we went inside, Radhika told us, 'Everything is alright. Code Blue was a false alarm. I noticed some bleeding. It was minor though. Not sure who pressed the Code Blue button; probably some nurse out of fear. There is nothing to be afraid of. Everything is under control. Why the Code Red? There is electricity in the operating room.' Fear was writ large on her face. She was repeating herself.

It appeared that the situation was under control. Was Radhika aware that the entire hospital did not have power and she was operating under the emergency light? How could she not be? The luminous lights of the TV crew that were hitherto shining were no longer there. Had none of these things come to her attention?

In the events that had unfolded, did Code Red lead to Code Blue or was Code Blue the culprit that led to Code Red? Whether there was an electric outage that led to a botch-up, resulting in Asha's bleeding or did Asha's bleeding make someone preemptively cut off the power supply to prevent the mishap going live on national television? Who is this someone? How is it possible that when an expert doctor like Radhika was performing a routine surgery, there was excessive bleeding? Even if there was, how could Radhika, being in the middle of the surgery, cut off electricity? Hadn't everyone seen her exclaim loudly on television?

Or had someone with a vested interest determined not to let these C-sections go live? Did someone mess up the transformer distributing the power to the hospital, without getting into the complex calculus of these Code Blue and Code Red alarm systems? I checked if Kuki or Mohammad Mohammad was around.

There was no constraint to thoughts floating in one's mind—untrammeled, and apocalyptic! If there was, in fact, a vested interest for someone to stop this live broadcast, would they stop here? What if something else were to happen? Does Amoka have the resources to provide the security we need? Where is Rick Jackson now? Does the hospital need to be evacuated? What do we tell everyone? Where can we evacuate them to?

Suddenly the lights came back in a flash! The moment the lights came on, the cameras started rolling without a moment's delay. I could not see the live telecast this time as I was inside the operating room.

Radhika said, 'Please everyone, the Code Blue and Code Red have been cancelled. Other than the operating room personnel, everyone else please vacate the area.' Possibly due to the ongoing chaos inside, the cameramen were a little frazzled. The cameras that were supposed to be focused on Asha and Habiba had every sundry medical staff and unrelated people in the frame. It was possible that these pictures were also being transmitted live.

I looked at Asha's face once. I thought that she looked somewhat pale. I could see Habiba's face also in the camera monitor next to me. I noticed intense fear on her face. Looking at Asha's pale face, I suspected that the bleeding may not have been as minor as Radhika made it out to be. Blood drenched surgical towels and heaps of blood red gauze pieces could be seen when I stood next to Radhika. 'Have you made any arrangements for extra blood, in case it is needed?'

Radhika was surprised to hear my voice. She could not immediately recognize me under the surgical mask that I wore.

She appeared a little shaken at first and then said, 'No, Guru. Everything is under control. Please leave me alone.' She tried to shield her eyes away from me.

'Radhika, I'm not here as the hospital's chief of staff. Please let me help you.'

I went to Saanvi and made my displeasure clear saying, 'Please stop this broadcast. Remember that you are showing this to the whole world. Use some discretion.'

'Guru, nothing is under my control now. This is a sponsored program. There are no full stops until someone gives a clear statement that there is something going on in this room that we should not telecast. Till then the camera will keep rolling. We have been given only a two-hour slot on TV. Do you think McDonald's and Pepsi would sponsor this slot to broadcast the same clichéd discussions, expert analysis and armchair debates? Let's show the world how you doctors navigate your way around these many hassles in doing what you do. Didn't Radhika say just a little while ago that there were no issues? Trust me. Everything that has happened so far is for everyone's good. We will get an amazing rating, way more than expected. I'm afraid that is how the cookie crumbles, my friend.'

I couldn't hold it any longer. 'What does it take for you to stop the broadcast? Do I need to give a statement to the public on what's happening here? I'll do it. I am still the chief. Please zoom the camera here.'

Radhika immediately came in front of me, facing the camera, 'We just finished operating. Asha has delivered a baby boy and Habiba has delivered a girl. Due to unforeseen reasons, there were some interruptions in our broadcast. Everything has been addressed now. The mothers and babies are doing well. We had no problems with the Cesarean sections.' After Radhika's statement, the camera was zoomed on Asha and Radhika. Asha smiled weakly.

Radhika continued, 'I will have them moved to the recovery room. After about half an hour, they will be ready for your questions.' Then Saanvi switched the camera off.

Saanvi was in such a murderous rage that it seemed quite likely she was ready to kill someone right then. Radhika was in the recovery room with Asha and Habiba. I was the unlucky one left with Saanvi.

'Guru, what kind of a hospital is this? How can there be a power outage at such a time? When the entire hospital is shrouded in darkness, what can we shoot? We were fully prepared for such emergencies and had brought our own generator. The hospital apparently does not allow outside generators and when we tried to explain why we needed it, your Rick Jackson, that self-righteous moron, brushed it aside by chiding us, "Do power outages ever happen in America?" And not just that, he rather pompously assured us that if there is any power cut, all the outlets in the operating room are powered by the hospital's generator and we didn't have to worry. Only the emergency lights in the operating room were working and even when we were ready to shoot with those lights, this damn Code Blue happens. If these many people barge into the operating room, where do we take our camera? How do we shoot? Who called this Code Blue anyway?'

It was apparent that for Saanvi, her program was the be-all and end-all. Nothing else was important to her. My patience had reached its limit and I could not hold myself back any longer. 'Shut up Saanvi!' I said. 'Your only concern is that you did not get your shoot done. Do you even know what Code Blue is? I do not know who called it. I also have no idea what happened. Please be quiet till I go inside and find out. You have got the footage that you needed. It has also been broadcast live. If you want, go ahead, edit and broadcast it again. Now I will go and have a word with Radhika.' Having said what I had to say, I went inside.

Radhika was sitting with Asha inside. She got up and came to the break room the moment she saw me.

I looked at her and said, 'What do you have to say about all these things?'

'Guru, didn't I tell you? It was a false alarm. I don't gain anything by hiding things from you. The moment my scalpel touched the uterus, blood gushed out. It was true I was nervous and on top of it I didn't know how many cameras were zoomed on me. Fortunately, there was this curtain between my hand and the camera. The nurse next to me reacted quickly and gave me the cautery to stop the bleeding. It was at this moment that the power went off. The electric cautery did not work. You are aware how our generators work, right? Whether there is power or not, the electric gadgets within the operating room should work. There is no margin for errors there. But other than the overhead lights, nothing worked. Finally, I had to look for the bleeding vessel and suture it manually. It may all seem minor now, but at the time it was a paralyzing moment. I almost had a brain freeze and did not know what to do. But I swear to god that I did not call for Code Blue. Nurse Hillary told me that it was the Anesthetist who did so. You can go ahead and ask him if you would like.' She went inside saying that she had some work to do and that Asha and Habiba needed to give press statements.

About two hours later, both Habiba and Asha Scott came before the camera. It appeared that Asha's pale lips were generously painted. Both thanked Radhika and O'Reilly. They held their babies to the camera and kissed them. They invited me to the group photo. When I refused, Srikantha nudged me to say, 'Why do you always prefer to get entangled in only the painful stuff? For a change, be a part of the joyous carnival.' I went ahead and posed for the picture.

I reviewed Asha Scott's chart before closing out for the day.

Since there was a Code Blue called, as the chief I had the legal authority to go over the chart without anyone's permission. Everything in there was exactly like what Radhika had told me except for one. Asha was transfused with two units of blood. I looked at the time when that was done, and it overlapped with the time when Radhika was with me in the break room. The puzzling fact was that Radhika herself had ordered the transfusion. Did she forget to mention it to me? Or was it when she went back to check on Asha after talking to me that it was discovered she was low on hemoglobin and then decided to transfuse?

I decided to have a chat with the anesthesiologist the next day. Jack Powell and I went home for the day, but only after ensuring that Asha and Habiba had safely retired to their rooms and their rooms were well-guarded.

***

That night, NBC beamed a thirty-minute special under the title, 'Live Cesarean section—A Success'. Radhika was on the panel answering viewers' questions. Jack Powell and Amoka's mayor were on it too. The Chair of the University of Pennsylvania's African Studies was also in the discussion via satellite. Once again, the same clichéd topics related to Sanghaala's internal and external strife, America's role in it, Sanghaali immigration to America were discussed for the first ten minutes. They spoke about how a routine procedure like the Cesarean section could present so many problems to such a community and how initiatives like the one Radhika had taken are relevant to solving such issues and they congratulated Radhika. On the same panel was a Bangalorean woman, Mangala Nagarkar, from Ohio University who had done a PhD on Sanghaali Cesarean sections. This was the same woman whose thesis Radhika had tried to borrow with no success. And now she had come all the way from Ohio to participate in the panel discussion! 'I wish Dr Radhika's initiative opens the eyes of many Sanghaali women. In the present situation, where Cesarean sections have been rejected by the whole community and there is fear and uncertainty that those who have got them done could lose their lives, it is commendable that Dr Radhika has done this operation on two Sanghaali women under the full gaze of the world. I offer my congratulations to her. I've worked with these Sanghaali women. There are several forces that control them. Despite all the hurdles and the challenges that they had faced, Asha and Habiba have come forward to get this surgery done. I congratulate them too.'

Radhika added, 'My thanks to everyone who has helped and lent their cooperation to our program. It is my wish that this program dispels all the wrong beliefs among the Sanghaali women about the Cesarean sections.' She didn't seem to have much enthusiasm to add anything else.

Fox News and Al-Jazeera broadcast another program under the title 'A Song of Fire and Blood—Code Blue and Red'. In its report they showed a video clip taken from the other side of the operating room, behind Radhika's back. It was clear that someone had shot it on a mobile phone standing behind Radhika. This was only a fifty second clip, and in it we could see the blood-soaked gauze pieces and the blood red towel, the ones that I had seen before. And not just that, I could see my back in the video which meant that this video was taken after we had responded to the Code Blue. The incision on Asha's belly and other parts of her body was blurred.

This video clipping left no doubts in my mind that it was not Saanvi alone who was doing the filming in the operating room. The fifty second video clip was played repeatedly with a ticker below proclaiming, 'Is the Cesarean section a safe surgery?'

The voiceover in the TV channel took a hard line: 'Until

now the Sanghaalis have their own reasons for opposing the Cesarean section, which is accepted as a routine procedure by many of us. Now when we viewed this surgery being performed, it frankly looked quite scary to many of us also. If you see here, the camera is showing us pictures of the operating field. We can only see blood-soaked towels and bloodied gauze pieces. Does a routine Cesarean section always cause such bleeding? Why was the Code Red called while the surgery was in progress? Isn't Code Red, a protocol for emergencies such as fire and smoke? Until now, no representative from the hospital has clarified as to who called for the Code Red. Dr Guru, the hospital's chief of staff has stated that Code Blue was called by the anesthesiologist with the assurance that there will be an enquiry about it. What do our medical experts say?'

The chief of the San Francisco General Hospital's obstetrics department weighed in, 'Amoka General Hospital is one of Minnesota's smallest hospitals. What were Dr Guru and Dr Radhika trying to accomplish with this live Cesarean? They need to clear this up for us because it is quite apparent just by looking at this video that let alone a live C-section, this hospital is not sufficiently equipped for performing even minor surgeries. I have never seen a Code Blue and a Code Red in succession just seconds apart in any hospital. Shouldn't there be some minimum preparedness, at least when you are performing a surgery live on TV? At least something as fundamental as preempting any power cuts? It's a Quixotic experiment and in my opinion, a botched attempt. In fact, the whole show was a big failure in every sense of the term.'

After having seen both the programs, I switched off the TV.

The following day, all newspapers had a field day feeding off the Amoka News. The headlines from their front pages were vivid and sensational: 'Successful live Cesarean from Amoka's doctors'; 'Dr Radhika's live Cesarean section on two Sanghaali women'; 'Live Cesarean: DONE. What next?'; 'A drama of live Cesarean amidst Code Blue and Code Red. What next—Code Black?'; 'Live Cesarean section—What really happened?'

The whole spectrum of print media, from local newspapers to the tabloids, had written about this experiment. They devoured and regurgitated this news like a hungry python. While Radhika and I felt that this entire coverage by the news media was not completely accurate, we also acknowledged that whatever they saw and experienced may be subjective but not false. It was quite possible that the person who had captured the video of the surgical field standing behind me was alarmed and even scared looking at the blood-soaked gauzes, After all, isn't it true that there was heavy bleeding? Otherwise, why would Radhika order blood transfusion for Asha?

The Minnesota Electric Corporation had issued a statement: 'The probable reason for the power outage at the Amoka General Hospital yesterday was an internal malfunction. Generally, our distribution transformer at the hospital is rated for taking the load from the power required to run the emergency electric lights and other surgery related equipment only. It is not designed to take on the consumption from the TV camera lights, the camera gadgets and other sundry equipment of the media channels, not to mention the air conditioners operating in the tents pitched outside the hospital. This overload led to its failure and the power outage. We subsequently fixed the issue in only five minutes.'

Jack Powell had given a rebuttal on behalf of the hospital. 'We gave the electric company a heads-up that we shall be organizing a project like the one we did and written to them asking for steps that we need to take. They did not respond at all. Yet, to be proactive, on the advice of our electricians we did not draw any additional lines from our hospital's transformer. As far as our studio and media personnel are concerned, they had made their own power arrangements and did not tap into the hospital's main line. The hospital's management is not aware of the nitty-gritty here. However, our electrical engineers have worked closely with them. There will be further enquiry and we will keep you informed as soon as we uncover more information.' We knew he was only telling a half-truth.

In summary, according to the Minnesota Electric Corporation, consumption overload caused power failure which led to the failure of the electric cautery that Radhika was using, and this also likely caused some sparking or burning with smoke. This is what they thought was the real reason for the power outage of the entire hospital.

A picture of a shocked Radhika's 'Oh my god' moment went viral on social media. Another picture of a couple of dead geese hanging from the power lines near our hospital's transformer was also circulating all over the internet. Additionally, someone was circulating pamphlets claiming that the real reason behind the hospital's power failure were the Jihadi Moms. Mohammad Mohammad had shared both these pictures on his Facebook page. And he had tweeted the same as well. It would have made no difference even if he had not done so; Radhika was a household name by then!

Radhika had received a letter from the American Medical Association saying, 'Doing a TV program like this is not within the defined scope of your medical license. We have to conduct an enquiry in this regard.' When she showed this letter to me, I directed her to Jack Powell and Rick Jackson. Rick asked Radhika not to worry about it. He said he will write a letter to the American Medical Association on behalf of the hospital.

Apparently, the Association has not contacted Radhika even once.

PART 2

Two Years Later...

25. Black Life's Matters

Nusrat comes from a small village near Dahir-Bar in Sanghaala. It has been twenty-two years since she came to Amoka. She founded and runs a restaurant called Nusrat's and looks after all aspects of the business. Her husband doubles as the chef of the restaurant. She has nine children. Now, she is pregnant with the tenth one. The first one Samira, a girl, is studying in medical school. The second one is a boy, Mohammad Igal. Then there is Hamdi Ahmad, who was previous year's Minnesota Wrestling Champion. The fourth one is a girl, Nazafi, who won the third prize the previous year at the National Spelling Bee Championship.

Nusrat speaks very good English. All her children were born and raised in Amoka. Nusrat had her children once in every two years as if she was on a schedule. Radhika had told me that two years ago, when all young Sanghaali mothers were killing themselves, she had considered Nusrat for the live Cesarean section, but unfortunately Nusrat was not pregnant at that time. Apparently, Radhika and Saanvi had even visited her restaurant to discuss this matter.

She sees Radhika now for her prenatal checkups. Radhika says that it is not clear yet, if she will have a C-section or have a natural delivery.

There is however one problem of concern in Nusrat's family. Her son, Mohammad Igal, has not been living in Amoka for the past six or seven years. Igal was a troubled young man.

He apparently had fled home when he was fifteen years old. According to the FBI, he'd fled to Syria and registered with the Islamic State. Now his name is on the FBI-Minnesota's 'Most Wanted' list. As per the FBI, during the past two years eleven Sanghaali young men including him, had registered with terrorist organizations based out of Iraq and Syria.

Nusrat's son had a track record of serial crimes; he had joined a gang in Minneapolis and was arrested several times for activities like stealing car parts, armed robbery of grocery stores and gas stations, assaults, and peddling drugs. He had spent some time at a Juvenile Detention Center. These were all petty crimes and not enough to indict him for longer and harsher sentences. One day, after his release, he had shown up at Nusrat's restaurant suddenly and purloined nine thousand dollars in cash and had disappeared. Last year, the FBI's Minneapolis bureau chief had released a statement that they had reliable information that he was in Syria. This was after six years since he left home. There was also some information on Wikipedia that he was one of the masterminds of an explosion that rocked Turkey last year.

Nusrat had given statements everywhere asserting that she had not seen her son for the last seven years. The Bureau and the police had interrogated Nusrat on this very question several times. So far, Mohammad Igal had not tried to contact either Nusrat or any of the other family members.

It was said that three months back, suddenly, there was a parade of agents in spiffy suits from the Minneapolis Bureau visiting Nusrat's restaurant. Apparently, they had some leads that Mohammad Igal was in Minnesota and was planning for a big strike on the Mall of America. They therefore had suspected that he may visit Amoka to meet his mother on some day or the other. They were making regular visits to the restaurant and had even interrogated Nusrat's husband. Now that Igal was on the

FBI's 'Most Wanted' list, there was news across the town that the Bureau would always have an eye on Nusrat's house. But Mohammad Igal had so far not visited Amoka at all. He was the phantom right in the middle of it all, waited for by his family, sought out by law enforcement agencies, and followed with interest by the Sanghaali diaspora. None had any luck so far.

The code name that the FBI had assigned to Mohammad Igal was *Black Eagle.*

***

Martin Luther King was a resident of the Minneapolis-St Paul twin cities region. While he was born in Chicago, he had moved to St Paul when he was three and was raised there. For the past two years he had been working as a supervisor in the Nutrition Services Department of St Paul's M.M. Mill Montessori School. Shaniqua Reynolds is his current girlfriend. They had met each other four months ago. They may have gone out just about six times since then. She was the mother of a child from an earlier relationship. According to the students at his school, he was a mensch, always smiling, altruistic and an honest man. They all had the same kind words for him: 'He always fed us, he was very hospitable, and he was like our gramma, may be grandpa sometimes,' and so on.

Martin Luther King is not related in any way to the American civil rights leader, but he is proud to share the same first and last names with the leader.

The world first became aware of the existence of another Martin Luther King on November 8th.

November 8th was like any other day, nothing out of the ordinary. It was a Tuesday. Since it was just past Halloween, orange, carved pumpkins stood in front of many homes. It was turning cold. Trees stood bare, stripped of their leaves. It had not snowed yet. Martin served meals for the school children at noon. He did not have much work that afternoon. He usually eats at school after serving food to all the children. Today, he felt like eating outside. He went alone and ate a steak sandwich with Diet Coke in a deli. He went to a nearby salon and got his haircut.

It was only two in the afternoon and he was finding it hard to kill time. He called his girlfriend Shaniqua. She did not work on Tuesdays.

'What are you doing?'

'Nothing much. I'm watching TV. The baby is sleeping.'

'Shall we go out somewhere?'

'Where?'

'Nowhere specific. Let's drive around for some time and do some shopping in the evening. Can you come over to my apartment tonight?'

She thought for a couple of minutes, 'I'm not doing anything either. I can certainly make it. Can you pick me up from my place? I will have the baby ready by then.'

'Sure.'

He picked her up from her apartment. Shaniqua seated the baby in the child seat in the back and sat next to Martin. The baby fell asleep barely ten minutes after settling down in its seat. Martin saw the sleeping baby in the rearview mirror. He stretched out his hand backward even as he was driving and wiped the drooling saliva from the baby's mouth. He straightened its cap and its head. Shaniqua, pleased at his gesture, squeezed his hand and asked, 'Where are we going?'

'If we drive north on the highway, there is not much traffic by Lake Minnetonka. It's great fun to sit by the lakeside and drink beer,' he said wistfully.

'We have work tomorrow, don't we?'

'We shall be back soon. It's only 2 pm now. The lake is an hour's drive. If we spend a couple of hours there, we can be back by seven. Why don't you stay at my apartment tonight?'

She smiled and said, 'Okay.'

The car raced on the highway. Shaniqua started changing the radio stations. She liked none of them. She switched it off and asked, 'Is there any good CD in the car?' She reached out to the glove box and opened it. There she found a brand-new silver-plated Smith & Wesson Governor model pistol. She was aghast.

'Why do you have a gun here?' She asked.

He smiled and replied, 'I have the license to keep it.'

'Of course, I know that, silly! You and I had gone to get the license.'

The one thing they had done together in the past three months since they started dating was to get his gun license renewed. They had both joined an amateur shooting club that was rather unimaginatively called 'Target Shooting'.

Shaniqua expressed her concern. 'Whatever, you should not have kept it in the car. The baby will be playing around and moreover, these aren't good times. What if the cops stop us?'

'Why would the cops stop us?'

'Have you read the bumper stickers on your car?'

Martin Luther King drove a 1989 Chevrolet Impala. There were two stickers on its bumper. One had the famous 'I Have A Dream' line from King's iconic speech and the other, a more recent one, was a 'Black Lives Matter' sticker.

Martin was in the forefront of the Black Lives Matter movement in the Minneapolis-St Paul region. He had coordinated several peaceful protests. He had even gone to jail for a day after his one-man protest sitting outside Minnesota's world famous Mall of America.

Martin did feel a little shaken for a moment after listening to Shaniqua's words. He had completely forgotten about the gun in the glove-box. He had three more guns and a 22 Magnum Pistol in his house.

For some unexplained reason, ever since he took an active role in the Black Lives Matter movement, Martin had felt a need for keeping a gun in his car. He felt more secure with a gun in his glove box.

The car exited out of the Highway onto Larpenter Avenue and was moving along slowly. Shaniqua turned around in her seat. The baby was still asleep.

'I forgot to get formula for the baby. There is none if he wakes up.'

'Just a minute. I'll get it right now.' He stopped in front of a grocery store and bought baby formula, diapers, a six-pack Miller Lite beer and a couple of condom packets, *just in case*. He kept the beer in the car's trunk and continued driving for about an hour.

Shaniqua asked, 'Do you know the way? Let's not get lost. Remember, we have a gun in the car.'

Almost as if they overheard her, a police car started following them with its loud siren blazing. Martin checked his speedometer. It did not look like he was speeding. He drove over to the shoulder and stopped his car tentatively.

The two police officers, John Mendez and Matthew Whitaker, who were parked on the side monitoring traffic violators had apparently received a message from the Central Dispatch to look out for a red Chevy Impala and do an ID check on the person inside. It was suspected that Black Eagle maybe inside the car.

The news that Nusrat's son Mohammad Igal aka Black Eagle from Amoka may be planning an attack on the Mall of America was in the FBI chatter and this in turn had generated a great deal of buzz and put the Minneapolis-St Paul twin cities as well as Amoka on high alert. All traffic and CCTV cameras—in stores, gas stations and restaurants—were closely monitored. The internet and the social media did not escape this security regimen either. There was tight monitoring of emails with names such as Mohammad and Ahmed and social media posts that looked suspicious.

Apparently, when Martin was paying at the counter in the grocery store on Larpenter Avenue, an agent had noticed him on the store's CCTV and had sent his picture to the state's FBI Office. On that day, Martin was dressed in blue jeans and a white Under Armor t-shirt. He wore the local team Twins' baseball cap. Only the profile of his face could be seen on the store's CCTV.

One of the agents at Minneapolis's FBI field office compared the profile picture of Martin Luther King with that of Igal and concluded that the pictures were of the same person. Nobody knows how such a glitch can happen in this day and age of state of the art facial recognition technology. Immediately a message was transmitted to all dispatch stations: 'High-valued suspect Black Eagle spotted at the junction of Larpenter and Maryland Avenue. Stop and search.'

Officers Mendez and Whitaker were doing the beat on Larpenter Avenue. They were regular police officers and had no clue about the Black Eagle. When they got the message, they responded with the standard protocol questions: 'Copy that. Is the suspect armed? Did you run his license plate? Can you check for the registered owner?'

The Minnesota bureau chief who was listening to the conversation decided that it was not appropriate to discuss Black Eagle over the police radio and called Mendez directly on his mobile. Hurriedly he went over with him who Black Eagle was and how dangerous he could be and promised to send additional forces and assured him that he would also come along in the helicopter as soon as he could. He promised

Mendez that he would be in constant contact with him. He also made it clear that it was Mendez's responsibility to ensure that the car does not go out of the neighborhood.

Dispatch announced: 'Suspect presumed highly trained and dangerous. Running license plate now.'

After a couple of minutes there was another message on the radio which said: 'The car is a Chevy Impala and belongs to one Mr Martin Luther King.'

Apparently both Mendez and Whitaker were stunned. They felt a small surge of fear inside. Mendez came to his senses and asked, 'Martin Luther King? Is this a real name or an alias?'

The dispatcher said, 'How am I supposed to know? I have no idea. I'm more confused than you are.'

Mendez grumbled, 'What the fuck do these dispatchers know about our problems? They say he is very dangerous. Other than a handgun each, we have nothing else. His background is very scary. His name is Martin Luther King! Which terrorist would give himself a name like that?'

He spoke over the radio. 'We need backup. Are you one hundred per cent certain that this is your guy. Is he the Black Eagle?'

Even before there was a response on the radio, the bureau chief called Mendez to say, 'I cannot guarantee one hundred per cent. He resembles the suspect from a certain angle. Stop the car and do a search only. I repeat, search only. If he has proper ID, then let him go. We are also sending you the feed from the closest traffic camera. The face is clearly visible there, but we still cannot confirm the identity. There is also a woman with him. It is advised that you be on your guard. Additional force is on its way. Follow him and wait till the backup arrives'.

They followed his car for ten minutes and cursing their department for not sending backup yet, they stopped Martin's car when he was making a right turn at Maryland Avenue, worried that they may lose him.

Since it was the month of November, it would get dark as early as four in the evening. Martin's face was not clearly visible. Mendez went to the car's window, 'License and registration please?' Martin was well prepared to handle circumstances like this. He was, after all, the trainer at Black Lives Matter to young black kids on how to face such situations—'Always keep your hands visible while raising them up in the air. Keep your hands empty. Do not hold even your wallet. Don't get off the car unless they ask you to. Whatever they might be asking you, always keep your hands raised and empty such that they are visible to them.' And so on…

How can he forget the very lessons he taught others?

He addressed Mendez keeping his hands raised, 'Officer, my wallet is in my back pocket and my license is in it. Would you like to take it out yourself or shall I do it?'

Mendez glanced at Shaniqua and the baby sitting in the back. Whitaker was standing ready behind Mendez with his hand resting on his holster.

Martin's face was clearly visible now. Mendez had no idea what the Black Eagle looked like and to what extent does he resemble this Martin Luther King in the car. He browsed the FBI website on his mobile and looked at Igal's picture there. Frankly speaking neither Mendez nor Whitaker had any previous experience of dealing with these kinds of situations. They spent their time writing speeding tickets or taking drunks on the streets to the hospital, or at the most keeping high school kids under control during rowdy football games. As police officers in a very safe area like Minnetonka, they had never, even in their wildest dreams, expected to have to stop a terrorist's car. This made both of them very nervous.

Mendez said, 'Could you please take off your cap?'

Martin complied without uttering a single word.

'What is your name?'

'Martin Luther King.'

'Junior?'

'No. Just King.'

'Why?'

'What do you mean why? How can I explain my name! You should ask my father, officer.' Even in that situation, Mendez tried to act cool.

Looking at Shaniqua he asked, 'What is your name, baby?'

'My name is Shaniqua.'

Martin thought that the situation was getting back to normal though he didn't quite like Mendez addressing Shaniqua as baby.

Truth be told, Mendez was more than a little nervous. He did not know if Martin bore any resemblance to Igal. He says his name is Martin Luther King as if it is a commonly christened name. Who names their child Martin Luther King? Mendez had never so far come across anyone with that name. He suspected that this guy is pulling a smart one on him.

'Do you need to see my license?' Martin tried to pull his wallet from his back pocket.

'Did you not understand what I said earlier? Keep your hands where I can see them.' He shouted at him and held his gun to Martin's head.

'Easy, officer. I know what my rights are. I had asked you earlier, but you did not respond. You can take my license yourself,' and raised both his hands. Mendez bent down, thrust his hand into his pocket and pulled out his wallet. He checked his license. It did show his name as Martin Luther King. He handed the license to Whitaker who was standing behind him and asked him to check its validity from the Motor Vehicles Records on the computer in the car.

Five minutes passed, and Whitaker was still in the car. Mendez asked Whitaker on the walkie-talkie, 'Is there a problem?'

'Yes, I've got nothing on him yet. Nothing is working. I have a blank screen.'

'Send it to the backup crew. Let them look him up on their computers. Where the fuck are they? The Bureau guy even said that he will fly down here in a chopper.'

Whitaker continued stubbornly, 'It's not working. No line is working'

'If it is not working, come over here. Take a picture of this Martin Luther King and message it to them.'

Whitaker said, 'That's not our protocol.'

'Fuck your protocol. Let's finish the job fast.' He was tired of holding the gun to Martin. Whitaker sat in his car watching the upload of Martin Luther King's data in progress. While he was doing so, his gaze fell on Martin's 'Black Lives Matter' bumper sticker. He thought the more they held this fellow the more trouble they would be in. It was in their interest to get him out of there somehow. When the public image of the police force was already at an all-time low after shootings in different parts of the country, they did not want to apprehend this fellow who appeared like an organizer of some sort for this Black Lives Matter group. If something goes wrong here, the blame will fall squarely on them.

Five more minutes passed by. Nothing was showing up on the computer screen. Whitaker was also losing his patience. Forget about a chopper, other than them there was not even another police car in sight.

'Get his car's registration. It is still 4 pm and the Motor Vehicle Department will be open. If he has a valid registration, we can let him go. I don't think he is our man.'

Mendez was stubborn. 'Negative. I won't let him go without double-checking his ID. Let's release the girl and the baby. Let's take him to the station.'

Martin was holding his hands up for nearly fifteen minutes,

by now. His hands were tired. He was angry when he heard what Mendez said to Whitaker on the radio.

'Officer, what is my crime that I need to come to the police station? I'm not coming anywhere.'

'Shut up. Listen, I'm not taking you anywhere now. Keep your mouth zipped and don't you dare talk so much!' Mendez had completely lost his patience. His situation was such: here he was, in the middle of the road, pointing a gun at a black man. What if somebody sees this? Everyone these days moves around with a camera. What if someone takes a picture?

Shaniqua who was quiet till then spoke up, 'Ok, officer, he is only trying to tell you that what you are doing is wrong. Why are you scaring him?'

'Shut up now. Ok. Please cooperate. Mr Martin Luther King, please show your car's registration.'

'A copy of the car's registration is in the glove box. Would you like to take it out from there yourself or do you want me to?'

'You take it out. At no moment, should your hands go out of my sight.'

Martin was not certain if he should open the glove box or not. What if the officer sees his gun? He is only asking for the registration. He knows exactly where it is in the glove box. He will be fine if the officer does not see the gun. Or should he tell the officer that he has a gun in his glove box? After all he has the license to carry the gun. He hasn't broken any law. So he decided to tell him.

'What are you doing? Even if I had asked the real King for the registration, I would've had it by now.'

Martin looked at Shaniqua. She seemed to have read his mind and shook her head suggesting not to.

It was not clear if she indicated 'no' to opening the glove box or to telling Mendez about his possession of the gun.

He decided to go ahead and open the glove box. This was a

fatal mistake. The Smith & Wesson revolver popped out of the glove box as soon as he opened it. Mendez had not expected this. Martin froze with fear. He tried one last time to prevent the tragedy waiting to happen.

'Officer, I've the permit to keep this gun. The permit is also here,' he turned around to fetch it.

Bang... bang... bang, Mendez fired in succession. The first bullet got his right arm, the second went to his chest and the third one got his tummy. Martin collapsed right there.

Shaniqua was in shock. The irony of it all hit her like lightning. Both of them had protested police atrocities at St Louis, Miami and Florida in the incidents of Michael Brown, Eric Garner and Trayvon Martin. Now the same tragedy has come calling into their own life, inside their own car! Is this an atrocity or should Martin have told the cop about the gun in his glove box? Do all shootings occur as a result of such confusion and misunderstanding?

The baby had woken up due to the sound of the gun shots. He started crying loudly.

She did not have much time to think and react. She heard Mendez say 'Shit,' and call out on his radio, 'Shots fired on Maryland Avenue. Suspect down. Send medics.'

It was not clear what was on Shaniqua's mind. She paused for a minute and started recording on her phone. Her courage was astonishing. It was possibly because she did not see the likelihood of two blacks being shot by the same cop at the same spot.

Then the whole world got to see what transpired next. Shaniqua started streaming this video live on Facebook.

'Officer, he was about to tell you that he had a gun with him. You asked him to get his registration from the glove box. He has the permit to keep the gun with him.'

'Shut up ma'am. Whitaker, is he still alive? Check his pulse once.'

Whitaker came running. 'What happened Mendez? You fucking shot him? You are always in a hurry.'

'Whitaker, shut up. She is fucking recording us. Ma'am, please stop recording.'

'I'll stop recording. Martin is not breathing. Start doing a CPR on him.'

Mendez told Whitaker, 'Start the CPR.'

'You fucking do it.'

'Whitaker. I'm your senior officer. This is an order. Do the CPR. I've called the paramedics. Till they get here, I've to secure this place.'

'Securing? Only the girl and the baby are here.'

'And the gun there?'

Whitaker saw Martin Luther King's gun near Shaniqua's leg. 'Ma'am, please stay calm. Do not move. I'm bending now to pick up your gun.'

Shaniqua did not speak. She was streaming everything on Facebook. In about three minutes there were a monstrous number of likes for her post. This video was visible only to her friends and those who followed her. By then someone had commented: 'Make this Public.'

Shaniqua felt that Martin's breathing which was already feeble had almost stopped. She turned the camera towards her and said on the camera, 'Someone please help him.' She placed the camera such that Martin Luther King's face was fully visible and started doing the CPR herself.

'Ma'am please sit down. Do not move.'

She sat down quietly. Everything felt surreal. She was not sure if these events were real or if this was a nightmare. The fact that she was still recording was a reality check for her. Meanwhile the tsunami of likes and comments that her video was garnering made it difficult for her to keep the phone aside.

By then, she had recorded for about seven minutes. The medics who came in the ambulance started the CPR right away.

'Ma'am, please switch your phone off. Is he your friend or your husband?'

'Friend.'

'Ma'am, are you aware that it is inappropriate to stream graphic images on internet? Please switch your camera off.' He grumbled, 'Ever since these phones started having cameras in them, things have become messy.'

Mendez asked, 'Is he still alive?'

'Please officer, let us do our job. Ma'am, if you don't switch your camera off, we must stop our work. Officer, how did you let her record?'

Mendez said, 'Can you just do your job? We will get her phone. He had a gun with him and so it was tough for us to manage both. My partner was trying to get the gun. I was keeping an eye on the road. And there was the baby in the rear seat crying loudly.'

He only knew that the camera was recording the events going on. He was not aware that the video was being streamed live.

A few more police cars arrived on the scene then, and all the police officers circled around Martin Luther King. Mendez was trying to explain the turn of events to everyone.

The bureau chief came next, apologizing for his delay. Apparently, his chopper landed in the football field of a school nearby and from there he had to summon a police car to drive down to Larpenter Avenue. He said that he had heard everything on his radio and had a hard time calling from the chopper.

Shaniqua's friend's friend is a reporter at a news channel in Minneapolis. She was logged on to Facebook when her phone pinged 'Shaniqua Reynolds is now live.'

Barely seven minutes after Martin Luther King was shot, Shaniqua's video had been broadcast on a local TV channel.

In fact, she was made aware of this broadcast only through a comment on her post. She switched her phone's camera off as if her job was done.

Mendez demanded, 'Give me the phone.'

She gave it with no protest whatsoever. Within thirty minutes after being shot, Martin was brought to the Hennepin County Hospital in Minneapolis. His chest was filled with blood and his pulse was very weak. He was barely breathing.

Fifteen minutes later, Martin Luther King was dead.

By the time he was taken to the hospital, many media vehicles were already parked outside jostling for space in the parking lot. Shaniqua had already given the world images that their cameras could never capture. In just about thirty minutes the video that Shaniqua had streamed on Facebook had gone viral. Many had shared this video on their Facebook pages. CNN did a primetime story on the incident. Wolf Blitzer gave his commentary: 'This is a new twist to the ongoing tension between the police and the African Americans. Till now, all these reported atrocities did not have a clear eye witness and most of the stories were based on "he said, she said" anecdotal reports. There was no clear evidence. This girl Shaniqua, has now captured on video, the footage of what happened after the shooting. There is no doubt that the video will throw more light on this issue.'

'This video was taken after Martin was shot. Who knows what led up to that shooting. According to Officer Mendez, Martin Luther King was trying to pull his gun out.'

'All police shootings have these accusations and conflicting opinions. It is rumoured that they are going to hand this case to the grand jury. Let us wait and see.'

'So far in the last couple of years there have been cases of police shooting on fourteen young men of colour. Many such cases have also gone to grand juries. How many of them have delivered justice to African Americans?'

'Zero.'

'Does this directly point to a defect in our system? We are only a news agency. Let us wait and watch what happens next. The victim's name is said to be Martin Luther King. Is this true?'

'Don't know. He is thirty-four years old. He was born many years after Rev. King died. All of this is pure coincidence.'

'Granting that someone can choose a name like this, how does such a name even occur to anyone?'

'Anything is possible in this world. Let's go to the next show.' A commercial break came up.

The tabloids and the yellow press feasted on this news. One tabloid published an article under the headline, 'Shaniqua's pleas go in vain as St Paul's police officers refuse to do the CPR.' Another tabloid criticized Shaniqua for choosing to take the video rather than doing a CPR, and published their critique under a big headline, 'Shaniqua, the girl who took the video of her boyfriend dying.'

Four days after Martin Luther King's death, a GoFundMe account in Facebook was set up in the names of the Pastor of Martin's Church and Shaniqua. Three hundred thousand dollars were collected in just four days!

The same tabloid published another article under the headline, 'Shaniqua makes a killing out of a killing.'

On the seventh day, Facebook deleted the video from Shaniqua's account citing graphic content. Mendez and Whitaker are both at home now on administrative leave. Mendez gave a statement which read: 'I got a message from dispatch that a man resembling the terrorist Mohammad Igal is in the car. I stopped his car and checked his driver's license. It had his name as Martin Luther King. If someone has a name like this, how can we leave him without checking carefully? Unfortunately, we could not cross-check his name on our computer system. Meanwhile he opened his glove-box and tried to grab his gun from there.'

Four days later, in the march organized by Black Lives Matter in Minneapolis downtown protesting the killing of Martin Luther King, a sniper shot and killed three white police officers from the top of the Renaissance Tower. Black Lives Matter immediately clarified that they had nothing to do with this shooting.

There was no news about the whereabouts of Mohammad Igal. No activities of his could be tracked on FBI circles either. FBI released a press statement that he has gone underground.

26. Where the River Joins the Sea

A month after Martin Luther King's death, Nusrat's restaurant was vandalized. All the window glasses, tables and chairs were smashed and destroyed. There was graffiti on her restaurant's walls: 'Where have you come from?', 'Go back to Sanghaala', 'There's no place for terrorists in Amoka'.

Days after the FBI added Mohammad Igal to its 'Most Wanted' list following his joining the Islamic State and the official confirmation of his involvement in several attacks and explosions, Nusrat established 'Moms against Terror Recruitment'—a voluntary organization of the Sanghaali mothers. Every time the news that a Sanghaali young man had joined an organization like ISIS or Al Tewagi became official, she would conduct Town Hall meetings in Minneapolis. No matter how difficult it was, she would gather the neighbours, the local police officers, and the office bearers of the school board for a meeting. She would organize discussions and workshops with experts on topics like terror recruitment and its prevention. She had apparently confided in Radhika and lamented that even though it has been twenty-two years since she came to America, she has been unable to comprehend the problems of the newly migrant Sanghaali community.

The news that Martin Luther King, who succumbed to Officer Mendez's bullet this past month, resembled Mohammad Igal made her sick to her stomach. Officer Mendez's statement that he thought he was stopping Mohammad Igal when he stopped Martin Luther King upset her even more. More than the fact that her son was a terrorist, what made her very sad was that someone else who had a resemblance to him fell to the police's bullet.

Her children consoled her by showing the CCTV picture from the grocery store that allegedly confused the police. 'Mother, look, there is no resemblance whatsoever between the two. This is a lie that the police are concocting to cover-up their error.'

After Martin's death, Nusrat had conducted another Town Hall meeting. Apparently, she was convinced that between Martin Luther King and Mohammad Igal, even if one were to be a white person, Martin would have lived. Minnesota Governor and the state's Attorney General also attended this meeting.

It was when she was at this Town Hall meeting that her restaurant was vandalized. The next day, *Amoka Daily Herald* ran the news of the attack on Nusrat's restaurant on its cover page. In the same edition of the paper, an op-ed column was published. It was written by Amoka's Mayor, David Wagner.

My Beloved Amoka

> My town is a small town on the banks of the Mississippi. My little Amoka, where all the four seasons of the year manifest prominently. My town with a population of mere ten thousand is a white town just like its winter. Fifteen years ago, we were 92 per cent white with Norwegians, people of Scandinavian descent, some Irish and Germans. Three-fourths of the town were catholic. We believed our celebration of Cinco De Mayo was being liberal. Ours is a small town, a small community. In here is one mill, one paper factory, and one hospital. Those young men and women of the town who did not want to work here migrated to Minneapolis and St Paul. A few more adventurous ones

moved to Chicago. Our world had not extended beyond Chicago.

Later, everything changed.

Possibly, due to the liberal policies of the Minnesota State, my town that had not seen any non-white faces started witnessing many blacks walking on its streets. That they were Muslims was something we came to know later. To be honest, we came to know about the existence of Muslims only after September 11. We believed that they only lived in cities like New York and Chicago. But now they are right here in our town. Today Amoka has a Sanghaali population of three thousand six hundred. On most of its streets we can see hordes of women wearing hijabs. There is a mosque in the town. The prayer calls of 'Allah-hu-Akbar' can be heard three times daily. States like Minnesota, North Dakota, Montana, and Nebraska have started seeing Mohammads and Ahmeds in their little towns. Ten years ago, the only high school in the town had one English teacher. Now there are six. A whole herd of Sanghaali translators can be seen in the school's parent–teacher conferences. This is something new, something that we had never seen in our town before.

By asking for an additional half hour for their prayers, the Sanghaali kids have messed up the school schedule. For the only reason that the pledge must be on 'god', our secular school system has not included pledges or prayers of any kind but now we have an exclusive room for Sanghaali students to pray.

Two years ago, a circus was staged in our town: Two Sanghaali women who had their Cesarean sections in our hospital committed suicide. Nobody, till now, knows the reason. They were supposedly jihadi mothers. By their suicides they had cautioned the hospital not to perform any more Cesarean sections on other Sanghaali mothers. If performed, there would be more suicides. I had believed that jihadis take others' lives but here these women were taking their own lives. It was at this time that Amoka

General Hospital, by performing a live Cesarean section on TV, became famous all over the world. By performing the Cesarean sections on two Sanghaali women live on national TV, they sought to demonstrate to other Sanghaali mothers that Cesarean section is a very safe procedure. May god bless Dr Radhika and her team for their courage. More than highlighting that Cesarean section is a safe operation, this was a kick on the ass of those goons who were instigating these suicides and roaming around Amoka calling themselves terrorists. In these two years, there has not been a single suicide of a young mother in the entire state of Minnesota.

But now in our town, we have the notorious Mohammad Igal!

We do not know you all. You write as jihadi mothers in the newspapers. Al Zarqawi from the Islamic State is a friend of this Mohammad Igal. Police kill Martin Luther King for his alleged resemblance to Mohammad Igal. This guy left Amoka a long time ago and currently is on the FBI's 'Most Wanted' list. Fifteen years ago, could anyone imagine that our town would become this notorious?

Since your arrival, our youth have left the town. Their jobs are gone. Are you doing their jobs? No! You have been busy killing others or yourselves.

Please do us a favor. Get out of here. Go to Syria or Iraq. Fight and die there. Or go back to Sanghaala. Allow this small town to be a small town again.

Good Bye.

Can someone who holds a responsible office like a Mayor's, write in such a way? Can he use words like 'ass' in an op-ed? Even if he did, what kind of newspaper publishes it? Isn't there a time and context for everything?

The moment I read the word 'goons', I thought of Kuki. I had totally forgotten about him. Is he alive? If so, where is he? Like Igal, has he also left for Syria or Iraq? I checked if his name also figures on the FBI's 'Most Wanted' list. However much I tried, I could not recall his real name. None of the pictures resembled Kuki's.

What kind of write-up is this? At a time when a woman like Nusrat from this town has lost her only restaurant, can Amoka's Mayor write and publish a piece like this? And if a newspaper like *Amoka Daily Herald* publishes it, what does it convey to its citizenry?

The very next day, the editor apologized and admitted his mistake for publishing this op-ed: 'Since the op-ed column was written by the Mayor, it was printed in advance. The restaurant was vandalized at midnight and it is cover page news. We will fix this on our website.'

But on the internet, where contents are read by clicking on what one is interested in, who would bother about the sequence of events?

The Mayor also had written a small one-line letter condemning the attack on Nusrat's restaurant in the 'Letters to the Editor' section: 'Nothing can be accomplished by violence. We regret Nusrat's losses.' He had not made any reference to the contents of his column.

Someone had reacted to this news rather poetically. 'Where a river joins the ocean, the ocean also joins the river. In this union, who can say which the river is and which is the ocean? What's the nature of this confluence? Union or separation, what should we call people like Mohammad Igal or Kuki? Are they being swept in by the river or are they swimming against the current into the river? Why this swim against the current? Are they domestic terrorists? Or foreign extremists? They are all American citizens. Is there a border for terrorism? Would folks like Kuki and Igal end up as dregs in a big melting pot because of their beliefs?'

I opened Facebook and looked for Mohammad Mohammad's name. His Facebook account was closed.

27. Afrcan Women's Voice

It was a cold night in December. Minnesota had its more than usual share of snowfall. Christmas was in the air, and there were celebrations everywhere. Since the snow was heavy, kids played outside in the yard, fighting with snowballs and making snowmen. The snowmen stood there with their frozen smiles, surveying the sea of white around them. Colourful lights could be seen all around.

I was working the night shift in the emergency department. The hospital's Christmas party was scheduled for the following week. In the corner of the hallway, stood a large Christmas tree. There were twinkling lights everywhere. Santa Claus on his sleigh pulled by reindeers, gift boxes and candy canes scattered all over the festive faux snow inside. There were stars placed on each leaf and branch of the Christmas tree with post-it notes on them. Each post-it note had a staff member's name on it. The star at the apex of the tree had Dr Smith's picture. He was retiring that year. Below the picture was a handwritten note, 'We will miss you Dr Smith.' In the branches underneath, Radhika, Srikantha and I were also there.

After Smith's retirement there would be no other doctor in the obstetrics department other than Radhika. Since she would be on call every day after he retires, she may not have much vacation time left. She had taken a week's vacation and gone to Florida's Key West along with Kristina and Saanvi.

I felt that I simply didn't understand girls. I could see

Saanvi and Kristina going together. They were a couple. Why Radhika, though? Srikantha and I never went out together even to a restaurant.

It was an ice cream social day. The entire staff got free ice cream from the hospital. For those working the night-shift, the hospital's board members showed up at around 10 pm to personally serve them ice cream. Rick Jackson wore a chef's apron and pushed an ice cream cart around the hospital serving ice cream to all. He was persuasive in his hospitality, 'Guru, have another scoop. I don't think you will ever put on much weight.' He served two scoops and handed me a gift box thanking me for my services to the hospital.

It was a golden coloured box loosely tied around with a blue ribbon. I untied the ribbon and opened the box. In it there was a Movado watch with an inscription on its back that read, 'For successful completion of five years'.

I kept the watch in my desk drawer. Eleven people were there in the waiting room of the emergency department. I was the only doctor on duty that night. There were two injured in a traffic accident. One had a broken leg. I was putting a cast on him when a nurse asked me to see his girlfriend right away since she had severe difficulty breathing because of a punctured lung. I evaluated her and inserted a small chest tube to help her lung expand. A child was crying from diaper rash. Another one had ear infection. In between this running around, we were preparing to transport a patient who had a heart attack to the Minneapolis Heart Center. Due to bad weather, there was no ambulance available to transport him. When we tried to get a chopper, they too expressed their inability due to poor visibility. Even though his condition was stable, it was important for him to be evaluated by a cardiologist for a stent placement as soon as possible. We had no choice but to keep him in the hospital till the weather improved. That night, Srikantha was the admitting physician. After briefing him about the details of this patient, I convinced Srikantha to manage him till morning. I had the patient admitted to the ICU and informed the patient's family about the plan. The family was on board.

When Srikantha came to see the patient, he asked me, 'Did you check your messages?'

'Not yet,' I said and looked at my phone. There were two messages. He had sent the link to David Wagner's letter published in the *Amoka Daily Herald* and an audio clip of Nusrat's interview on the public radio. There were also some pictures sent by Radhika from Key West.

I opened the pictures first. She, Saanvi and Kristina were all dressed in bikinis with towels wrapped around the head and another fastened around their waist. They wore large sunglasses. I had never seen Radhika in a bikini before. If I were to guess, she must be around thirty-five. It is not so much of a big deal to have a comely and sexy figure to wear a bikini, but it is important to have the attitude to carry it off. I have seen many Indian girls trying to cover their bare knees even while wearing something like Bermuda shorts. But here, I saw no hesitation or self-consciousness. She held a tender coconut in one hand while showing thumbs up with the other. I was tempted to look once more but being aware that I'm in the hospital, I saved the picture and texted Radhika, 'You look beautiful.' The moment I pressed send, I realized that there were Saanvi and Kristina also along with her. Immediately I sent another message, 'I meant you all.'

The second message I presumed would put the first one in a more proper context, but I realized that the second message would emphasize that the first message was intended only for Radhika. I got a smiley emoji from Radhika and then a mischievous question, 'Saving lives?'

I responded, 'One at a time.'

A smiley with another naughty question followed, 'One Sanghaali at a time?'

I tried to end the chat with a smiley face and the message, 'Duty calls'.

'No more gunshot wounds, right? Get them out ASAP. Don't be a cowboy. Stay away from the TV cameras. Take care.' She went offline.

Two Sanghaali girls were registering at the front desk almost as if they heard her. I let them continue with their registration and sat there listening to Nusrat's interview.

'You are listening to News Hour, from Minnesota Public Radio. Last night there was a town hall meeting in Minneapolis on "Afrcan Women's Voice". The meeting was organized by a group called "Moms against Terror Recruitment and Racial Profiling". Nusrat, a prominent member of Minnesota's Sanghaali community conducted it at the Town Hall. She is the founder of "Moms against Terror Recruitment"—a voluntary organization of Sanghaali mothers fighting against recruitment by terrorist organizations. She has been doing a phenomenal job of identifying and educating vulnerable young Sanghaali men from getting recruited by terror organizations. This town hall echoed the sentiments of the Minnesota Muslim community, which according to Nusrat was at the center of the nation's attention for the wrong reasons.

'Last year Minnesota witnessed the eleventh incident of one of its young Sanghaali men register with the Islamic State. The FBI has alleged that this young man has helped the ISIS with money and other resources. He happens to be Nusrat's son, Mohammad Igal. Tragically, a black man by the name of Martin Luther King whose facial features were said to resemble that of Igal died in a police shootout. In the melee of protests and unrest that followed, three police officers lost their lives.

These events have put Amoka, this small town in Minnesota, at the center stage of media attention. Mohammad Igal's mother Nusrat has been running a restaurant in Amoka for several years now. We spoke to her a little while ago.'

Interviewer: 'Welcome to News hour. Were you ever suspicious that your son Mohammad Igal had contacts with terrorists?'

Nusrat: 'No. Never.'

Interviewer: 'Isn't your son an American citizen?'

Nusrat: 'All my children were born here.'

Interviewer: 'Now another is on its way. Congratulations!'

Nusrat: 'Yes. Thank you.'

Interviewer: 'Whenever we speak of Amoka and pregnant Sanghaali women in the same sentence, people always ask this question. Before I do so, I would like to remind our listeners that most of the news media has dismissed this as a non-issue. Did you have Cesarean sections for all of your other babies and if so, is the next one also going to be a Cesarean?'

Nusrat: 'I had my last three babies by Cesarean section. My doctor, Radhika, has said that this one is also most likely going to be one.'

Interviewer: 'Is this the same Dr Radhika who did the live Cesarean section on TV?'

Nusrat: 'Yes, very much. Don't you worry. I'll not commit suicide (laughs).'

Interviewer: 'Let me directly come to the heart of the issue. Sanghaalis quite understandably oppose racial profiling. But now there is an allegation about your son being associated with terror organizations. And you are aware that these allegations are not without any basis. There are enough reasons to profile him. Of course, I don't need to spell them out. In such a situation how can Sanghaalis get away from being racially profiled? In this fight against terrorism, what strong reasons do Sanghaali mothers like you have, to oppose profiling?'

Nusrat: 'It's a good question. Thank you for asking it. Sanghaalis share three general characteristics. We are all immigrants, we are all Muslims and all of us are blacks. The moment we step into America, we are profiled. The finger of suspicion of any wrongdoing or illegal acts always points at our children. I consider myself a good mother and I believe I've raised my children well. But, Igal failed me. I wish that nobody in the world goes through this kind of turmoil. If there is any evidence that my son is a terrorist, I believe that he should be punished appropriately. If, in fact, he comes to my house, I will hand him over to the authorities. I have also raised nine other children and they are all good citizens. But the joy of raising these nine to their full potential is negated by one Igal. My family is a perfect example of why racial profiling is wrong. Our family has only one Igal. Apart from him there are his brothers, sisters and his mother. We are all Sanghaalis, Muslims and Blacks too, but that does not make us Igal. A person is more than a sum of his parts and acknowledging them just by colour and physical appearance can be tragic. Take the example of Martin Luther King. You have seen his pictures. Is there any resemblance whatsoever between him and my son? If he were to be a white person, would the police have shot him?'

Interviewer: 'Do you know why young men like Igal are radicalized this way? Why are they influenced, in fact brainwashed, into making these life choices especially when they are nurtured by good mothers like you. FBI has declared that another ten young men just from Minnesota alone have registered with terrorist organizations in countries like Syria, Iraq and Sanghaala. FBI does not publish statements like these or post the list on its website with your son in it without enough evidence. Why do Sanghaali American kids like Igal have to make this devil's choice between making a future for themselves here or die in countries like Syria as terrorists? What drives them to this stage, to this point of inflexion?'

Nusrat: 'Our organization is not just working with the state's Attorney General. We also work with the local police. We should all join hands and try to find the root cause of why kids like Igal get into this fatal courtship with terrorism. According to the FBI all these kids get recruited through social media. It's been seven years since Igal abandoned us. Who knows when he went to Syria and when he turned into a terrorist? What's the point in blaming Facebook? We have a lot of work to do in our community. Our community has a small presence in Minnesota. We are not in millions but just about twenty to thirty thousand. Whenever there is news of a suspicious death in our community or news of a young man running away to the Islamic state, I personally go to their family and talk to them. Everyone tells me the same thing—that they had no clue about it. I did not believe them. I suspected that the mothers and the other family members were not telling me the whole truth. Now that the story has played out in my own family. I must believe these mothers.'

Interviewer: 'Finally, is there a solution to this problem?'

Nusrat: 'All of us, the Sanghaali community, the Minnesota Police and the Attorney General's Office must work together. We should collectively be on the lookout for who contacts our young minds and how do they do that. These are all school going kids. Some of these kids don't return home after school. It is tough for many Sanghaali mothers to monitor their children closely since they have as many as six to eight children each. We should provide them opportunities for after-school activities and provide jobs for those who have graduated from high school. All these call for money and other resources. We need the government's assistance and the cooperation of the police.'

Interviewer: 'What do you mean by cooperation of the police?'

Nusrat: 'Cooperation to monitor and discipline our children on the streets. The problems always start in our homes or on our streets.'

Interviewer: 'Do you think the contemporary American society has failed to restore goodwill between the police and the black youth?'

Nusrat: 'I don't think so. There are lots of African Americans who are successful here and are leading a decent life. In fact many of them serve in law enforcement.'

Interviewer: 'Well, let me ask you, is there any relationship between the shooting of blacks by the police and Sanghaali young men gravitating towards terrorist organizations?'

Nusrat: 'You have quite an imagination! This issue of police shootings is more of an internal issue of America. It is way too simplistic to conclude that police shootings of blacks have provoked the Sanghaali youth to turning into terrorists. So far, the police have not killed a single Sanghaali young man.'

Interviewer: 'What about Jihadi Moms? Where are they now?'

Nusrat: 'I am disappointed that the media keeps going back to this issue again. Nobody knows that Jihadi Moms existed. Everyone knows about young Sanghaali mom's suicides that happened in Amoka two years ago. The media labelled these suicides as jihad. Somebody thought that a live Cesarean section on TV can address this issue. Coincidentally, two years since then none of the Sanghaali women who have had Cesarean sections have killed themselves. Labeling these suicides as jihad and concluding that our doctors reformed these jihadi mothers by performing Cesarean sections on TV is oversimplifying everything.'

Interviewer: 'But then isn't it a fact that the incidents of suicides have stopped? What may be the reasons for it?'

Nusrat: 'First of all, we do not have an answer yet on why these suicides happened. In my opinion, there are more educated Sanghaali women now than there were two years ago. Their worldview has changed and is demonstrably more independent. The very fact that they have come forward and got their Cesarean sections done on TV is a big development; a watershed moment. One of my daughters is a doctor. I can assure you that come what may, she will not commit suicide.'

Interviewer: 'Do not duck the question. After the live operation on TV, there has been no suicide either in Amoka or Minneapolis. What do you suppose is the reason?'

Nusrat: 'I'm neither a policewoman nor a detective. However, if in fact someone has brainwashed these innocent women into committing suicides and given it a jihadi tint, then this TV Cesarean has given the right answer to them. And the Sanghaali women have sent out a strong message to the world not to take them lightly, not to take them for granted! The live Cesarean has helped to address the issue to that extent. The Sanghaali women will be grateful to Dr Radhika for making that happen. Change does not happen in a day. Sometimes it may take generations. We should do what we can under the circumstances. We should guide and educate the next generation well. That is all we can do from our side.'

After I was done listening to Nusrat's interview, I opened the next patient's chart in the computer. I thought that Nusrat spoke quite well. Her pristine experience as a youth had acquired a civilized edge due to her stay in America. She was able to introspect and articulate well on topics like war and terrorism within the context of her experience.

I thought everyone spoke well in interviews these days. For the question on why a young man like Igal gets radicalized, Nusrat had given an evasive response, with an answer that was not really an answer, by mentioning that to stop such things from happening, everyone—the government, the police and the Sanghaali community—should work together. What else could she say? These interviewers were indiscreet and didn't seem to have anything else to ask when it came to Sanghaali women. They keep coming back to their pregnancies and suicides. Overall, the interview pleased me. I messaged Srikantha, writing 'Very insightful', and sent the interview link to Radhika also.

28. Me—A Good Racist, an OK Racist

I looked at the picture that Radhika had sent me. I remembered the kiss she gave me at the hospital's parking lot on the day of the board meeting. I smiled in my mind. She is at Miami Beach with Saanvi and Kristina. Cities like Miami and Las Vegas are sin cities. They can tempt even saints and renunciates into wrongful acts. I didn't want to guess what they will be up to and what kind of fun they are having. Now that Giri is out of her life, Radhika is a free spirit and an unfettered bird. I hope that she comes back safe and in one piece.

It was three years ago that Radhika had planted that kiss on me. No matter how much I tried I could not entirely recall what went through my mind as she kissed me in the parking lot. Later, my wisdom had prevailed, and I had thought it was a simple gesture of thanking me. But, during that moment, did I have the wits to resist it if I wasn't thinking about Giri? What if she did that now? I decided not to stretch myself too much.

I saw an envelope from the Department of Homeland Security in my mailbox. I opened the envelope. It was my green card!

I couldn't control my curiosity. I looked in Radhika's mailbox too. Sure enough, there was a similar envelope sitting there. I placed my green card and her envelope next to each other and took a picture. I messaged this picture to Radhika. I got a response from her within a couple of minutes, 'Please open my envelope and tell me what's in it.' I opened her envelope, and her green card was in it. I placed our green cards next to each other and took a picture and again messaged the picture to Radhika.

She messaged me back saying, 'Yay!'

A couple of minutes later, I received a selfie with the three of them toasting with tequila shots.

I responded, 'Have fun' and opened the next patient's file.

My phone buzzed again. This time, it was a message from Saanvi. 'Hi Guru, you sent picture of both of your green cards kept side by side like you are trying to say something. What's up buddy? She is enjoying being single again. Leave her alone for now.' The message came with a smiley face.

***

The Sanghaali woman who had checked in was complaining of abdominal pain. She spoke at the reception in a raised voice that her stomach pains were severe and could not wait in the waiting room. She demanded that she be let inside immediately. Nurse Stephanie took her to a room. She stunk of alcohol. I couldn't get to her right away as there were five patients ahead of her. To make her happy, I ordered her blood and urine tests and went to see other patients.

I could not free myself for the next half hour. Meanwhile Stephanie came up to me and said, 'That Sanghaali girl is rambling all kinds of nonsense. It is not clear if she is really in pain, but she is insisting that she wants to see a doctor right away.'

I decided to see her and checked her chart for blood and urine results. Her urine test showed that she had smoked marijuana. Her pregnancy test results were yet to come. There was no infection in her urine. Her blood alcohol level was more than the legal limit.

I went into the examination room and asked, 'Name?'

She replied, barely looking at me, 'Fadhuma Hassan. I've a severe stomach pain.'

'What did you say?' I was surprised for a moment.

'I said I have a severe stomach pain.'

'No. Your name?'

'Doc, my name is Fadhuma Hassan.'

'Can you speak English? Do you need an interpreter? How many months?'

'You must be kidding! Are you joking, doc? I was three years old when I came to America. Now I'm a sophomore at the University of Minnesota's Business School. I can probably speak better English than you. And how many months? I'm twenty-four years old.' She had a perfect American accent.

'Sorry. My bad.'

'What?'

'I made a mistake. I'm sorry'

'How about "My apologies", like a gentleman?'

I was both surprised and a bit amused. 'Ok. My apologies.'

'Good. There is a difference between "My Apologies" and this hackneyed "Sorry". Don't get me wrong. I'm not sure if anyone else has mentioned this to you. You have a very thick accent. I may even need an interpreter to understand your English.' She laughed.

I looked at her, stunned. It was likely that my mind was primed for certain thoughts with certain names. The name Fadhuma Hassan invoked thoughts of pregnancies, interpreters, and suicides. This had made me ask her: 'How many months?' Also, did she not understand my accent or was she making fun of me?

'Sorry, what brings you to the hospital tonight? How may I help you?'

She said again, 'I cannot understand your accent. I need an interpreter.'

Hospitals generally provide interpreter services for patients who can't speak or understand English. All doctors who come to America do know how to speak English. Of course, they all have different accents depending on where they come from. But for the accent, patients understand them for the most part. At least that is the assumption. For the first time in my professional life, here I was, being asked for an interpreter just because I had an accent! I said to her, 'Alright, we can provide you with the interpreter services, but it is not clear from what language to what other language you need the interpreter for. You are speaking in English and so am I.'

She was stubborn, 'I can only speak English. There must be interpreter services to interpret your Indian English to American English.'

Nurse Stephanie who was with me, came to my rescue and added, 'The doctor's accent is perfectly fine. I've been working with him for five years now and there has not been a single instance when I've not understood his English.'

'Be honest. Do you understand every word that he speaks?' She challenged her.

'There is no need to understand every word. I can understand enough to be able to work with him.'

I looked at Stephanie. She said, 'Sorry,' and addressed Fadhuma. 'Which part of the conversation did you not understand?'

'I don't want to talk about it now. I cannot bear the pain. Get the interpreter right now.' She gave us no choice.

'I've been living in America for the past eight years. I'm this hospital's chief of staff. I've sat in many meetings and done press conferences too. Till now, nobody has told me that they could not understand me. Let me know what it is that you are not able to understand. Stephanie was also raised here in Minnesota. I think both of you speak the same accent. She can act as an interpreter between you and me.'

Stephanie said, 'Sorry doctor, as per the hospital's policy, interpreters have to be neutral and should have no vested interest. We both work for the same hospital. If tomorrow something goes wrong, she might say that she did not understand you and that my interpretation was not good enough. We are on the same side, doc. I don't want to lose my job or license. I'll call for the interpreter services. Why don't you talk to them?' She skyped for the interpreter services.

The service representative Julio Fernandez came on the Skype screen. 'Hello, this is Northwest Interpreter Services. For what language are you looking for our services?'

His English had a distinct Spanish accent. I looked at Fadhuma.

I said haltingly, 'Do you have interpreter services from Indian English to American English?' I was certain that he would say 'No'.

Without any hesitation Julio said, 'One moment, let me get that interpreter for you,' and got an English to English interpreter named Sunil Joshi.

'Hello, my name is Sunil Joshi. I am your interpreter. I'll introduce myself to the patient. Please speak directly to the patient. Speak slowly and clearly. My job is to directly translate from your language to the patient's language. Also, to be clear, I'll be interpreting your conversation only. I will not be adding anything that is not in the conversation and definitely not try to consciously bias either party with ideas of my own.' He set his interpreter's disclaimer.

If anybody had told me before that there are English to English interpreter services, I would not have believed it.

I said hesitatingly, 'My name is Guru. I'm speaking to a person by the name of Fadhuma. Fadhuma, what brings you here? How may I help you?'

He repeated exactly what I said, 'Fadhuma, what brings

you here? How may I help you?' I didn't think that his accent was any different than mine. But Fadhuma answered directly, 'I've been having stomach pain for the past three days. It starts from my lower belly and moves to the front of my upper belly. The pain waxes and wanes. I took some over the counter pills, but it did not help. My mom gave me a cup of cold milk mixed with saffron. That did not help either.'

The interpreter repeated, 'I've been having stomach pain for the past three days. It starts from my lower belly and moves to the front of my upper belly. The pain waxes and wanes. I took some over the counter pills, but it did not help. My mom gave me a cup of cold milk mixed with saffron. That did not help either.'

It was virtually a comical skit. Did she really have any pain at all or was she trying to take me for a ride?

'Are there any chances that you might be pregnant?'

'Sure, there is always a chance. You have my urine, don't you? Did you not do a pregnancy test?' She answered without waiting for the interpreter's translation.

'I did. I have not got the results yet.'

'Then why are you asking this question? Wait till you get the results.'

'There are traces of marijuana—meaning pot—in your urine.'

'I know what marijuana is. Traces? Had you asked me, I would have told you. You talk like you have made some important discovery. Does smoking pot cause stomach pain?'

'No, but I'm supposed to share the test results with you.'

'Doc, do you test for marijuana, alcohol and whatever other shit you test for everyone who comes complaining of stomach pain?'

The conversation was happening directly between the two of us by then. Fadhuma had insisted on an interpreter, now not only had she completely forgotten about him but was ready to fight with me. Meanwhile Sunil Joshi, on Skype, tried translating our conversation for some time and then gave up.

'Not for everyone. If there are enough medical reasons to do those tests, then we do them?'

'Why did you think I needed to be tested for pot, medically?'

'Not like that. It is a protocol.'

'What protocol, doc? Do you test everyone with stomach pain for drugs? Would you have done this test had I been a white person? You are a racist. Are you profiling me because I'm a black person?'

'Excuse me, do you really need our interpreter service or not?' Sunil Joshi asked.

I decided to do some talking and put the hospital's perspective before the pendulum starts swinging the other way completely. 'Look, this is a general test that is done in any hospital. If anyone older than sixteen comes in complaining of stomach pain, it is common to do a urine pregnancy test. Moreover, you are drunk and so, we need to test for other recreational drugs in your body. We do that because it helps us determine that the medicine we give does not interact with the drugs already present in your body and cause more harm. There is no question of white, black, brown or any other colour here.'

'Excuse me,' Sunil Joshi tried to ask again.

'Oh, shut up!' Fadhuma shouted.

'Ma'am, I'm only doing my job. There is no need to get angry.' The poor guy said.

'Don't you understand what shut up means? Which part of that did you not get? Do you understand English?'

'Ma'am, I'm an interpreter.'

'That is exactly why I asked you. I don't need your services.' She got up.

'Ok, ma'am. Thank you for using Northwest ...' Fadhuma

disconnected Skype before he could complete his sentence. She slumped back on to her bed.

It was apparent looking at her face that she was in pain. I put an order in the computer for starting an IV on her as well as doing an ultrasound and moved on to check on the next patient.

I felt a little gloomy for some reason. Fadhuma needed an interpreter only to prove that she is smarter than me. She had used my English accent to dent my self-righteousness and the sense of authority over a patient that came with my job.

Am I really a racist like she had accused me? How can a simple test done to a patient make one a racist? Did I profile her? Did my ordering for a drug screen amount to profiling? Would I have done all these tests before my examination if this was a twenty-four-year-old white girl?

I'm a doctor. How can I be a racist?

I was reminded of my days when I was new to America. I was doing my residency in a New York hospital. Once, a woman came to the hospital complaining of abdominal pain. I was fresh from India back then and the first question that I asked that woman was, 'Are you married?' When she said no, I had ordered a CT scan of her abdomen. To which she responded immediately, 'I'm twelve weeks pregnant. Who in their right mind does a CT on a pregnant woman?' and she had fired me as her doctor. I didn't know at that time that my patients could fire me.

In my innocence, I believed that if not married, there is no chance that she could be pregnant. This was the pure naiveté' of a young man displaced from his nurtured land and its values—the good-natured innocence of a novice.

I had learnt my lesson the hard way.

The first thing that I do now whenever women of any age between thirteen and forty-nine, come to the hospital complaining of abdominal pain is their urine test, especially urine pregnancy test. Many had complained that I suspect every female patient to be pregnant. Once, someone had complained that I had gotten a pregnancy test done for a lesbian woman, the hospital board members had also had a word with me about it.

I blamed my profession for all these missteps. I had argued that it had destroyed my innocence and made me a die-hard cynic. I had tried to prove myself to my colleagues and administration with examples of women testing positive for pregnancy after they had sworn that there is no way they can be pregnant, even lesbians.

If I were to be observed without the halo of a physician, do I do things differently based on the skin colour? Do my prejudices, values and experiences drive me towards this kind of behaviour? Do I order more and unnecessary tests to Sanghaalis in comparison to white patients? If a white person and a black person are badly injured in a road accident, who would I try to save first?

'Doc, hey dude. Are you going to give any medicine for my stomach pain? What kind of hospital is this?'

Stephanie came over and helped me out of Fadhuma's room and asked me, 'Guru, just order some pain medication for her. It's not worth it.'

I asked her, 'Stephanie, you have been working with me for the last five years. May I ask you a question?'

'Now?'

'Yes. A very quick question. Am I a racist?'

She thought for a moment and then said, 'No. Not really. Wait, one moment. Tell me, who isn't? You are not that kind of racist. Even if so, you are a good racist, an okay racist. You are on the right side.'

I looked at her stunned.

29. A Long Night

Stephanie called me. 'Doc, come here quickly. We have a full term pregnant Sanghaali woman. This is her tenth pregnancy. The baby is ready to come out anytime. Precipitous delivery. Radhika's patient.'

Radhika is in Key West. There's another Fadhuma in the emergency department. And on top of that, I must deliver a baby of a Sanghaali woman with no help from anyone.

For some reason everything felt like déjà vu. Deep inside, my instinct told me that this patient is likely to be Nusrat.

And yes. It turned out to be Nusrat. She made no noise, no loose talk, and no crying. It was obvious that she was in pain. She was wheeled to the room next to Fadhuma's. I excused myself from Fadhuma saying, 'Sorry there is another emergency.' Seeing me leave her room she began to swear, 'What the fu …' and then stopped midway upon seeing Nusrat. Nusrat's mere presence silenced her. 'Asalaam walekum,' there was respect laced with fear in her voice.

I did not know Nusrat personally. I introduced myself. I told her that Radhika was not in the hospital today. And that I could only deliver her baby if it was a normal delivery but if there were any complications, I may have to send her to Minneapolis.

Nusrat said, 'Doctor, this is my tenth baby. Since I had the last three babies by Cesarean section, Dr Radhika had told me that this baby too would most likely be by Cesarean. She has given me her phone number in case I need her. I had called her just a little while ago. She advised me to get to the hospital immediately.'

I decided to examine her. By the time I was ready, the baby was ready to come out with its head crowning. I told Stephanie, 'We do not have time to move her to the labour ward. Please set everything ready for delivery here in the emergency department.'

My heart was beating fast. Nusrat is not just another average Jane. She is a well-known personality, not just among the Sanghaali community but in all of Minnesota. And she is the mother of the notorious Mohammad Igal! Why in the world did Radhika even agree to deliver her baby?

I asked Nusrat to lie down on the examination table and after placing her feet on stirrups, I examined her. I could feel the soft spot on the baby's head. The bedside monitor indicated that the baby's heartbeat was normal. Stephanie started an intravenous infusion.

Nusrat tried to push a couple of times and stopped. 'I'm not feeling any pain,' she said when I looked at her. I increased the infusion rate, 'You have to push only twice.'

She pushed twice and stopped again.

There was no further screaming from Fadhuma in the next room. I was sitting there waiting for Nusrat to deliver her baby. Apparently, her water had broken quite a while ago and I was concerned about infection because of ruptured membranes.

I told Nusrat, 'If it is ok with you, let me call Radhika.'

Nusrat said, 'Isn't it one am for her now?'

'That should be ok. She is anyway aware of you coming here, isn't she?' I called Radhika.

Radhika seemed to have not slept at all. I could hear loud music blazing in the background. I informed her about Nusrat being in the hospital with labour pains and briefed her on what I had done so far.

'One minute,' she said and stepped out of the bar. 'Increase the dose of the infusion some more.'

'I am at the max already.'

She asked, 'Where is the baby?'

'What do you mean?'

'Tell me the position. I mean the station of the baby in the cervix.'

'Probably three or four.'

'Guru, what do you mean by three or four? Is it three or is it four?'

'Radhika, I don't know. This is not my expertise, not my job.'

'Ok. Ok. Never mind. How is Nusrat doing?'

'She is doing fine.'

'I'll come on Facetime. Let's get that baby out.'

I had no time to think about anything. Nusrat looked at me approvingly.

I took the phone near Nusrat's bottom, near the baby's head.

This was a discomforting situation for me, but I really had no choice. Nusrat on her part showed no discomfiture.

Radhika said, 'Guru, can you put the ultrasound probe on her abdomen. Let me look at the baby.'

I did as directed.

Radhika continued, 'The baby is too big. Possible shoulder dystocia. Nusrat, your baby's shoulder is much bigger than its head. Therefore, the baby may not come out easily. If I were to be there, I would take you for a Cesarean section right away. There is no doctor there who can do a Cesarean section now. So, I will walk Guru through the procedure and get the baby out. You have to be patient for a while.'

I asked Radhika, 'Shall we send her to Minneapolis? I can get the chopper here in ten minutes.'

Radhika said, 'If we don't take the baby out in ten minutes, the baby will die. Whatever we need to do, we have to do it now, and we have to do it right here.'

Nusrat's pain was getting worse. Yet she seemed to be in a world of her own. It looked as if she was not aware that she was delivering a baby. But her pain showed on her face.

Radhika was giving me instructions on the phone. 'Guru, try some vacuum.' I immediately applied suction pressure using a vacuum extractor on the baby's head and tried gentle traction. The baby's head came out fine, but as Radhika predicted, the shoulder posed a problem. No matter what I tried, the shoulder was stuck. The baby's face had swollen like a potato and its colour was changing.

I looked at Radhika.

'Ok Guru. You have only one option now. Fold both of Nusrat's knees and bring them all the way up—as in a missionary position. Insert both your hands fully inside, and hold the baby by both the shoulders and then pull it out gently but firmly… that is good… now press your thumbs firmly against the baby's collar bone. Keep in mind that we may have to break the collar bone. That should be ok and that is the only way we can save the baby.'

Nusrat said, 'Is there no other way?'

'There is another very difficult procedure. We need to push the baby all the way back into the uterus and then do a Cesarean section. That is very dangerous. And as it is, there are no doctors there who can do a Cesarean now. So, we must do it the way we discussed before. And we must do it right now.'

I was passively following Radhika's instructions. Both my hands were inside Nusrat and I pressed and held the baby's shoulders while pressing the collar bone with my thumb. Soon the shoulders loosened enough to touch each other, and the baby folded up almost like a newspaper. I broadened Nusrat and slowly and firmly pulled the baby out.

It was a boy.

The baby was not breathing. Two minutes of ventilation,

a couple of injections and a vigorous massage on the base of his feet later, he started crying loudly. It was the robust cry of a healthy baby.

But he didn't move either of his arms. Radhika was explaining to Nusrat over the phone. 'Sorry Nusrat, I should have been there. But what is important is that the baby is alive. You don't have to be concerned. He is not moving his arms probably because of the pain in the collar bone. Another very rare possibility is that pieces of the broken collar bone may be pinching the nerves that control the arm muscles. If it stays that way, the baby's arms will not work temporarily. If the baby does not move his arms for a long time up to a year or so, then we need to worry about permanent damage. I am almost certain that this is not likely to happen. But if it does, there are lots of treatment options.'

Nusrat picked up the phone next to her, 'Dr Radhika, thank you for your help. I've to sleep now,' and she went to sleep.

I came out to the break room and poured myself a cup of coffee. I stretched my feet for about half an hour on the recliner. Stephanie knocked on the door and came inside. She gave a quick report of the emergency room status—that Fadhuma had signed herself out against medical advice, Nusrat had been shifted to the labour ward, there were no new patients in the emergency department except for a couple—one person waiting for his CT scan results for his abdominal pain and a child with an allergic reaction for which she had given Benadryl injection.

My phone buzzed. There was a message from Radhika, 'Turn on CNN.'

I switched on the TV. There was some breaking news.

A twenty-two-year-old young man having links to Al Tewagi was shot dead in a gunfight with the police in the northern Minnesota suburb of Robbinsville. The young man,

Mohammad Igal, was from the town of Amoka. He was on the FBI's 'Most Wanted' list. It is believed he was involved in last year's bomb attacks in Turkey and Paris. Many explosives and firearms were seized from his Robbinsville home. FBI has also seized a laptop and several mobile phones from there. The rest of his family members live in Amoka. Our reporters have tried to contact them many times and have had no success. One point of significance is that Igal's mother, Nusrat, who is very active in Minnesota's Sanghaali community had recently organized a Town Hall meeting about 'Sanghaali mothers fight against terrorism and racial profiling'.

I switched the TV off .

To the north of our Amoka Hospital one can only see the vast expanse of the sky. I was looking out through the window. Everything thus far had unfolded like filmy melodrama. Did Nusrat know about Igal's death? He was dead before she came here for her delivery. Does that mean she knew about his death before she came here? And despite that, did she check in to deliver the baby?

It was a crazy, almost senseless thought. What other choice did she have? When she starts having labour pains, she does have to come to the hospital, doesn't she? Had Igal called her? During the shootout, when he was mortally wounded and aware of his imminent death, did he think of calling his mother once?

I suspect I watch too many movies.

There were no patients in the emergency room. The kid with allergic reaction felt better and had gone home. The man with abdominal pain was found to be constipated. He went home happily after having a huge bowel movement, thanks to Stephanie's enema. I heard him yelling on his way out 'This is the most expensive crap. You've got to do a CT scan to tell me that I haven't pooped for a week. That's the reason I came to the hospital. I ain't paying no fucking two thousand dollars for taking a shit in your ER.'

There were three more hours to go on my shift. I tried to sleep. I could not. I was tossing around on the bed.

I heard a loud brouhaha in the emergency room. Stephanie banged on the door of the call room. I came out. The police had brought a man in handcuffs. He didn't have even a shred of cloth on him. He was completely naked from head to toe. He had a smooth shiny body with hardly any hair on it.

He yelled at the top of his voice, 'Motherfuckers! I will do whatever I want in my house. Is that a crime? I know my rights. I'm telling the truth. Someone is spreading fake news about me. They are trying to poison my food. After I ate the muufasos in that Sanghaali restaurant, I could not get up for three days. When I got up this evening and watched the TV news, the FBI had shot dead that Igal from our town. The other day, the muufasos I had was at his mother's restaurant. God bless our FBI. Yo Igal, go, get lost to the land of seventy-two virgins. Goodbye!' Fortunately, Nusrat was not in the emergency department.

He looked at me and said, 'What is your name? Are you the doctor here?' He was disgustingly rubbing his penis with his cuffed hands. I did not bother to answer.

A child who had come to the emergency department looked at him, 'Yooo! You are not wearing your clothes. Who are you?'

He answered, 'I'm god.'

He looked weird. Possibly seventy years old. Strongly built and tall, around six feet four inches. His face was heavily botoxed.

He addressed me again, 'Where are you from? Bangladesh? Pakistan?'

Stephanie and I looked at the policeman.

The policeman said, 'Cocaine doc, cocaine. It was all over his house. He was sitting on top of his roof, butt naked in this cold.' Stephanie made a sign with her finger across her neck in a cutting motion and gestured to me with her eyes not to talk to him or answer any of his questions.

But if I don't talk to him, how can I even treat him?

I looked at him and said, 'Hi.'

He ignored me, looked at the child and waved bye with his hands. His hands were disproportionately small compared to the rest of his body. He held his penis with one hand. His penis was so large that when he walked, it dangled up to his knees.

His hair was tousled by the breeze of the corridor fan and it had a strange colour. It was not clear if the colour was natural or fake. It was the colour of pure undiluted saffron or orange. The colour of Baji Rao's flag.

The police took him to the special room meant to treat psychiatric patients and laid him on the bed there. He was given the hospital's clothes to wear. He did not so much as even look at them. The walls of that room were padded with soft cotton wool. Even if he does try to bang his head against the wall, he will be safe. More than anything, we will be safe if he tries to attack us. After checking that it is safe to go inside, I entered his room. A security guard from the hospital was sitting there. The orange-haired person was lying naked on the bed. There was a picture of the Washington monument hung on the wall. He was trying to get his manhood straight enough as if to put the tall monument to shame. The seventy-year-old organ curved at the end. He held his handcuffed hands as if he held a camera and took a fake selfie of his erect Willy.

I tried to ask him, 'What's happening? Are you doing ok?'

He held his fingers like a gun, pointed at me and said, 'Dishum.' Then he looked me in the eye and said, 'Let's chase these Mohammads and Ahmeds away. Let us build our own America. Let us make America great again.'

I ignored his shenanigans and examined him. My hands felt something gooey. I felt nauseated.

'Stephanie, give him ten milligrams of Haloperidol, get him dressed no matter how difficult. If the medicine does not work and if he is still up to his antics, page the psychiatrist.'

I ran to the restroom. I could not puke properly either. Perhaps because I had too much of coffee, I could only spit out bitter bile. My throat felt bitter. I pissed copiously. I sat on the toilet bowl with my eyes closed.

Om BhoouH,
Om BhuvaHa,
Om SuvaHa,
Om MahaHa,
Om JanaHa,
Om TapaHa,
Om Satyam,
Om Tat Savitur Varenyam
Bhargodevasya Dheemahi,
DheeyoyonaH Prachodayat,
Om Apo Jyotiraso Amrutam Brahma Bhoorbhuvassuvarom

It had been so long since I recited the Pranayama chant. I was not even aware that I still remembered it. I could recall it very well. I continued reciting sitting there.

It is strange that we came to this anonymous town only with the desire of getting our green cards, never to be a part of its history, its social fabric or its cultural identity.

How can a town this small, this modest, hold so many things inside her—anger, love, hate, sacrifice, frustration, suicide, deaths, pregnancies, politics, sympathy, guns, fights, terrorism, Sanghaala, India?

Is this the real America? The melting pot and the land of opportunities? Is this the American dream that we came after? Or is this simply my dream—my sights and sounds—circumscribed by my work at the emergency department, my patients' diseases and the anger and the frustrations that came with them.

Where had I seen the America beyond my work? I did not have contact with anyone here other than Srikantha, Radhika and Saanvi. I lived in a bubble. Not once had I ever gone to a co-worker's house. Be it Smith, Rick or Powell, none of them had ever invited me over to their home for a meal. Whenever I have had time, Srikantha and I would go out to the Minneapolis temple. Beyond an odd comment about family, pastime and politics, our social life in America is dotted by our own rituals, and Indian food in the Udupi restaurant in Minneapolis. Our awareness of Amoka is limited to the outer layer of its outer skin.

Today, I had delivered Nusrat's baby against many odds. Yes, the baby's collar bones were broken but he survived the ordeal. Nusrat will be discharged either tomorrow or the day after. A baby is born, and a son has died. Other than these, what do I know about her? If I see everyone's life in such a cross-section how close to the truth can I get?

Is the way I see and perceive, wrong? There are lots of other people living in Amoka, who don't come to see me in this hospital. Why is it that only things like suicides, drugs, murders, anguish, and terrorism come to my attention? Why only the dark side? The orange-haired man started screaming profanities again. I closed both my ears and eyes.

Had I known answers to all my questions, would I be sitting on the toilet bowl in the middle of the night chanting Pranayama?

I came out of the room and stood by the window. There was not a single star in the sky. I stared at the sky and even as I did so, I felt that there was something going on there. Sure enough, suddenly the sky turned purple as if someone was painting it in broad brush strokes. Disneyland's 10 pm fireworks came to my mind. I thought I was in the middle of a dream. I pinched myself and confirmed that was not so. It was almost as if someone was projecting the sky with luminous purple from a projector. Five minutes later, the sky turned dark green and yellow. Five more minutes later, it was pink in colour.

The sky was a cacophony of colours. It seemed as if a game of Holi was being played in the sky. The pervasive jumping lights came through the window and reflected on my face. I did not know what it was or what exactly was happening. The whole show seemed like a large-scale replica of a Jeetendra–Sridevi movie song set. I stood there witnessing it.

I had seen a rainbow in the sky but never seen the sky bathed in rainbow colours one after the other. Stephanie who was standing behind me said, 'Aurora Borealis. Northern Lights. Doc, how fortunate are we! People go to Cook County and wait all night to watch this.'

People from all over the country come to Minnesota to watch the beauty of Aurora Borealis. They wait for hours to get a glimpse of its magic. Apart from Iceland, it is only in our town that the majesty of this natural phenomenon can be seen so well. I had heard that our eyes do not do justice to these lights caused by the convergence of sun, air and the earth's gravitational field. I was witnessing it for the first time.

The whole expanse of the sky turned into a fabric of purple, green, yellow, pink and red. It felt as if I was transported to a divine world. I was pinching myself hoping that this should not be a dream. I went on YouTube on the phone in my hand and searched for 'Northern Lights'. There were some videos that came up. But it felt that none of these high definition videos did any justice to the feast of colours that I was witnessing.

Stephanie said, 'Doc, keep the phone aside. Trust me. By

the time you try to confirm if this is an illusion or real, this beautiful spectacle will be over. Just enjoy.'

I picked up my phone again. My camera did not have enough pixels to capture this beauty in all its glory. I took a picture. It was slightly hazy. I sent the same picture to Radhika with the message, 'We have an Aurora Borealis happening in our town.'

I got her reply, 'What is it? Looks very hazy.' She had obviously not seen the picture I sent. I did not bother to explain. She also had perhaps not slept all through the night.

The sun had risen outside. I washed my face and poured myself another cup of coffee. As I was leaving, I thought of talking to Nusrat once, in the maternity ward upstairs. I went to her ward. She was also awake and was speaking to someone in Sanghaali. As soon as she saw me, she disconnected the phone and smiled, 'Come doctor, have a seat.'

She looked tired. The baby born just a few hours ago was sleeping in his crib.

I didn't quite know what to say. 'Nothing really. My shift has ended, and before I go home, I thought of talking to you once.'

She smiled weakly, 'When will they discharge me?'

'Usually after such complications, they keep you for a minimum of three days. If you recover quickly, we can perhaps discharge you even earlier.'

'Oh ... alright.'

'Do you have something important that you have to do?'

Nusrat looked at me strangely implying if this was even a question to be asked.

I was embarrassed and immediately tried to change the subject, 'Didn't anyone from your home visit you to see the baby?'

She did not answer that question either.

The baby woke up and started crying. She picked him up for feeding.

Both the arms of the baby dangled by its sides. The collar bone probably pulled a bit and he started crying loudly.

She gently moved the baby's arms to the side. She placed two soft pillows on her thighs as a support to the baby's arms and started feeding him.

I glanced at the label on the crib. It had the baby's name on it: 'Mohammad Igal'.

I looked at Nusrat, surprised.

'Don't worry, doc. He shall not be a terrorist. He cannot, even if he wants to.' And then she started sobbing loudly.

I kept looking for some motion—a twitch, flicker or even a small muscle fiber to fibrillate from the little fellow's tiny fingers peeping out of his blanket.

Acknowledgements

Our sincere thanks to

M.S. Nataraj, Professor Narayan Hegde, Uday Datta, Pranita Kaginele, Prajwal Kumar, Rachel Fedorchak and Anjum Hasan for their valuable feedback.

Kanishka Gupta, our agent without whom this book would not be possible.

Sayantan Ghosh, our commissioning editor for meticulous editing.

Team Simon & Schuster India for production, marketing and distribution.

Vivek Shanbhag and Arunava Sinha for their nice words.

Guruprasad Kaginele
Pavan N. Rao